JOLIE BLONDE

Amanda hoped the music would go on forever. Alcée's bow moved effortlessly across the violin, the notes of the song of a man pining for his blond love who has left him. He begs her to reconsider, to not listen to others and return to her family. He vows his complete love for her, adding that death would be welcome if she will not come back to him . . .

Amanda imagined that René was singing the song for her.

But when the song was finished, and she glanced at him, he rose and pulled her gently from her chair. "Perhaps it's time you went to bed," he said.

The two walked up the stairs in silence. Once inside the threshold to René's room, a wall would separate them. Amanda looked up at René and her stomach tightened. She had to ask him.

"Well, good night," he said quietly, handing her the lamp.

"Good night," Amanda answered, feeling amazingly disappointed. What had she expected, a kiss good night?

Yes, her heart responded. But she entered the bedroom alone, closing the door behind her. As she moved to undress, she could hear René doing the same in the room next door. She sat down on the bed, chastising herself for being a coward and a hopeless romantic. *If I'm not mistaken, Amanda Rose,* she scolded herself, *wishing for kisses in the moonlight is what got you into this mess.*

"Go away," she told her emotions, but they refused to budge. She placed her head inside her hands and took a deep breath. She had to tell him.

She had to have an answer . . . .

BOOK YOUR PLACE ON OUR WEBSITE AND MAKE THE READING CONNECTION!

We've created a customized website just for our very special readers, where you can get the inside scoop on everything that's going on with Zebra, Pinnacle and Kensington books.

When you come online, you'll have the exciting opportunity to:

- View covers of upcoming books
- Read sample chapters
- Learn about our future publishing schedule (listed by publication month *and author*)
- Find out when your favorite authors will be visiting a city near you
- Search for and order backlist books from our online catalog
- Check out author bios and background information
- Send e-mail to your favorite authors
- Meet the Kensington staff online
- Join us in weekly chats with authors, readers and other guests
- Get writing guidelines
- AND MUCH MORE!

**Visit our website at
http://www.zebrabooks.com**

A CAJUN DREAM

Cherie Claire

Zebra Books
Kensington Publishing Corp.

http://www.zebrabooks.com

ZEBRA BOOKS are published by

Kensington Publishing Corp.
850 Third Avenue
New York, NY 10022

Zebra, the Z logo and Splendor Reg. U.S. Pat. & TM Off.

First Printing: July, 1999
10 9 8 7 6 5 4 3 2 1

Printed in the United States of America

Chapter One

Franklin, Louisiana
Lower Bayou Teche
1848

It was the hottest summer to date.

Amanda Rose Richardson gripped her gardening basket and searched Main Street, absentmindedly tugging down on her bonnet in an attempt to keep the noonday sun from scorching her forehead. The midmorning breeze from the Gulf that had offered a hint of respite had dissipated, leaving the harsh Louisiana sun alone with its victim.

Had she mistaken the time? Perhaps it was later than she realized. It was close to lunchtime and still he hadn't come.

She dared not wait much longer. Another few minutes and her clothes would become pasted to her skin, outlining her figure for all who walked the busy streets of Franklin.

What would her father say to that? she wondered, the familiar anxiety taking hold of her usually calm demeanor. She could see him now, criticizing her actions in his dark, heavily paneled study. Likening her to her mother.

Glancing back at the stately house she had called home for the past ten years, Amanda knew what she had to do. It wasn't her fault she was born a female, or that her mother had run away with the French Opera Company when Amanda was less than twelve years old. Today was Amanda's birthday, a landmark date, and she would cross into adulthood an experienced woman.

She knew it was doubtful her father would finally agree that some man in the great state of Louisiana was well-bred enough to marry his only child. Suitors Amanda had liked were quickly discarded as incompetent loafers, even the ones from the finest families in Franklin. Rich men from important families Amanda had met in surrounding cities such as New Iberia and St. Martinville—on the rare occasions she had been allowed to accompany her father on business—were rejected for everything from "poor breeding" to "bad judgment in obtaining wealth." By the time Amanda had reached nineteen, she'd become convinced she would live her life as an old maid.

Today she turned twenty-one, and there was little hope of her marrying. When once her dance cards were filled with names, now Amanda sat out between numbers, watching as one by one her friends entered into matrimony. Only Sally Baldwin remained, but she was scheduled to marry in the fall, just before sugarcane harvest.

It was Sally who suggested she consider Henry Tanner. Amanda's father's plantation overseer was notorious for romancing the ladies. Henry Tanner had blatantly kissed Katharine Blanchard, who everyone knew was engaged to Bernard Mann, on a buggy ride home from a dance. According to Sally, Katharine was outraged at the dapper man's actions, but cherished them all the same. She couldn't stop talking about his feathery kisses along her neckline, the way he held her hand and the romantic sonnets he recited to her in the moonlight.

If he could offer Katy Blanchard, who was promised to someone else, a quick glimpse of romance, surely he would be willing to offer Amanda, a single woman of social standing and wealth, something to remember when her youth faded into spinsterhood.

With Sally's help, Tanner had agreed to secretly escort Amanda to the public ball that evening at the Franklin Exchange. Amanda's father would be gone on business, and he sternly forbade her to leave the house in his absence, even though she would be surrounded by all of her closest friends merely blocks from her home. Amanda had never defied her father before. But situations being what they were, she had to do something drastic. She couldn't spend her whole life not knowing the romantic advances of a man.

A droplet of perspiration trickled down her back. Her friend wasn't coming, Amanda thought, or he had arrived too early and she had missed him. She knelt down and gathered up her gardening tools, placing them neatly into her handbasket along with the rows of cut roses. She would try again tomorrow.

"Good morning, Miss Richardson," came the familiar accented voice from above her head.

Gazing up and over her white picket fence stood René Comeaux, his chestnut eyes peering down at her intently from beneath a wide-brimmed planter's hat, its crest accented by a bright scarlet sash. He lingered at the fence's gate as he had every morning the past month, his tall, imposing figure casting a welcoming shadow over Amanda's smiling face, one boot resting amiably against the lower fence post.

For not the first time during the past few weeks, Amanda felt the butterflies taking flight inside her stomach.

* * *

René Comeaux had spent the morning convincing himself not to walk down Main Street past the Richardson house. It was useless, a waste of time. Yet here he was staring down at the flushed, smiling face of an angel. His angel. Amanda Rose Richardson possessed the most impressive sparkling blue eyes framed by curls of the brightest, blondest hair he had ever seen. Her heart-born smile literally radiated warmth throughout her face, and its heat poured over him like the wild prairie brush fires common to southwestern Louisiana.

She contained all the grace, elegance and warmth he imagined the perfect woman would have. She was charming, intelligent, friendly and kind. And from their first meeting in her front yard, when she unhesitatingly offered her hand in greeting after he tipped his hat to her from the street, he'd been hopelessly in love with her.

Still, she was an American. Not from a working-class American family that had moved into the new state hoping to carve out a place for themselves as his family had when they were exiled from Canada by the English. Amanda Rose Richardson was from one of the finest American families in Virginia, descendants of American revolutionaries. In Louisiana, her father had made a name for himself as an intermediary between New Orleans's French population and its newly formed American government after the Louisiana Purchase. For some reason René had not understood, the Richardsons had chosen to move from New Orleans to the small, yet booming southwestern Louisiana town of Franklin, where James Richardson served as the parish judge.

Through a series of successful sugarcane ventures, in addition to his political career, James Richardson had become one of Franklin's richest and most influential citizens.

None of this mattered to René. He had seen his share of

rich, influential citizens, be they French, English, Spanish or American. Like most Acadians, he vowed allegiance only to his family and his land. Political authorities were not to be trusted or admired. His people had realized that during a century of oppression when almost every government they encountered had treated the Acadians with disdain or neglect.

Still, Amanda Rose Richardson was not an impossible dream. Among his people, René Comeaux was a rich and influential man as well. He would make a fine husband, able to care for Amanda in the way she was accustomed. Or close to it. He was formally educated—the first in his family to be so—and was successful in his father's cattle business and his own ventures, and he spoke English fluently.

But James Richardson had refused to allow him to call on the girl.

"No child of mine will ever be married to a Frenchman," the elder Richardson had bellowed in his suffocating study. "My Amanda Rose would never even consider an offer from an Acadian, no matter how much money you make. You can take your immigrant concerns elsewhere."

Frenchman indeed, René thought, feeling the anger burn at his temple. The fool man didn't even know the difference between René's people and those who arrived directly from France. He might speak the mother tongue and be descended from the French, but René was an Acadian, now and forever.

And an immigrant! The man surely was confusing René with *les americains.* Amanda was native-born to Louisiana, but her father certainly wasn't. René was the third generation of the Comeaux family born in the Louisiana Territory.

Looking down into the deep, blue eyes of the woman who had cast such a spell upon his unawakened heart, René wondered what he was doing there. Despite all of her father's threats, he couldn't stay away.

Yet he couldn't remain either.

"I see you're visiting town late today," Amanda said, breaking the silence that had lingered uncomfortably between them. "I was just about to go inside, to escape this sweltering heat."

Why was she smiling? René wondered. Why was she consistently friendly to a man her father had said she despised? If it were true that she would never allow an Acadian man to call on her, why was she always so agreeable when they met on the street every morning?

"Mr. Comeaux?" she asked, gazing up at him with those eyes the color of robins' eggs. God, she was beautiful. He felt perspiration trickling down his back.

Perhaps she had been mocking him all these weeks, greeting him with pleasure at her fence, then denouncing him to her friends when he was out of earshot, using that awful pronunciation of his nationality: *Cajun*. "Did I tell you about that *Cajun* man who thinks I am good enough for him, who actually asked my father if he could call on me? He actually had the gall to think I would consider marrying him!"

"Is something wrong?" Amanda asked, her smile replaced with a frown.

René had endured enough torture for one morning. At any moment now he expected her father to step out of the house, further humiliating him by publicly sending him away. One last look and he would move on.

"Good day to you, Miss Richardson," he said proudly, tipping his hat. "I will not let an immigrant impose on your time any longer."

Amanda had not seen him leave, but she knew Monsieur Comeaux had left the front gate when the sun he was blocking blinded her eyes. She turned to escape the sun's piercing effect, and found no one on the street.

"Amanda," she heard her father call from the porch. "Who was that?"

Still holding her gardening basket, Amanda turned and walked slowly toward her father and the house. The intense heat sucked the breath from her lungs. "Monsieur Comeaux," she answered quietly.

"What on earth did he want?" her father demanded, towering over her in his usual formal blue suit that outlined an older, but trim and muscular, man. His slightly curly blond hair accented by hints of gray fell about his forehead as his tone grew stern. "And why are you talking to men off the street?"

Amanda sighed. Must she constantly endure the sins of her mother? Genevieve Richardson, one of the world's most famous opera singers, had left one night on the arm of a French tenor and because of that infamous night, Amanda was turning into an old maid. Couldn't her father realize he was destroying her future as a happy, fulfilled woman by constantly "protecting her from the evils of men"?

"He wishes me good morning when he passes, Father," she answered, her dislike of the subject apparent. "I doubt he plans to make love to me over the front fence."

"Amanda," her father said, brushing his hair away with an aggravated movement of his hand. "How dare you say such things, use such language? Who has been teaching you such filth?"

"No one has been teaching me anything, Father. I am barely allowed to leave the house."

James Richardson grunted, staring out at the street. Amanda knew this conversation would not last long. "I am your father and it is my job to protect you," he said. "I don't wish to hear any more of it."

Knowing he would quickly exit both the porch and the painful subject she had brought up, Amanda opened the front door and watched her father disappear into the inner sanctum of his study. Whatever anxiety she felt over the night's meeting with Henry Tanner, her father instantly dispelled. She would get her kiss, of that she was sure.

What lingered in her mind, however, was Monsieur Comeaux and his talk of immigrants.

"Amanda dear, come into the house. I need your help with lunch so we can get to the butcher before this heat melts everything in sight." Virginia O'Neil's lilting voice broke the spell, and Amanda turned her gaze from the street.

"He called himself an immigrant," she said absentmindedly. "What do you think he meant by that?"

"Who called himself an immigrant? Dear, you really must get out of the sun or you shall be fainting over lunch."

Amanda let her nanny, housemaid and companion of the past ten years guide her into the house. Within seconds the bright light of the outside world was replaced by the dark, oppressive interior. Amanda felt, as she did every morning, that a heavy drape had been drawn over a window in her heart. Since two summers hence, when word came that her mother had died of a lung infection while on tour in Venice, her father had drawn the enormous curtains on his Greek Revival house— and his life—and left the family hovering in humid twilight.

If only he would speak of her, Amanda thought. *Tell me what she was like, why she ran away.* Father was always blaming the Frenchman she disappeared with that night, but Amanda knew there was another side to the story. What few memories Amanda had of her mother in New Orleans were not happy ones. She remembered Genevieve Richardson pacing the parlors in her finest gowns and jewels, arguing with Father about his refusal to attend the annual Carnival ball at the Labordes mansion in the nearby Vieux Carré. She had stormed out that night, and returned three days later, refusing to speak to anyone on the matter.

Once Amanda had found her mother crying hysterically in

the kitchen in the middle of the day. Amanda had thought her heart would break at the sight. She had thrown her arms around her mother's neck and begged her to stop. Her mother had muttered something about watching her career slip through her fingers, all for the sake of her family, and pushed her away.

"I must leave," she would forever remember her mother saying that fateful afternoon. "If I cannot sing, I will surely die."

Amanda had tried numerous times to discuss the scene with her father after the scandal broke, but he refused even to mention her name. Her mother became dead to him the night she walked out.

Or so she thought. When the news of her mother's death arrived that hot August day, her father fell apart for the second time in his life. He kept to his room and refused food for days. Amanda knew he never would have come out had it not been for dear Virginia. She slowly coerced him into eating something, then joining Amanda in the dining room. Within a month's time, Father was back at work and serving the people of Franklin. But he was forever changed. And the house was always dark.

"Do you think Father wishes that I never marry?" Amanda asked.

Virginia stopped short and sent her a concerned glance. "Why do you say that, child?" she retorted in an Irish accent that had not weakened since her arrival in America. "Your father wishes only the best for you."

"I don't know," Amanda answered, knowing how strange the words sounded. "I'm not getting any younger, Gin, and he doesn't approve of anyone. Pretty soon there will be no others, if that time hasn't already arrived."

Virginia huffed as she opened the door to the back pantry. "I was a year older than you when I married," she said good-naturedly, sending her a wry smile. "Are you saying I'm an old woman?"

"Of course not," Amanda said as she placed her basket down on the pantry table and began to remove her bonnet. "But you *were* married. I don't see why . . ."

"Give it time, Amanda Rose," her take-charge nanny insisted.

"Time for what? For the men in this town to become Catholics?"

Virginia silently turned and began collecting the dishes for lunch. "Who said he was an immigrant?" she asked, changing the subject.

"Monsieur Comeaux. He said something about not letting an immigrant impose on my time any longer."

"Why would he say something so queer? He comes from an old Acadian family."

"Yes. His family raises cattle on the prairie near St. Martinville. They've been in Louisiana for decades, which is why it's so strange he would say such a thing."

Virginia turned from her job to gaze intently on Amanda.

"What?" Amanda asked, wondering why she was suddenly receiving Virginia's infamous eagle eye.

"How come you know so much about this Mr. Comeaux?"

A smile stole its way across Amanda's face, even though she fought hard to suppress it. "He walks by every day on his way into town. Sometimes he stops and we talk a little."

The eagle eye persisted, and Amanda felt another trickle of perspiration travel down the cleavage of her bodice. The sun's torture had been avoided, but the heat permeated every inch of the back room. After lunch, she would retire to her bedroom to attempt to sleep through the hottest part of the day.

"It is hot today, isn't it?" Amanda asked sheepishly. "If you like, I'll go into town and get the meat for dinner."

Virginia returned to her task, but continued her inquisition. "You haven't answered my question, Amanda."

Wiping the back of her neck with her handkerchief, Amanda sighed. "You're as bad as Father. We talk, is all. He politely mentions my health. I comment on the weather. It's all very formal and proper, I assure you."

"Knowledge of where he comes from and what his family does is hardly what I call commenting on the weather."

"All right," Amanda acquiesced, placing some of her cut roses into a crystal vase. "I asked him one day how the Acadians came to Louisiana and he told me his family history. Did you know the English exiled them from Nova Scotia and sent them to the Colonies, where some of their children were kidnapped or sold into slavery?"

Virginia grunted. "Is that what he told you?"

Amanda twirled a fading rose between her fingers, wondering whether to place it in the bouquet or throw it away. "It's true, Gin. I've heard others speak of it. All because they were French and Catholics and refused to swear allegiance to the British crown."

Amanda inwardly smiled when her auburn-haired nanny stopped stacking plates and sighed. It was a sign she approved. What Irishwoman, whose family had suffered a similar fate, wouldn't?

"Well, I guess he's a gentleman. I've noticed his dress and he doesn't look like a Cajun."

"What does a Cajun look like, dear Gin? How many have you seen in your lifetime?"

Virginia smiled a little. "Not many, but I've heard tales. They were peasant farmers in Nova Scotia—or Acadia, if that's what they called it. They're mostly illiterate. Even their French language betrays their class. When some of them were sent to France by the English, the French couldn't do anything with them because they had lost touch with the modern world. They lived off the crown, you know. And refused to go to work.''

''Monsieur Comeaux says that was because they had been independent all those years in Acadia. Most of them had their own farms for over a century. France was still under a feudal system, and the Acadians refused to live under it.''

This time, Virginia laughed. ''Only talked about the weather, eh?''

Amanda gazed down at the flower in her hand. She decided to place it in the center of the bouquet, despite its faded glory. ''I like him, Gin. He's my friend. At least, I think he is.''

A silence almost as stifling as the heat fell upon the back room. ''Beware, my dear,'' Virginia said. ''Don't give him ideas.''

Amanda could hardly believe her ears. ''For goodness' sake, Gin, he's just an acquaintance. We barely know each other.''

Virginia waved a hand between them. ''Perhaps you should keep it that way.''

With those final words, Virginia moved into the dining room with her stack of fine china, leaving Amanda alone with her thoughts.

''Ideas indeed,'' Amanda said to herself. Monsieur Comeaux would hardly think of her in the romantic way. He was an Acadian and she was an American. He would marry a nice Acadian girl and have a lot of French-speaking children. And she . . .

Amanda didn't know if it was the unbearable heat or the smothering darkness, but a pain settled on her heart and took hold. Suddenly she could no longer make out the bright yellow rose in her hand. This time it was tears that dampened her gown.

* * *

James Richardson would have worked straight through from morning till dinner had it not been for the attentive Miss O'Neil, Amanda's former nanny and the household's all-around life-saver. He had hired her years ago when he and Amanda moved to Franklin, and it was one of the finest decisions he'd ever made. In addition to maintaining a household of servants, she made sure that every midday James settled down at the lunch table with Amanda, despite his repeated objections.

The way conversations were headed these days in his house, James preferred the peace of his study where a case against the new sugar tariffs awaited him. Girls were supposed to go through these stages when they turned twelve or thirteen, or so he was told by other fathers in similar situations. Amanda had been a pillar of strength when she was twelve, the year her mother ran . . .

As quickly as the thought entered his mind, James dismissed it. He would not think of his wife. He couldn't bear it.

Looking over at his daughter, he was thankful she resembled his side of the family. She would have been more fortunate to have inherited her mother's dark, seductive looks, but the torture of seeing Genevieve's face every day would have been more than he could have borne.

Irritated that thoughts of her again infiltrated his mind, James grabbed the napkin and hurriedly placed it in his lap. "Miss O'Neil, where is lunch?"

His tone startled Amanda, whose eyes met his for the first time since he sat down. Had she been crying? He knew she was unhappy, but he dreaded finding out why. Every time they approached the subject, she began inquiring about marriage and men. Sometimes she even mentioned that dreadful night.

"Are you not well?" he asked her, forcing his mind to other things.

"I'm fine, Father," she answered meekly.

James sighed. Why couldn't women just speak their mind

and not make you pull it out of them? "Is this any way to spend your birthday? You should be beaming. After all the money I spent on you."

"The dress is beautiful, Father. You know I love it."

"But?"

"But what use is it if I can't wear it to the ball tonight?"

A slow pounding began behind James's temple. "We have been through this all before. I don't wish to speak of it again. You are not to leave the house when I am out of town."

Amanda stared at the salad placed before her by one of the servants. Without moving to eat, she said, "Do you realize how old I am today? I am twenty-one, the age most women enter spinsterhood."

James threw down his spoon. "Amanda, I do not wish to speak of this. I have heard it all before."

"But you haven't heard me, Father. I keep trying to talk to you about this and you keep refusing me. Why do you not approve of any men in town? Do you really wish for me to spend the rest of my life alone?"

The pounding that had started as a slow beat began to increase in intensity. James rubbed the bridge of his nose, but to no avail. He wanted the pain to disappear as much as the subject.

"Your . . . mother," he continued, physically cringing at the sound of the word, "insisted you be raised a Catholic. You must have realized that there are no men in town from the families we socialize with who are Catholics."

"There are some families who are . . ."

"There are no families," he answered a bit too harshly. Since Franklin was a town born of Americans straight off the boats and wagons of other states and territories, most were Protestants. But regardless of any religion, James approved of none of them as suitors for his daughter.

Amanda's sad gaze returned to her uneaten salad. James

knew Amanda always thought the best of everyone. She was by far the most unprejudicial person he had ever known.

And naive.

He remembered how easy it was to trust people, to let one's heart love freely, and he'd be damned if he'd let his daughter make the same mistake.

"There are well-connected Catholic families in New Orleans," Amanda added, refusing to let the subject drop. "But you won't let me enter society."

"I don't want you away from home," he retorted, stabbing his fork into the plate of lettuce before him.

Amanda turned her startled eyes on him. "I spent years in an East Coast finishing school."

James thrust the salad aside with disgust, his headache getting the best of him. "Why didn't you find a proper husband then?"

Amanda laughed. "Well, if there aren't many good Catholic men in French Louisiana, there certainly aren't any in the Commonwealth of Virginia."

"Take my word for it, Amanda," James said, hoping to end the distasteful conversation. "There are no decent Catholic American men in the city of New Orleans."

James watched as the corners of Amanda's lips tightened into a grim smile. "But there are French families," she said quietly.

He had had enough. Damn Miss O'Neil's lunch. Damn women. Throwing down his napkin, he stormed from the room.

Alcée Dugas couldn't find enough to talk about as they walked down the waterfront to the market. First the weather and the heat scorching acres of Jean Bergeron's corn, then Widow Pitre's new hound dog, now the price of steers. If René didn't know better, he would have thought the man was trying to slowly drive him insane.

"Have you managed to breathe all this time?" René finally asked his uncle.

"What?" Alcée asked, then began to recant his conversation with Father D'Arbyville, who was hoping to raise enough money by fall to build the new church.

René had suffered enough. Grabbing his lifetime companion who, thanks to being his mother's youngest brother, was only five years his senior, he shook him long enough to shut him up. His uncle indeed stopped talking, but his deep brown eyes staring out of a kind, yet stern, countenance made it clear he didn't approve of being rebuked.

"I know you're trying to help, but I'd rather you didn't," René said, attempting to smooth the wrinkles he had caused in the shoulders of Alcée's waistcoat.

Alcée sighed and followed René to the market. Catching up with long strides, Alcée muttered under his breath, "Just trying to get your mind off your *jolie blonde*."

René stopped abruptly, causing Alcée to practically trip over him. "She is not my *jolie blonde*," René said sternly and a bit too harshly. "And I'd prefer if we didn't talk about it again."

Before René could return to his hurried gallop across town, Alcée grabbed his arm. "My friend, I have known you all my life, have I not?"

René stood in silence, but refused to turn around.

"Have I not stood in the very shoes you stand in today?"

Again, René did not speak or turn around.

"It may be a long time before you forget her, but you will forget her, *mon ami*. She is an American and she will marry an American and that will be that. And soon you will go home to that wonderful family of yours and marry that Dupré girl your *maman* keeps writing you about."

The familiar pain stabbed at his heart, but René refused to grant it refuge there. "Of course I will," he answered.

René waited for Alcée to keep talking, to reassure him that

he would indeed forget, that time would heal his persistent need. Instead, Alcée put a fatherly arm about his shoulder and led him away from the market.

"How about I buy you a drink?"

A drink was what he needed, René thought. A good drunk would cure him of this incessant aching. But there were people waiting for him to return home with provisions, his widowed cousin and her children who needed food to eat that night. He had responsibilities.

"After dinner," he said. "Then I promise we will gaze at the bottom of the best bottle of rum."

"Bon," Alcée replied. "But I will hold you to it."

René knew this to be true. Alcée hated drinking alone. Many nights the two had spent visiting the pubs along the coastline of nearby Côte Blanche Bay.

Turning Alcée back toward the direction of town, this time René put his arm around the older man's shoulders in a paternal gesture. René was a good two or three inches taller than Alcée, even if he was twenty-nine and Alcée thirty-four.

"I promised Colette I would pick up some oysters for dinner," René said. "It will only take a minute."

The two entered the Franklin Market House and found it bustling for a Friday afternoon. Alcée leaned lazily against the front wall, tipping his hat down over his forehead while René pushed through the crowd to get to the counter. There were too many people in the tiny space, and the heat had made the air unbreatheable. Noticing that the selection was slim, René quickly decided he would purchase what he could and make a hasty retreat back to fresh air.

As he made his way to the newly opened space at the counter, he heard a familiar voice. Perspiration dripped over his eyes, clouding his view for an instant, but it didn't matter. He would have recognized that heavenly voice anywhere.

Searching for its owner, he spotted a pair of sky blue eyes

staring vacantly at the butcher. If René wasn't mistaken, Miss Richardson appeared as if she was ready to faint.

Before he could tap her elbow and inquire as to her health, the woman next to her bumped her basket on her way to the door and Amanda looked over in his direction. She appeared first glad to see him, then apprehensive. René moved to her side to study her further.

"Miss Richardson," he said with a tip of his hat, "are you well? You look very pale."

At first, Amanda acted as if she hadn't heard him speak. Then she nodded slowly and gazed over to a chair in the corner of the room.

"A glass of water, Johnson, if you please," he shouted to the man behind the counter. With an afterthought, he added, "And a pound of oysters."

René led Amanda to the chair and helped her sit down. He crouched down next to her to get a better look at her condition and, he admitted to himself, another glimpse of her angelic face.

Amanda's eyes were swollen and red, and her lips were trembling slightly. Had she been ill that morning? he wondered. He really hadn't noticed, he had been so focused on her father's hateful words and the realization that she had thought nothing of him after all this time.

"Are you ill?" he asked her.

Amanda shook her head and continued to study him. René stared back at a loss for words until the butcher broke the silence between them.

"Is she all right?" he asked, handing her the glass of water. "Perhaps you should take her outside for some fresh air."

"Yes," René answered, taking the opportunity to break the spell she was casting on him. "Good idea."

When the butcher was out of earshot, Amanda finally spoke. "Why did you call yourself an immigrant this morning?"

René couldn't believe his ears. Miss Richardson was on the verge of fainting and she wanted to know about his use of words? Then a hopeful thought entered his mind. Was she crying because he had slighted her that morning?

"Forgive me," he said, "but I was not myself this morning."

"Have I offended you in any way?" Amanda asked earnestly.

Hope that René had not dared imagine filled his heart. "No. I have behaved rudely because of something your father has said. It has nothing to do with you."

But it had everything to do with her, he reminded himself. Didn't her father make it clear *she* would have nothing to do with Acadians? Still, the concern in her voice made him doubt she could be so prejudicial, especially after all their warm conversations over her front picket fence.

"Why on earth did you have words with my father?" she asked.

The reality of her statement erased all of René's hope. Why on earth indeed would an Acadian such as himself be talking to the father of one of the most prominent American women in town? Discussing the weather and the history of Louisiana over rosebushes was one thing; asking her father for the right to court her was yet another.

"You're right," René answered sternly, rising. "Why would I have reason to talk to your father?"

Amanda quickly placed the glass at her feet and rose. The sudden movement drew all the blood from her face, and René thought for a moment she might faint for sure. Instead, she placed her hand lightly on his arm.

"I have offended you again," she said in a tone that touched his heart. "And I don't know why."

His lips moved to speak, but he could not find the right English words. Confused, he could only stare at the woman he had dreamed of relentlessly. He reached for her hand, but before he could place his fingers over hers, he heard a shrill female voice calling her from behind.

"Amanda," the voice practically yelled over the room's noise, "I have been looking for you everywhere."

René turned to find an impeccably dressed woman standing before him. After she had taken René in from foot to head, she grabbed Amanda's elbow and quickly led her away. As the two women disappeared through the market's front door, he heard the woman say, "What do you mean talking to that man? Don't you know he's a Cajun?"

René felt the bag of oysters being pressed into his hand and he heard Alcée mention bringing the wagon around, but nothing else seemed to register. The humid air pressed at his lungs and again his sight blurred from the sweat on his brow. He imagined himself drowning, standing straight up in the Louisiana heat. Drowning in the pain of a broken heart.

Henry Tanner adjusted his cravat and sleeves, knowing well his attire was as close to perfection as any man would come. His evening clothes had been meticulously chosen, down to the solid gold cuff links he had won in a New Orleans poker game. If he played his cards right tonight, he would soon be a very wealthy man.

Women were always willing to be seen on the arm of dapper Henry Tanner, he thought with a smile, and he was more than willing to offer his services. So when that trite Sally Baldwin had explained how poor Amanda Rose, the only daughter of rich Judge Richardson, was slowly entering spinsterhood, he knew his charms would come in handy. For both of them.

Amanda was hardly a beauty, but not unpleasing to the eye. What feminine attributes she possessed were enough to keep Henry entertained, he was sure. And if he should become bored with her, there were plenty of women to be had in New Orleans.

Yes, Amanda Rose Richardson would do nicely. Her father owned enough sugarcane to pay off Henry's mounting gambling debts, and then keep him in the manner to which he had been accustomed before losing his family's estate. Perhaps, he might even enter politics. The thought was enticing.

What had that insipid Baldwin girl said? Amanda wished for romance, perhaps he could be of some assistance? He knew what Amanda wanted, and needed, and it certainly wasn't another ball and a simple kiss in the moonlight. Tonight, he was going to show her what a real man was, and her father would pay handsomely for the lesson.

Chapter Two

Amanda stared at her image in the mirror, but failed to see the beauty in it despite the exquisite gown her father had ordered from New Orleans. Its petite blue flowers against a background of white accented Amanda's ivory complexion and sea-blue eyes. She carried the fitted garment at medium height, not short and stocky like many of the women in her father's family, nor tall and Junoesque like her mother. Her bosom filled out the bodice only adequately and her waist diverted in only slightly. The curves her mother had boasted were sadly lacking on her daughter.

Her mother. What a beauty she was, Amanda remembered with both fondness and envy. She had inherited nothing of her mother's dark, cosmopolitan looks, growing up instead ordinary and mediocre. She certainly didn't turn heads when she walked the streets of Franklin. Men didn't lurk outside her door waiting for her to emerge onto the street as they had for her mother when they lived in New Orleans. Amanda recalled how conversations would cease when her mother gracefully entered the room.

Perhaps her father was being kind when he said there had been no fit suitors. There must have been some Catholic Americans in town her father would have approved of. They just weren't interested in Plain Jane Richardson.

The Catholic church in Franklin was still in the planning stage, so Amanda traveled with Virginia every Sunday to Indian Bend to attend services at Immaculate Conception Chapel. From what she could remember, most of the other worshipers were French-speaking residents. She thought of the Wilsons, a prominent family from Pennsylvania, but their men were either too young or too old. The McKinleys had two eligible bachelor sons, but they were too poor for Father's approval.

Amanda sighed and sat down on the chaise longue. Was she so desperate that she had to count out the available men inside her head? Was marriage all that mattered, and not the man involved?

Of course, the man mattered, she reprimanded herself. She didn't wish to marry just for the sake of marriage. She desired romance, love, children, a family of her own. And a house where the sun shone in.

As if self-reproach and anxiety weren't enough for one evening, now guilt was showing its familiar head. She hated herself for wanting to leave her father, but she couldn't help admitting she desperately wanted to rid herself of her suffocating circumstances. If only he would talk to her. If only they could put the scandal behind them. Then maybe, in time, her father would heal his broken heart.

"Amanda," Virginia called from the hallway as she did every night before retiring. "Can I get you anything?"

Amanda forced herself to breathe. "No, thank you, Gin," she answered to the closed door. "I shall turn in myself."

"Very good," she heard Virginia say, and then heard her

door close at the end of the hallway. Amanda would wait ten more minutes and then quietly leave the house.

Sally had been quite thorough in her instructions. Henry Tanner would meet Amanda at the nearby corner, waiting inconspicuously in his carriage underneath the broken street-light. He would escort her to the ball, where Sally assured Amanda he would be attentive, then drive her home later that evening.

It seemed harmless—except for the silly part about feigning headaches. Amanda was to flirt with the man during the dances, then announce she had a headache and wished to be driven home early. Sally assured Amanda that Tanner would know this was a code for wanting to be kissed.

How she knew this was a mystery to Amanda. When did Sally Ann Baldwin learn such things? She was always on the arm of Jeffrey Trowbridge or Peter Rogers, and Amanda doubted either one would dare take advantage. But in a few months Sally would marry one of the richest sugar planters in the region, so obviously she knew something about courting men.

Amanda dreaded the pretense, the childish games women played, but she wanted her kiss nevertheless. She would attempt to flirt with the man, and if she felt inclined, complain of a headache. If the ball proved enjoyable, however, she saw no reason to cut the evening short. Perhaps Tanner would kiss her on the ride home regardless.

Checking to make sure Virginia had indeed gone to sleep, Amanda ventured into the hall. Virginia's light had been extinguished, so Amanda continued down the stairs and out to the back porch. Exiting the house to the deserted street, she made out a buggy lingering underneath a darkened area. Her heart beating dramatically in her chest, she fought the desire to return to the safety of her home.

No, she thought. *I can't live inside this darkened cave any longer.*

"Forgive me, Father," she said softly to herself. "I will never defy your wishes again, I promise." Taking a deep breath of the humid, but slightly cooler, night air, Amanda forced herself through the back gate and toward the waiting buggy.

Amanda met Tanner's carriage, entering cautiously while he gallantly kissed her hand and offered her a seat a bit too close for polite company. The driver bolted the horses to action, but they never made it to the Franklin Exchange. While Tanner romanced Amanda with Shakespearean sonnets, distracting her from the scenery, his servant raced the carriage out of town. They were a good mile from Franklin when Amanda became wise to his actions.

"You didn't really want to go to the ball," Tanner said, drawing uncomfortably near. "I know what you want. Your friend told me all about it, and I will be more than happy to be of service. After a quick visit to your father, you and I will have everything we desire."

He started kissing her then, the one thing Amanda had hoped for when she secretly left the house, but his kisses were anything but romantic. Tanner thrust his mouth upon hers, and his hands grabbed at her waist, pulling her hard against him. Amanda fought him, pounding his chest with her fists, pushing his advances away. When it became clear to him that she would not relent, he angrily shoved her to the side of the carriage.

"Damn you, woman," he shouted. "Don't tell me this is not exactly what you had hoped for."

Amanda started crying, and begged him to turn the carriage around. Instead, Tanner urged the driver on toward Port Cocodrie, where the small seaside town would conceal them until he found her father and demanded a payment in return for their marriage.

"He'll never allow it," Amanda said between sobs. "You'll never get a penny."

Tanner only laughed. "He'll pay me what I want, even at the thought of his lovely daughter marrying his poor overseer. After all, we don't want a scandal, do we?"

Amanda knew then she was trapped. A single woman out of town in the middle of the night was ruined. She could not return without a husband or risk losing her good reputation forever. Even if she managed to escape from Tanner and get back to Franklin by other means, God only knew how long that would take. Arriving home by morning's light would be disastrous. Someone was sure to see her.

As the hours and miles dragged on, Amanda's hope faded. By the time they reached Port Cocodrie, Amanda lost all consciousness of time and place. Tanner purchased a room at the local inn, and left her there while he traveled to Berwick in search of her father.

Amanda paced the room for what seemed like hours trying to fathom what to do. She prayed endlessly, begging God to send an answer. All she received were drunken shouts from the nearby tavern.

If only she could reverse time and start the day over, she thought. If only she were standing in the front garden once more, cutting roses as she did every day, waiting for her friend to turn the corner and recount more tales of his Acadian family. Amanda stopped pacing and sat down on the bed, defeated. What would René Comeaux think of her now, she wondered, and she felt as if her heart would break. She valued their friendship and knew he would no longer respect her.

Could she blame him? She had wantonly walked into the arms of a gambler against the wishes of her father, secretly meeting him in the middle of the night, hoping the awful man would grace her with a kiss.

She would never forgive herself. And her father would banish her from his life forever.

Not knowing what else to do, and fearing Tanner's return, Amanda left the room and wandered down to the docks. She found a quiet spot with a bench, and decided that it was as good a place as any for God to grant her a pardon. "Please," she prayed earnestly, "send me an answer."

The dark brown rum left quite a satisfying trail down the back of René's throat. A good drink was definitely what he needed. He signaled the waiter for another round.

"Slow down," Alcée said with a smile. "We just got here."

"And it took us two hours to do so," René snapped. "I don't understand why we had to ride all this way to enjoy a bottle of rum."

Alcée shook his head as if the logic was lost on his nephew. "We enjoy ourselves tonight, maybe find a woman or two. Then we pick up the supplies at the port tomorrow morning. Michael promised the supplies would be waiting for us by sunrise."

"At sunrise, the horses will need exercise." René adored his uncle and took his advice to heart, but his lack of business sense irritated him.

"I told you T-Emile will do it," Alcée said, visibly upset that René had continued their argument.

"The Vaughn horse hasn't been eating well," René insisted. "I promised Jack I would look after him myself."

"I explained all this to T-Emile and he knows what to feed him," Alcée said, slamming his glass a bit too hard on to the table. "It's all taken care of."

"T-Emile is a boy, Alcée. I don't feel comfortable leaving the horses in his hands."

"You don't feel comfortable leaving anybody with your precious horses."

René knew he had insulted his uncle, but Alcée's constant demands to let others do more of the chores angered him. René and Alcée had built the Franklin horse stables and racetrack years before, but it was René who had turned it into a money-making operation. The area's horse owners trusted René to take care of their investments, and he never disappointed. He exercised the horses daily at sunrise, managed the stables, oversaw the races and meticulously kept the betting books. René was the chief reason Alcée, his cousin Colette and her children were living as well as they were. It was René's handling of last year's fall races that had brought in enough money to buy the neighboring ranch and house that the family lived in. It was René's keen business eye that had enabled them to purchase cattle and several acres of sugarcane land.

Which was precisely why he had moved to Franklin in the first place. He and Alcée had envisioned the racetrack as a source of entertainment for the incoming Americans, and their foresight had proven fruitful. The new gregarious residents had eagerly embraced horse racing, and Acadians and French Creoles traveled across the entire Bayou Teche region for a chance at the Comeaux/Dugas racetrack, including a few hardy souls from New Orleans. Even Porter Neese, one of the prominent, wealthy residents of Franklin, began breeding English racers to try his luck at the track. René rented stable space to the horse owners, charged entry fees for the races, awarded purses to the winners from the gambling revenues and kept the remaining funds for himself.

Alcée enjoyed the business at first, and was equally thrilled at its success. After a few years had passed, however, he became restless and talked of returning home to Loreauville, a small town miles up the bayou near the French Creole city of St. Martinville. The Comeaux and Dugas families lived in Loreauville, and the two planned to make enough money to improve their families' *vacheries,* or cattle ranches, then return home.

Since their arrival in Franklin, each of the family estates had been enlarged and more cattle purchased. But René didn't wish to return. Making money intoxicated him. Counting out the American dollars after every race was too much of a temptation to resist. He had to continue. A few more years and they would be wealthy beyond their wildest dreams. Why couldn't Alcée see that?

"Please, Alcée, let's not argue about this again," René said, suddenly feeling very tired. "Let's have a few drinks and go home. We can send T-Emile over in the morning to pick up the supplies."

"My friend," Alcée began, his voice already thickening from the effects of the rum. "You're not listening."

René tossed back his glass of rum and slowly counted to five in his head. He didn't want to have this conversation again, especially tonight, but he didn't want to further insult his uncle.

"You work too hard," Alcée continued, motioning for the waiter to return with another round. "Life is too short to be spent working endlessly. Have we not everything we ever wanted? Isn't it time to say enough and go home?"

When René didn't answer, Alcée leaned forward so his words would only be heard at their table. "There are prettier girls in Loreauville."

René slammed the glass on the table, causing most of the pub's visitors to look over. Hastily grabbing his coat, he headed for the door.

"Where are you going, *mon ami,*" Alcée asked, sounding worried. "Let us talk about it."

Pulling the store-bought waistcoat over his *cotonnade* shirt and decorated *carmagnolle,* which his mother had lovingly created with homegrown cotton and hours of spinning and weaving, René silently headed for the bay. As much as he loved his uncle, he couldn't bear talking about the business another minute. More importantly, he couldn't bear talking about *her*.

He walked pensively down to the waterside, leaving behind the lights and noise of the Port Cocodrie establishments. There, at the water's edge, sat the fishing boats, pirogues and skiffs used daily in collecting the bounty of the Gulf waters and carrying supplies into the heartland of the Louisiana prairie along the sleepy Bayou Teche. The boats sang a rhythmic cadence as the waves brushed against them. The night was absent a moon, but the thousands of stars lit up the sky and their reflection illuminated the bay.

René pushed his hands inside his trouser pockets and rested his right boot against a cypress knee and his shoulder against the trunk. The solitude of the night comforted him and he felt the rum warming his veins. For the first time that day, he started to relax.

Gazing down toward the water, he realized he was not alone. A solitary figure sat on a nearby bench, seemingly mesmerized by the water's repeating motions. René realized the person was a woman by her delicate posture and the sounds of what seemed to be weeping.

He decided to be of service, in case the woman needed assistance, and headed down to the water's edge. As he quietly made his way toward the bench, the woman's features slowly became visible. There, in the soft starlight of the humid Côte Blanche Bay night, sat the woman he had been dreaming of relentlessly for the past few weeks.

Amanda watched the small, constant waves washing up on the shore at her feet, but she comprehended nothing, paralyzed by fear and the overwhelming feeling of being completely out of control of her situation. All she could do was numbly watch the repetitive motions of the dark, solemn water.

She didn't know how long she had been sitting there when the voices inside her mind again urged her to take action. She must think about what had happened, what was going to happen. She must find a solution to the horrible circumstances that had befallen her.

Amanda remembered the optimistic advice Virginia had given her when she came to live with the Richardsons, the week after her mother had left for Paris. "There is never a problem without a solution," Virginia had told her, gently stroking her hair and wiping away her tears. And until this moment, Amanda had found that always to be true.

She had learned to live without a mother's guidance. She had adapted herself to the American settlement of Franklin, doing without the French food and culture of her native New Orleans. She had comforted her father, helped him with his work and avoided all mention of everything that reminded him of his wife.

Was that why she was sitting here at Côte Blanche Bay, the dark body of water that emptied into the nearby Gulf of Mexico? Did her desire to move beyond her mother's scandal and into a family of her own blind her to the kind of man Henry Tanner was?

"God help me," she prayed. "I don't know what to do."

For not the first time that day a voice stirred her from her thoughts. A warm friendly voice boasting of its French heritage awakened her from her lethargy.

"Miss Richardson?"

Turning around, Amanda found René Comeaux standing before her.

"Miss Richardson?" René said again, startled to see her sitting in the dark at the base of the deserted dock. "What are you doing in Port Cocodrie?"

When Amanda didn't answer, René hurriedly sat down next to her, trying to examine her in the dim light. "Are you ill?" he asked, picking up her hand as if to check for life. "Are you hurt in any way?"

Again Amanda refused to answer.

"Are you with your father?" René continued. "Is he here?"

Amanda swallowed hard and shook her head. René stared back, at a loss for what to do, watching her eyes for a sign. Something was terribly wrong, but how could he discover what it was when she sat before him in shock?

"Tell me, *mon amour,*" he whispered gently as his thumb softly stroked her small hand lying placidly in his.

Something he said awakened Amanda, and tears began to replace her vacant stare. As a lone teardrop fell upon her cheek, she whispered so quietly he almost didn't make out the words. "I have done something terrible," she said.

"How could that be, *cher?*" René asked, not believing her capable of doing anything wrong, except perhaps refusing his hand. The pain of their earlier meeting returned, but his concern for her instantly sent it away.

"I am in a great deal of trouble," Amanda answered, again so quietly he wasn't sure he'd heard right.

René tightened the hold on her hand. "Why don't you tell me why you're here."

Tears began to fall, and René knew Amanda was fighting back a sob. "I am here with a man," she began. "He has gone off in search of my father so we will be married."

René felt his breath leaving him, and he dropped her hand back into her lap. So, she loved another man. Why hadn't he figured that out, after all the questions he had asked others about Judge Richardson's daughter? Until now, no one had ever mentioned it, not even her father. Perhaps her father had not approved, which was probably why Amanda had eloped with the bastard.

The pain gripping his heart was more than he could stand. René forced himself to look away. He couldn't bear gazing into the azure eyes that had haunted him so for the past few weeks, knowing they would never be his.

"He has compromised me," Amanda said in between the waves breaking the lonely silence.

Suddenly, the meaning of her words became clear, and René turned back to find Amanda sinking back into a state of shock. "What did you say?" he asked her, but she had tightly wrapped her arms around herself and stared off into the night.

"Amanda," René said, grasping her arms with such a force that she immediately stared back at him in alarm. He never would have dreamed of using her first name, but the gesture had made a difference. She could hear him. She was paying attention.

"Tell me what happened," René began. "Has he hurt you in any way?"

"No," she softly said, seeming to grasp his meaning.

"Then how has he compromised you?"

Amanda gazed up at her friend's caring brown eyes and wondered why the tall Acadian thought so well of her. She had always heard the Acadians were private people, living in clusters of their own kind and avoiding rich Americans like herself. After all the mistreatment his people had experienced from the British, it was no wonder they distrusted authority and kept to themselves. But René had become her friend. And despite everything she had just told him, he was still here, hoping to help, giving her encouragement like a big brother. Suddenly, she felt very safe.

"He brought me here against my will," she told him, wanting desperately for René to blame Tanner and not herself, even though she knew she was primarily to blame. "He has gone to Berwick in search of my father, to make my father pay him for the honor of marrying me and saving me from ruin."

"Is there anything I can do?"

Amanda shook her head. "I have searched my soul praying for an answer, but there is none. Either way, I have lost the only family I have. I cannot go home, my reputation is ruined. My father will certainly disown me for the scandal. If Tanner speaks to my father, he may pay him the money and we will marry, but my father will never speak to me again."

"Tanner?" René asked, disdain clearly showing in his voice. " 'Enry Tanner?"

Under ordinary circumstances, Amanda would have smiled at the way René eliminated consonants in English too difficult to pronounce, but no matter how the name was spoken, it sent chills up her spine.

When Amanda didn't answer, René let loose a series of French expletives. "Do you have any idea who he is? What kind of reputation he has?"

"I heard rumors."

"Rumors?" he practically shouted at her, running his fingers through his fine brown hair. "*Mon dieu.* Forgive me, my dear, but you have played with fire tonight. The man is notorious with women. There is word around town that he owes some powerful men a lot of money from gambling. He has been banned from the racetrack because no one can trust him."

Guilt settled in around Amanda's heart. Her father always considered her naive, and she resented the label. She knew now she wasn't just naive, she was remarkably stupid.

Tears began to emerge, and Amanda wondered how there could be any water left inside her. "I am ruined," she cried.

René abruptly stood and began to pace the waterfront. "I will take you home," he said.

"It's no use. Father will beat us to Franklin."

"How is that possible if he is in Berwick tonight?"

"Berwick," Amanda announced, remembering why the name had sounded so strange. "Tanner said he was going to

Berwick. My father changed his business meeting this morning. He went to Charenton with plans to return in the morning.''

René sat down next to her and looked into her eyes eagerly. ''That's good,'' he said, almost smiling. ''That will at least buy us some time. Berwick is in the other direction.

''If Tanner is going to Berwick,'' he continued, ''we will go toward Franklin and be home by midmorning, arriving there before Tanner. When your father returns, we will explain to him what has happened. He will have to understand.''

''We will be seen coming into town and he will blame you. He will think *you* have compromised me,'' Amanda said quietly.

René looked as if she had offended him yet again.

''We'll explain,'' he said sternly.

''He'll have you hanged,'' Amanda said almost to herself. Saving her reputation was one thing, but no one crossed her father, especially when it came to his daughter and especially when it concerned a Frenchman.

René self-consciously adjusted his shirt collar and frowned. ''There has to be a way.''

''I can see none,'' Amanda answered, relegating herself to failure and feeling the tears falling on her cheeks once again.

René studied the horizon for several moments as if searching for meaning behind the dark bay waters. Several silent minutes passed between them, except for the boisterous singing of a drunken man leaving the pub. Amanda wished with all her might that she could remain in that position, never leaving René's side, never returning to the harsh reality that awaited her.

Suddenly, René's countenance changed. He turned and gazed intently upon her as if something miraculous had come to him.

''What is it?'' she asked.

René reached down and softly grasped Amanda's hand. His

eyes were not as gentle, and Amanda feared what he might suggest.

"I want you to stop crying," he instructed sternly like a father. "I want you to understand perfectly what I am about to ask you."

His tone unnerved her, but she shook her head in agreement. She trusted him.

"You must also promise to listen to everything I have to say. Promise?"

Amanda drew a deep breath to try to dispel the tears. She had to concentrate. "I promise."

A few moments passed before René stated his intentions. Amanda hardly breathed while she waited for his instructions.

"There is a way out of this," he began. "If you were to marry me instead."

Chapter Three

Was it love or revenge that made René propose? Surely, he adored Amanda Richardson, but he had to admit the thought of returning to Franklin to tell the Judge his daughter had become a Comeaux overnight was too much a temptation to refuse. He couldn't wait to see the look on the face of the old American, the same one who had determinedly decided his daughter would never marry a Frenchman.

In the end it would solve Amanda's problems, and keep her from marrying that bastard Tanner.

First, he had to convince Amanda. She sat there staring at him with eyes the size of picayunes.

"You must hear me out," René insisted when it appeared as if Amanda would protest. "You have promised."

Amanda remained silent, her eyes never leaving his face. René began to feel like a guilty man being pierced by the eyes of his victim. He again drew his hands through his hair and looked away.

"I'm a devoted bachelor, Miss Richardson," he began. "I live with my uncle and my cousin's family. I work at the racetrack day and night, every day of the week. I have never had time for a family."

He glanced back to see how she was reacting to his explanation, but her face never changed expression. She appeared to be in shock once again. René's feeling of guilt grew heavier.

"My home would be yours," he said, less confident than before. "I make a very good living. You will never want for anything. My family and I will take very good care of you."

Amanda must have begun to absorb the meaning of his words because she turned away pensively. René began to doubt she would accept. After all, their nationalities were miles apart.

"As I said before, I am hardly at home. You will never have to worry . . ."

Amanda looked up at him when he failed to find the proper English words. Taking her hand in his once more, René added quietly, "We will be married in name only. I will not ask anything of you that you do not wish. We could have a family later when you become more accustomed to being married to me."

A long silence befell the couple, and René thought he heard the pub owner calling for last rounds. He wondered if Alcée had become worried over his absence. In all probability, Alcée was half asleep at his table, one arm hugging the bottle of rum.

"What about you?" Amanda asked quietly, breaking the solitude.

René frowned at the question. Was she referring to his intentions?

"Do you not wish to marry someone else?" she clarified.

The question almost caused René to laugh out loud. The only woman he loved, the only one he dreamed of marrying, was sitting before him. "There is no other," he said with a grim smile. "I work too much to be bothered with such things."

He wanted to dispel any worries she had over his intentions. He wanted to assure her he would be the utmost gentleman as her husband. "Are we not friends?" he asked.

Amanda nodded.

"And don't friends help each other when one is in trouble?"

When she smiled, René knew he was winning her over. He could read it in her eyes. Amanda was relenting.

"But I am Catholic," she inserted.

This time, René did laugh. He knew the Richardsons were Catholic. He had seen Amanda in church when Colette had talked him into attending an occasional Mass.

"I think I can live with that, *cher*," he said still smiling.

Amanda appeared to have realized her mistake, and smiled slightly again. "Of course," she said softly, looking down at her hands.

Once more René feared he was losing her. "Father Breaux lives on the other side of the bay, at Bayou Attakapas. He could marry us tonight and we will be able to arrive in Franklin by noon tomorrow. I will then approach your father and tell him we have eloped."

"Do you think he will believe you?" Amanda asked, not looking up.

René grimaced at the thought of the last meeting between himself and the Judge. "I believe I can convince him that I talked you into it."

Amanda would never have thought of eloping with him under normal circumstances, René thought bitterly to himself, and the familiar pain flooded his heart. Perhaps this wasn't a good idea after all. Plus, he had failed to consider what his mother or Alcée would think or even where he would put his new bride. In the long run, could he live loving a woman as intensely as he did Amanda, knowing she would never love him in return?

He tried to shake off the painful premonition. "When I meet

your father, I'll make sure there's no rope handy," he said with a wry smile.

"All right."

René stared down into the eyes that had been his undoing, wondering if she was referring to the rope or the marriage.

"I will," Amanda said calmly, staring back.

"Are you sure?"

"Yes," she said with a confidence that gave him hope. She wasn't faltering; she knew exactly what she was doing.

"*Bon*," René said. "Then we should leave as soon as possible."

Alcée drew a deep breath as the Franklin courthouse's bright white marble, shining in the early morning light, came into view. Only a few more miles and he would be home. Their farmhouse and racetrack lay on the outskirts of town in the bend of the bayou, the home a simpler dwelling than the elaborate monstrosities lining the street he now rode. René had always admired such wealth, but to Alcée the enormous houses and plantations represented products of slave labor, a peculiar American institution he openly despised.

René echoed his feelings on slavery, but never expressed his views to *les americains*. Bad business, he said, to cause rifts with clients. Better to keep quiet on matters of politics and religion, René had told him. Better to simply do business with the Americans, and not get involved in their private affairs.

Alcée grimaced at the last thought. Even with all his best intentions of staying clear of the flame, René had thrown himself full force into the fire.

Old Man Wilkinson waved from his porch as Alcée cantered past, beckoning for him to ride over. Alcée knew what he wanted. Wilkinson fancied his horse the fastest in the parish, even though the poor mare was half blind and couldn't beat a mule. René always entered the horse in races whenever Wilkinson asked. As long as the old man was willing, René said, he wouldn't mind taking his money.

"Not today, Wilkinson," Alcée called to him from the street, urging his horse on to a faster pace.

The old man stood up as if to protest, but Alcée had no time to lose. He had more important problems on his hands than an old man's money. After he'd received René's message in Port Cocodrie, he couldn't get back to town fast enough.

When the two-story farmhouse finally came into view, Alcée spotted Colette standing outside, twisting her apron anxiously. For an instant, Alcée feared the worst. Had Judge Richardson, in an emotional outburst over the fate of his daughter, hurt or killed his nephew? Alcée felt the blood rushing to his chest, knocking the air from his lungs. He would never forgive himself if anything happened to René. He had promised his sister he would look after the boy. Even though René dealt better in business with the Americans, Alcée knew how vulnerable love made its captive. He should have been more attentive to his brokenhearted friend and less enticed by a damned bottle of rum.

Before the horse could come to a halt, Alcée jumped down and grabbed the reins. In French he asked, "Where is he?"

"Gone to town to speak to the girl's father," Colette answered, visibly shaken.

"I'll follow him," Alcée said, turning the horse back around and remounting. "Just in case anything happens."

"What will I do with her?" Colette asked, grabbing Alcée's shirtsleeve anxiously. "I can't speak English."

Alcée stared at the second story where four bedrooms were located. Colette and her children had moved in with the two bachelors when her husband had drowned in a boating accident years ago. René and Alcée had welcomed Colette and her family into their business venture, and were thankful for her home-cooked meals. The large farmhouse provided the family ample space, including a *garçonnière,* or attic quarters for the young boys. While Colette occupied one side of the upper floor, René and Alcée slept in the other two rooms.

"Put my things in your extra room," Alcée answered, still refusing to believe his nephew had married the girl. "Tell Miss Richardson, or whatever her name is now, that she can rest in my room."

Colette stared at Alcée as if she failed to comprehend the instructions.

"Just put her in René's room," he finally said. "He got us into this mess; let him deal with her."

With a quick kick to the horse's flanks, Alcée headed quickly back towards town.

Amanda couldn't decide who was more nervous or afraid, she or the cousin René quickly introduced as Colette. The sweetly plump, petite woman had actually turned white when René explained that he had married Judge Richardson's daughter. He'd used those words, she was sure of it. Her French may have lain dormant for ten years, but some of the words were beginning to come back to her.

It had sounded as if he were bragging, she thought, then instantly reprimanded herself for thinking such a thing of the man who had rescued her from a lifetime with Henry Tanner. Now the rest of her life loomed ahead of her, tied forever with Monsieur René Comeaux, the local Acadian who ran the horse track. Although she didn't fear René, the future appeared bleak and uncertain.

For the thousandth time, Amanda wished she could turn back time and start anew. A little more than twenty-four hours earlier her father had given her the exquisite evening gown she still wore. Virginia had wished her well by bringing her breakfast in bed. About this time yesterday she had stood in the front garden picking a half-dozen yellow roses for the lunchtime table, wondering why her friend René Comeaux was taking so long.

If only her evening with Henry Tanner would disappear and René would be standing again on the other side of her fence.

Looking around at her new home, Amanda felt the pain settle again in her heart. *This is what I wanted,* she thought grimly. *This is what I wished for. Now I'm married to René Comeaux.*

Colette must have sensed that Amanda was about to faint, for she was instantly at her elbow, urging her into a nearby seat. The woman began to talk incessantly, as if she hoped additional French words would be more comprehensible than none. Amanda knew she was asking for approval, but through the haze of exhaustion nothing made sense.

Finally, Colette pointed to the ceiling, then leaned her head to the side while placing her hands against her cheek and closing her eyes. Amanda smiled faintly when she realized the woman was asking her if she wanted to rest.

Amanda knew the proper response, but nodded instead. Then she accepted Colette's outstretched hand and followed her to the rear of the house where the staircase to the second floor was located. Amanda had heard of Acadians building staircases on the outside of their homes to save space on the inside.

The second floor was situated much like the first, with two rooms on either side of the center wall, which housed the fireplaces. On the second floor, however, one had to walk on the outside balcony to get to the other side.

"Alcée," Colette said as they stood in the first room.

Amanda nodded, realizing that this must be the uncle's room.

After they walked through a doorway leading to the next room, Colette announced, "René."

Again, Amanda nodded and glanced around her husband's sparsely furnished, yet extremely neat, bedroom. A massive dark mahogany bed occupied the center, with a mosquito net hanging from its canopy. Towards the front door, a small chest of drawers sat underneath the opened window that allowed a small breeze to enter. A comfortable-looking chair, next to a pile of books on the floor, completed the room's furnishings. The scattered books appeared out of place in the organized setting, and Amanda wondered if they were an indication of René's personality while the room's cleanliness was a result of Colette's. She made a mental note to check the books' titles.

What Amanda noticed most of all were the light, lace curtains billowing in the morning breeze as if welcoming her home. The twisted majestic oak trees surrounding the house fought off the intense summer sun, yet the house radiated a soft, diffused light. She inhaled the fresh air circulating through the open windows and doors, and felt rejuvenated despite her lack of sleep. As scared as Amanda felt standing in the strange man's bedroom, her heart felt ten times lighter. Somewhere in the deep recesses of her soul a voice told her all would be well.

Colette pointed to the bed and made a hasty retreat, closing the door behind her. The door to the front balcony remained open and air continued to stream through, teasing the sweaty curls gracing Amanda's forehead.

Amanda removed her wrap before cautiously sitting down on René's moss-filled mattress. It was then she noticed the painting. Above the fireplace hung a portrait of seven people, two seated in the center who appeared to be the parents of the group, with five grown children, who resembled each other, surrounding them. René stood smiling in the back, the tallest and oldest of the siblings. They were all smiling, Amanda noticed, one large happy family.

Suddenly Amanda felt fatigue creep back into her bones, and she lay down on the bed, facing away from the smiling people whose culture and language were so distant from her own. She had always envied people who came from large families. Now it was possible she'd lost her father, her closest and, as far as she was concerned, only relative. Her father had cut them off from her mother's family a long time ago. Her Protestant Virginia relatives were elderly aunts and uncles who didn't take kindly to Catholic children born from scandalous women. They had been little more than polite when she had boarded at the school near their homes. Only when she had agreed to attend church with them had they seemed vaguely interested.

Again, the images of the past few hours came flooding back—the conversation with her father over her Catholic upbringing and the lack of proper suitors; René being so disagreeable at the gate; the crowded market; and Tanner's intrusive mouth upon hers.

How ironic life was. She had wished for a kiss, and a kiss she'd received. But she'd never dreamed it would be one standing in front of a priest.

Amanda gently touched her fingers to her lips, and vividly remembered how René had gently kissed them after she had said her vows. He'd been the epitome of a gentleman throughout the ceremony, holding her right hand tightly in front of them and placing another arm around her waist to support her. He'd translated the priest's words when she failed to comprehend them, and when the priest said his final words, René had turned toward her and ever so cautiously leaned over and brushed his lips to hers.

It had been the most exciting thing she had ever experienced.

Amanda rolled over and gazed up into her husband's eyes staring at her from above the fireplace. His eyes, she determined, were her favorite feature. Although his broad shoulders, tall stance and feather-soft brown hair were enticing from a woman's point of view, Amanda preferred his eyes above all else. They spoke of a warm, friendly personality, sparkling like firecrackers when he broke into a smile. Those deep brown eyes her *grandmère* used to call "French eyes" seemed to announce that she was safe within their reach. Feeling their presence blanketing her, she drifted off to sleep.

It seemed that only minutes had passed when she heard two horses approach and the raised voices of two angry men, even though Amanda knew the sun had reached its zenith and was now cascading down towards the western horizon. René's voice she recognized immediately, but the other, throatier voice was a new one. It was he who argued heatedly with René, his voice reaching up to the second floor.

The French words came fast and furious, much too quickly for Amanda's unpracticed ear. She made out a few words and phrases, however, such as "imbecile," "reckless" and "you should have known better than to marry an American."

Had René told his relatives what happened? Were they critical of his actions regarding Henry Tanner, or just marrying an American girl in particular? She didn't imagine they would be happy about either.

Amanda quietly crept down the stairs, anxious to learn of René's meeting with her father. She peered into the living room until René and the other man came into view. René stood pensively at the fireplace, one hand grasping the marble mantel, the other hand inside his trousers pocket while a boot rested on a fireplace log. His jaw tightened at the other man's words and his face exhibited a diligent attempt to remain calm despite the anger brewing at his temple. Every few moments his hand balled into a fist, then relaxed as if he was fighting the urge to strike something or someone.

Amanda doubted René was listening. He seemed to be enduring the conversation more than heeding the other man's words. She suspected it was a repeat performance.

Staring at the now-worried brown eyes that had not seen sleep in two days, Amanda felt a desire to rush into René's arms and hold him tight, to shelter him from the unkind words this relative was inflicting upon him. Didn't this man realize what René had done, how noble he had been to marry a woman he barely knew for the mere sake of saving her reputation?

As if René read her mind, he looked up and noticed Amanda standing at the threshold. He stared emotionless at her for several moments before the other man realized her presence.

"Alcée," René announced calmly when the other man stopped talking. "Let me introduce my wife, Amanda."

The blood retreated from Amanda's face and she felt her heart quicken when the slightly older man turned. His gaze was critical and harsh.

"Madame Comeaux," he said with a short, stiffly polite bow, his voice colored with cynicism.

René rubbed his temples, visibly irritated that Alcée had made the introduction unpleasant. Amanda extended her hand to Alcée in an attempt to ease the tension between the two men. "It is a pleasure to meet you, Monsieur Dugas. I have heard a lot about you."

Alcée eyed her hand, then cautiously accepted it. "When did you hear these tales, between midnight and morning?"

His tone unnerved her, but Amanda fought to keep her ground. If René could take the beating for her honor, then she at least must stand the fight. "I have heard quite a few tales about the famous Comeaux and Dugas horse track, sir. And René has talked about you quite often at my house."

"You mean outside your house, don't you, Miss Richardson? If I'm not mistaken, Acadians aren't allowed inside."

Before Amanda could fully digest the words, Alcée angrily passed her on his way out the door. She took a deep breath and gazed up at René for support. The deep eyes that had held laughter in the portrait upstairs stared at her with a solemn intensity.

"I take it the meeting with my father this morning didn't go well."

René laughed, which startled Amanda more than his brooding. "No," he said with a sad grin. "It didn't go well."

"What did he say?"

René looked off as if pondering the right words. "What didn't he say is more like it. Let's see. There was a part about me being a treasure hunter, I believe is the right expression. Wanting to marry you for your hordes of money or something to that extent. Oh, no, I've got it. I'm a 'swindler of an old man's money and his only daughter.' There was also a delightful speech about me ruining such a chaste woman and being a father's worst nightmare. Did I mention the part where he insulted my family? No, I don't think I did."

"René," Amanda said, reaching out to touch his arm in an offer of sympathy, but he instantly moved away. "I'm sorry," she whispered.

"Sorry?" he asked, his voice rising. "Sorry for falling for that fool Tanner or for having to marry me?"

The guilt and shame over her actions resumed its ugly hold on Amanda's heart. "I'm sorry for hurting you," she forced out, hoping the words wouldn't turn into the sobs fighting to be released.

René grabbed his hat from off the mantel and straightened. "Well, it's too late for that."

When he placed the hat on his head, Amanda knew the conversation was over. Panic seized her. "Where are you going?" she asked.

"I've lost almost a day." René said. "There's work to be done."

"Then let me help."

René smiled cynically. "At a racetrack? Now what would the Judge say to that?"

"Please don't leave me," she pleaded.

"You won't be alone long. Your father's on his way. He wants to make sure you're well, that I haven't chained you to

the altar or beaten you into submission. Perhaps he's afraid
I've put you to work shoveling manure at the stables.''

"René . . .''

Pausing at the doorway, René turned, showing Amanda the
anger lurking beneath the surface. "I can stand being called
names. I can understand him thinking that an Acadian such as
myself might want to 'marry up.' I can even take his criticism
of my work. But I will never allow a man to belittle my family.
Do you understand?''

With those final words, René headed for the racetrack.

Alcée stormed into his bedroom and slammed the door. He
didn't know what made him angrier, his nephew's irresponsible
behavior or his own violent reaction to the news. He had always
been able to talk to René, always able to reason with him, work
things out. Instead, he'd unleashed a fury on his nephew he'd
never released before. When he'd learned René had approached
Judge Richardson regarding the elopement of his only daughter,
for the first time Alcée had imagined his beloved friend and
nephew in jeopardy. René gambling with his life so recklessly
had infuriated him.

Amanda was indeed pretty in a sweet sort of way. He could
see now why the boy had fallen in love with her. She had a
pleasant, cheerful, unpretentiousness about her that reminded
him of René. He could understand how the two had become
friends.

But marriage? They were cultures and worlds apart. Their
marriage had a slim chance of survival. Alcée could tell by the
confused look on Amanda's face that she didn't understand
French. Who was going to teach her the language? he wondered.
What would their children speak?

Alcée stopped pacing and sat on the edge of his bed. How
would she communicate with Marie, René's mother, and the

rest of their family? None of them spoke English, except for an expression or two.

As Alcée's heartbeat slowly returned to normal, he sighed. He was thankful René was all right. Amanda appeared unharmed as well. Perhaps, in time, they would work it all out.

A carriage approached the house, and Alcée moved toward the front balcony to see who was visiting. He watched Amanda walk toward the carriage apprehensively, standing a good yard or two away from its doors.

Who on earth? thought Alcée, until the doors opened and an angry Judge Richardson emerged. The two stood staring at each other in silence until the Judge raised his right hand and sent a scalding slap across his daughter's face.

Alcée jumped at the sight of the man striking his child. His first urge was to run to Amanda's side in case her father decided to harm her again, but he soon assessed that the worst was over. Her father began shouting and demanding answers, but Amanda stood still, much as René had when Alcée vented his anger. Alcée watched the blond head carefully, but it never flinched. Whatever anger or pain she was experiencing was carefully hidden away.

Finally, her father grabbed her by the shoulders, hoping to make her talk. Alcée again thought of descending the stairs, but his instincts warned against it. He would not let the Judge hurt Amanda, but he would equally not act in haste, causing more problems between the two families.

"Amanda Rose," he heard the Judge say almost in a pleading voice. "Tell me this is a mistake. Mistakes we can fix. I can have the marriage annulled in no time. Life will go on as before. It will be as if this nightmare never happened."

Amanda stared down at the ground by her feet, saying nothing. The opportunity was perfect, Alcée thought. All she had to do was agree and they would all go back to normal. Problem solved.

"And what about René?" Amanda asked.

"What about him?" the Judge answered between gritted teeth.

She looked up then, staring at her father proudly. "If I annul the marriage, René will be the laughingstock of town. He has a business to think of and a reputation. You're asking me to destroy everything he has built."

"What business? It's a horse track, for God's sake. No one's going to care if he failed at trying to marry into one of the most prominent families in town. People like him have nowhere else to go but up. They may laugh, but they'll soon forget it. He'll be free to marry one of his own kind."

"Like you did?" Amanda said, throwing her head back defiantly.

Alcée was surprised to see Judge Richardson flinch at the words. A look passed over his face that Alcée had never witnessed in the always solemn Judge. A look of vulnerability, perhaps. A hint of being human after all.

Alcée was equally surprised at Amanda's next words.

"I love René," she said with difficulty.

The Judge laughed cynically. "The hell you do."

"Why do you doubt it?"

"Because before this week René Comeaux never existed. If you had pined for the man and I had repeatedly refused, you might have done such a thing as elope. But you have never mentioned the man except for the fact that he greets you at the fence every once in a while."

"Every morning," Amanda inserted, which made the Judge pause momentarily.

"You never would have defied me," he insisted. "You always did as you were told."

"I turned twenty-one yesterday, or have you forgotten?"

The Judge removed his hat to wipe the sweat from his brow. "We said a lot of things yesterday, but nothing to incite you to this," he said, waving a hand with disgust toward the house. Alcée backed up a few steps, hoping he hadn't been seen. When the two resumed talking, he assumed he hadn't.

"Amanda, it's a simple procedure," the Judge pleaded. "You can come home with me now and all will be forgiven."

"At the expense of René."

"Damn René," he shouted. "He's a bloodsucker."

"No, Father," Amanda answered, lifting her chin bravely. "He's my husband. And I intend to keep it that way."

The two remained silent, again staring at each other in a war of wills. Judge Richardson, admitting defeat, slammed his hat back on his head and turned to enter the carriage.

"Don't expect my blessing or my support," he said without turning. "You will get neither."

Her resolve slipping, Amanda swallowed, then quietly said, "I would appreciate it if you would have Virginia pack my clothes for me and send them around. As it is, I have nothing to wear."

The Judge paused at the remark, but said nothing. He entered the carriage and motioned to the driver. The carriage bolted off toward the road.

Amanda stood silently, watching the carriage until it disappeared from sight. Alcée thought to go to her, but before he could reach the bottom floor, she was gone.

The emotions that raged inside her were dangerously close to the surface. Amanda knew she had to find a secluded spot soon before she lost all control.

Finally settling under the wide expanse of a live oak tree, far away from the house and its inhabitants, Amanda started to shake violently. At first the sobs seemed lodged inside her and all she could do was hug herself and rock slowly back and forth. Then, as if the pain manifested itself and rose up through her chest to freedom, she began to sob incessantly. She wrapped her arms around her knees, then buried her head inside her hands, but nothing relieved the choking emotions. All the guilt and fear of the past two days, coupled with her intense fatigue, were a weight upon her chest, dragging her down into an abyss of despair.

Amanda's hysterical sobbing drowned out all other sounds. She comprehended nothing but the relentless pain tearing at her heart. When the leather boots appeared at her feet and a gentle arm pulled her softly against his chest, all Amanda grasped was that God had taken pity on her and sent an angel to comfort her in her anguish.

"Go ahead and cry," she heard her angel say while he planted kisses on the top of her head. "I'm here."

Amanda buried her head into the soft cotton shirt and held onto her angel's lapel, fearing he might disappear as quickly as her former life had done.

"Things will turn out all right in time," the voice reassured her.

In between sobs, Amanda remembered René's image at the door and the haunting words her father had spoken. "But I have ruined your life," she whispered.

René laughed. "No, *mon ange*. My life has just begun."

The sun began to set when the sobs finally gave in to fatigue. René held Amanda close as she slept, softly stroking the blond curls from her forehead. When darkness settled around them like a soft quilt, René lifted Amanda into his arms and carried her to his bed. She slept peacefully now, but René couldn't find the strength to leave. After what seemed like an eternity, he left his wife's side and descended the stairs to try to make peace with his family.

Chapter Four

The pungent aroma of coffee entered Amanda's dreams, where she was again a small girl playing in the backyard of her New Orleans home. She could hear the kitchen servant singing *Mon Cher Papa,* a song they sang at birthday celebrations, and her mother joining in on the chorus, her distinct soprano voice rising above the others.

Her mother opened the back door and smiled down at Amanda, who immediately ran into her arms. When Amanda glanced up, expecting to find her mother's resplendent face and sublime smile, instead she found René gazing down at her. She then stood in the garden of her home on Main Street, and René peered at her from the street, his large planter's hat blocking the morning sun. He spoke French to her, words she understood, but when she opened her mouth to answer, the words refused to come.

It was then she woke up, remembering the house she now lived in and the man she had married the day before. She could hear Colette downstairs scolding the children, who were laughing, yelling and running up the stairs.

Remember, she instructed herself, *try to remember.*

The bedroom door burst open and a tow-headed boy Amanda figured to be about six years old bolted inside. When he realized Amanda was awake and staring at him, his courage faltered and he froze halfway to the bed.

"Bonjour," Amanda said cautiously.

The child instantly lost his nerve and ran out of the room as fast as he had entered. Colette threw him a stiff spank on the backside as he passed her on his way to the stairs.

Another child, this one about ten years old with curly auburn hair and deep brown eyes, peered around the corner, but Colette quickly dismissed him as well. Once Alcée's door to the back balcony was closed, Colette moved to Amanda's bedside, busily talking in French about what Amanda assumed was the impertinence of young boys.

When Amanda heard the word "cafe" mentioned, she almost leaped out of bed.

"I haven't had a decent cup of coffee in years," she told Colette in English before she realized her mistake. She attempted to recant the sentence in French, but failed miserably.

"Pardon," Amanda said to the petite woman. *"Ma français est trés mal."*

Colette immediately brightened at Amanda's admission about not knowing French well. "The sky is blue," she answered in English slowly and with pride.

Amanda smiled politely, but inwardly wondered how the two women were going to communicate. *Force yourself to remember,* she scolded herself. It had seemed so natural in her dream. The words had made perfect sense.

Colette grasped Amanda's arm good-naturedly and led her to the nearby dresser where a pitcher of water was placed. After she pointed to the pitcher, Amanda knew that Colette had brought her up some fresh water from the well so she could wash.

"*Merci,*" she told the polite woman.

Colette quickly moved to the door leading to the back balcony and pointed to a large object waiting there. When Amanda moved closer, she learned it was her trunk of clothes sent over by Virginia.

"*Merci,*" she said again, this time with added enthusiasm.

Colette nodded and began to push the massive trunk into her room. Amanda joined in, and within a few minutes the two women managed to maneuver it to the foot of the bed.

Again Colette mentioned something about coffee, and headed for the back stairs. The enticement of a cup of tangy, strong Louisiana coffee was too great. Amanda couldn't dress fast enough. Besides, she was enormously hungry.

When she entered the downstairs dining room, Alcée was seated at the table's head enjoying a plate of oranges, bread and what looked like a large cup of black coffee. He appeared to be about the same age as René, possibly a few years older, with little family resemblance, except for his deep brown eyes. Alcée didn't match René in height either, and his hair was much darker, his countenance more chiseled and defined. Yet Amanda sensed that Alcée, like his nephew, embraced a fondness for living, a *joie de vivre* that sparkled in his eyes when he smiled.

Unfortunately, Amanda had yet to see Alcée smile.

"Good morning," he announced sternly.

"*Bonjour,*" Amanda answered.

Alcée gazed up at her attempt at French, but eyed her suspiciously. "You don't speak French, do you?"

"I haven't in quite some time," she answered, wondering if she should sit down on her own or wait for him to invite her to dine with him. Alcée seemed to read her mind, and briefly stood while motioning for her to sit at his right.

"May I have a cup of coffee?" she asked meekly.

"*Bien sur,*" Alcée answered, then quickly added in English, "Of course." He called to Colette, who arrived smiling with a fresh pot, plus an overabundance of fruit and bread.

"René leaves early to attend to the horses at sunrise," Alcée explained. "We tend to the farm and have our breakfast here at the house."

"When does René eat?" Amanda asked, breaking off a piece of the baguette before her.

Alcée laughed. "He doesn't."

"But that's awful," Amanda said. "Every man should have a good breakfast prepared for him."

Amanda wondered if she had insulted Alcée, for he sent her a discerning look. "What did you mean, you haven't in quite some time?" he asked.

Amanda gazed at the black liquid Colette was pouring in front of her and wondered if there was sugar available. She had developed a taste for coffee as an adolescent, but it had been diluted with dollops of cream and locally grown sugar. "I spoke French as a child," she said.

Alcée leaned back in his chair and grabbed a sugar bowl from a nearby buffet. He handed it to Amanda, who smiled in thanks. "In New Orleans?" he asked.

"Yes, I grew up in New Orleans," Amanda said, grimacing at the memories so long hidden inside her. "My father was an intermediary between the French and American business communities."

"I had heard that, but I didn't believe it," Alcée said, sliding the creamer in her direction.

"Why not?"

"Because he is not what I'd call friendly to cultures other than his own," Alcée said dryly.

Amanda stirred in three teaspoons of sugar, despite Alcée's frown when she did so, then tentatively took a sip. The strong, hot coffee was every bit as wonderful as Amanda had remembered. She sighed and settled back into her chair. "My father has become rancorous over the years, but it has nothing to do with the French really. He's suffering from a broken heart."

Alcée put his cup down on the table and stared at her intently. "What do you mean, a broken heart?"

Amanda tried to think of the words in French, but stumbled through an English explanation instead. "He was in love, but then . . ."

"I know what a broken heart is," Alcée answered impatiently. "Why is he suffering from one?"

"I'm sorry. I wasn't sure you understood the metaphor." Apparently even a good night's sleep hadn't softened the chasm between René and his family. "My mother was a famous opera singer," she began. "She was extremely popular on both sides of the Atlantic. People came from miles around to see her perform. In New Orleans, she played at all the important theaters."

Amanda stared at her hands thoughtfully. "She was also breathtakingly beautiful."

When she paused, Alcée leaned forward. "Go on," he urged her.

"She quit singing to marry my father and rear me, but she must have missed the stage very much." The vision of her mother briskly walking out the front door that cold winter day returned, and Amanda felt as if the air had left her lungs.

"She left us to join the French Opera Company and, it was rumored, for another man, a Frenchman," she whispered. "Since then, my father would have nothing to do with the French. We left New Orleans for Franklin and he forbade us to speak French, speak of my mother or have anything in the house that reminded him of her. Even our French-speaking servants were dismissed. My housekeeper of the last ten years is Irish, and I have not been allowed to associate with the French families of Franklin.''

Amanda turned toward Alcée, softly placing a hand on his arm. ''But you must believe me, it has nothing to do with René or your family. He can't stand the thought of anything or anyone who will remind him of her. He adored her. He was devastated when she ran away. He was equally distraught when he learned of her death two years ago.''

Alcée's brows bent together and he whispered, ''My God, Genevieve Vanier?''

It was the first time in years Amanda had heard her mother's name spoken aloud. She bolted upright in her chair and tears filled her eyes. ''You knew my mother?''

Alcée placed his right hand passionately over his heart. ''Only in my dreams. I saw her perform in St. Martinville when I was twenty-one.'' He sighed. ''Words cannot express how I felt hearing her. She was magnificent—a diva. I could not speak for three days.''

Amanda had heard all this before, about the men who cried when her mother sang and the ones who refused to leave their front doorstep in New Orleans when her mother simply smiled at them on the street. But since her mother's departure ten years before, Amanda had begun to doubt the truth of these tales. It surprised her how disappointed she felt now. Alcée's confession reminded Amanda that she paled in comparison to her mother.

''She was quite a beauty,'' Amanda said softly.

''Beauty is such a meek word,'' Alcée answered. ''She was *formidable*.''

Amanda focused on finishing her coffee, hoping the conversation would end. The older she became, the more she despised hearing those glowing remarks about her mother's unlimited beauty.

''You don't resemble her,'' Alcée said, breaking the silence.

"No," Amanda answered quietly, the familiar pain lurking at her heart.

This time it was Alcée who placed a hand on her sleeve. *"Mon dieu,"* he said. "I certainly didn't mean . . ."

Amanda tried to act nonchalant. "It's all right. I'm well aware of my shortcomings."

"No, my dear," Alcée said sternly, like an older brother teaching his younger sister an important lesson about life. "Your mother was a beauty, that's a fact, but you must not compare yourself to her. Your beauty comes from the heart. René had said your smile could touch a man's soul, but I had merely thought it was a young man in love talking. Now that I have met you, I agree. Your mother may have had physical attributes you do not possess, but she certainly lacked your sweetness."

Before Amanda could fully digest his words, Colette entered, giving Alcée instructions in French. "Forgive me," he said, rising. "I must go. I have some important business to tend to in town."

"Of course," Amanda answered.

"If René doesn't make it back for lunch, then he will be here by dinnertime."

As Alcée grabbed his hat and headed outside, Amanda sat mesmerized while she sipped her treasured coffee. Thoughts of her mother vanished, replaced by the words "a young man in love."

It didn't take Amanda much time to realize that her presence at the house did not cause much of a disruption. The boys played their usual games by the side of the house, every few minutes demanding something or other from Colette, who quickly shooed them out of her way. The oldest son, T-Emile, a timid seventeen-year-old who looked remarkably like Colette,

performed his chores quietly, leaving every once in a while to
help out at the racetrack. Pierre, the youngest, demanded to be
with the other boys at all times, whining and crying whenever
they disappeared from his view. Alexandre, whose corkscrew
locks must be the envy of all his female classmates at school,
Amanda thought, was the typical middle child. He admonished
Pierre for following him everywhere, then trailed after T-Emile
at every possible chance.

All three argued incessantly, much to the constant chagrin
of their mother. Colette seemed to always be involved in some
sort of argument. From what Amanda could assess, Colette
would order the children to perform some task or chore, then
spend a good ten minutes arguing with them over why they
had to do it. After several explanations, Colette would raise
her hands in defeat and do the project herself or grab one of
the two youngest and land a good spank on his behind.

Amanda approached Colette and offered her services, but
Colette vehemently refused. Amanda began clearing the dishes
from the morning breakfast, only to have Colette grab them
from her hands and push her away from the washtub. When
Amanda spotted Colette washing clothes over a fire at the back
of the house, she again offered to help, but Colette would hear
none of it. "I must help. You must let me help out somewhere."

Colette shook her head sternly and continued stirring the
collection of dirty clothes in the massive pot. *"Non, merci,"*
was all she would say.

Not knowing what else to do with her time, Amanda decided
to tour the house. The sturdy two-story farmhouse was built
of cypress, brick and *bousillage* construction. Amanda had
heard how early Acadians mixed mud with Spanish moss to
create this unique insulating material for external walls.

The first and second stories mirrored one another, each containing four square-shaped rooms separated by a common wall
and fireplace. The second floor housed equal bedrooms for

Colette, Alcée, René and now Amanda. The three boys lived in the *garçonnière,* a finished space in the house's attic built specifically for adolescent boys. The area was connected to the second floor by a center, hidden staircase. Pierre and Alexandre seemed too young for the upper floor, but Amanda sensed they had followed T-Emile there and Colette welcomed the peace it offered.

There was a wide gallery across the front and back of the house, one for each story. The only way to access one side of the house from the other was by walking through the outside covered galleries. Access to the second floor was by the back gallery staircase. As was tradition, staircases were built outside the house to allow more space inside.

The right two rooms of the bottom floor were used as a dining room and work area. A massive, rough-carved cypress table and matching buffet filled the dining room, while the workroom offered no pretense of formality; there were wash-tubs, tools and horse and farming equipment stored in every corner.

The left side was kept open so both rooms could be used simultaneously as the living area. This part of the house was Amanda's favorite. Mahogany furniture, a settee and comfort-able chairs were arranged in a semicircle around the fireplace as if the chimney was designated as a theatrical stage. Along one wall of the front living room, the room that opened to the house's front gallery, stood an enormous cypress bookshelf filled with a wide variety of books, family mementos and two violins.

The house's most redeeming feature, Amanda noticed, was the wide windows in every room accented by delicate white lace curtains. The windows remained opened at all times, allowing a cross-ventilation of air throughout the house. The slight breeze brought little relief from the stifling August heat, but the house appeared ten times airier and brighter than Amanda's more formal home in town, where every window was covered by yards of heavy drapes.

Amanda chose a book by Voltaire and sat down on the settee. She tried to concentrate on the words and to decipher their foreign meaning, but her thoughts kept racing elsewhere. What was she doing here, she thought, in this strange man's house, in a culture she knew nothing about? How did she manage to get in such a pickle when all she wanted was a little romance?

Images of Henry Tanner entered her mind and she shuddered. "Stupid girl," she admonished herself aloud. "How could you have been so utterly stupid?"

Before the darkness could settle around her heart again, a pair of giggles arose from the outside gallery. Glancing around the corner of the room, Amanda made out two sets of feet peering from beneath the wide cypress door. She heard the mention of *"loup garou"* in a voice trying to appear scary, then another round of giggles. Amanda recognized the phrase from her youth. It was French for werewolf.

The voices resumed, this time louder and scarier. The boys were getting braver, and were possibly planning a charge through the room in an effort to frighten Amanda. When Alexandre leaned toward the threshold, looking as if he would dart through the room, Amanda jumped around the corner and landed on the gallery's stone floor with a cry. The boys screamed in surprise and took off toward the other side of the house.

Amanda followed them through the dining room, but found no one under the table or buffet. The workroom seemed deserted as well except for the brownish blond curls poking up over the back of a trunk. Amanda slowly worked her way to that side of the room, then quickly plucked the boy out of his hiding place.

Pierre screamed again and began to fight, his arms and legs flailing. Amanda held him close to her side, whispering what few phrases she remembered in French about eating young boys for lunch. Alexandre soon appeared, but instantly assessed the situation. He began to laugh, then act scared as he followed Amanda's lead.

"Let me go, let me go," the young boy cried, but Amanda refused to let him down. When tears began to fall, Amanda let him run into the arms of his older brother, who continued to laugh at his expense.

"I'm sorry," Amanda said in the best French she could retrieve. "I was only joking."

Pierre cautiously peeked around his brother's side, wondering if the blond *loup garou* would eat him after all.

"She's not going to hurt you," Alexandre said. "Now, get away from me." Alexandre pushed the young boy backwards, releasing his hold on his waist, then headed for the backyard. Stopping to look nonchalantly over his shoulder, he asked Amanda, "Aren't you coming?"

Amanda was surprised that she passed the initiation so quickly, and decided it was best to act on it. Pierre wasn't as certain as his older brother, but followed Amanda nonetheless. Walking single file, the trio made their way down a narrow, dirt path to the banks of the sleepy Bayou Teche.

"This is where we go fishing," Alexandre explained. "We catch a lot of big alligators."

Amanda widened her eyes. "Really?" she played along. "How big?"

"Big," the younger boy chimed in, holding his arms up from his sides as far as they would go.

"Will you show me? I want to catch an alligator too."

When neither one answered, Amanda figured she had spoken the wrong words. But the guilty looks that spread across their faces betrayed their lie.

"Actually," Amanda said, breaking the silence and getting them off the hook, "I could use your help in another way."

The boys seemed genuinely interested. "The last time I spoke French I was about your age," she began, pointing to Alexandre.

The older boy laughed. "Is that why you talk so funny?"

"Oui," Amanda said, instantly worried she had used a previous word in the wrong context. She began to understand their meaning when they imitated her French equivalent of "yes."

"How do you say it?" she asked when they were done making fun of her. The boys recited their version of *oui* in a more relaxed, informal pronunciation.

"Merci beaucoup," she said, and the boys again began to laugh.

"Now what?"

"You sound like a Creole," Alexandre said.

Amanda knew he was referring to the colonists of French descent born in Louisiana, particularly New Orleans. They had immigrated to Louisiana directly from France, and their French resembled what was currently being spoken in France, as opposed to the Acadians, who had been separated from France by an ocean for approximately two hundred years. She imagined the differences were comparable to American and British speech patterns. English dialects were evolving into a host of unusual accents on the American side of the Atlantic.

"All right," Amanda agreed in English, then attempted to imitate their accent in French.

The boys giggled. Then Alexandre took her hand, urging her to join him as he sat on the ground. Amanda made herself comfortable next to the base of an oak tree, listening to her new teachers. Watching the boys eagerly share their knowledge with an adult, Amanda realized two important things: Children's French was a lot easier to understand, and her heart was beginning to feel immensely lighter.

After an hour of language lessons, Teche exploration and then meticulous instruction in how to catch crawfish, the boys

lay down and almost instantaneously drifted off to sleep. When
Colette found them lying peacefully on the banks of the slow-
moving bayou, she stared at Amanda in surprise. Amanda raised
her shoulders as if to say she was as surprised as Colette to
see the two consistently active children sound asleep. Colette
sat down by Amanda and sighed. A look of contentment stole
across her face as she took Amanda's hand and said, *"Merci."*

Amanda smiled back, thankful for the warm, friendly feel
of the older woman's hand in hers. *"La Teche est belle,"*
Amanda said slowly in her simple French, remarking on the
beauty of the bayou.

Colette squeezed her hand and nodded. *"Oui, la Teche est
belle,"* she answered.

After the boys awakened, the group headed back to the house,
amazed to find the sun close to the western horizon. None
of the men had returned from the racetrack and dusk was
approaching. Amanda changed into dinner clothes and Colette
resumed her duties in the kitchen, applying the finishing touches
to a gumbo. By the time the boys washed themselves up and
Amanda made it downstairs to set the table, darkness had settled.

Amanda and Colette had been too busy to light all the lamps
before darkness came and a hungry swarm of mosquitoes
buzzed in the shadowy, damp corners of the house, picking at
everyone's feet whenever they chanced by. The insects became
so disruptive, Colette was forced to close all the dining room
windows, once the invading pests were extinguished, raising
the inside temperature considerably.

The intense heat failed to dispel the happy mood among
the children, however. They were both excited over the new
company and because the half-dozen crawfish they'd dug up
at the bayou's edge had made it into Colette's prized gumbo. To

encourage their gaiety, Amanda placed the discarded crawfish heads on her fingers. When Pierre or Alexandre let down their guard, she thrust the mudbugs at them, their beady red eyes bulging from her fingertips. Both boys squealed with delight.

Colette proudly produced a cauldron of thick brown gumbo filled with a collection of seafood and okra. The boys cheered when she made her entrance, demanding to see the crawfish tails Colette had added to the soup. In a few moments, everyone was happily talking at once.

Almost silently, T-Emile entered through the back door and motioned to his mother. The shy boy held his hat tightly in his hands while he passed on some information, looking up every once in a while as if fearing a reprisal from Colette. His mother said nothing, but appeared disappointed at the news. Finally she shrugged her shoulders, said a few words to T-Emile and began dishing out the gumbo.

Turning toward Amanda, she explained that a horse had damaged part of the stables and everyone was needed to repair the stalls. The men would not be home in time for dinner. Colette peered up at her curiously, as if hoping her words had made sense. Amazingly, they did.

"Je comprend," Amanda answered.

As Colette handed T-Emile gumbo to bring to the men, Amanda found herself disappointed that René would not return. She had looked forward to the evening, waiting anxiously to taste Colette's special dinner in honor of her arrival and for the chance to talk to her new husband.

The news of the men working late cast a gloom over dinner. Colette was clearly disappointed after spending the entire afternoon working on the gumbo. Amanda complimented Colette numerous times and asked for two second helpings, but her attention failed to lighten the mood. After everyone finished eating, they quickly brought the plates to the outside kitchen, glad to escape the sweltering heat.

The boys took turns playing some sort of game in the dirt while Colette washed the dishes. Again, she refused to let Amanda help, so Amanda took one of the lanterns and retired to her bedroom.

The night became ominously still, refusing so much as a whisper of a breeze, and the pesky insects invaded her bedroom. As fast as she could, Amanda changed into her nightdress, grabbed one of René's books by the bedside and crawled under the sanctuary of the mosquito net. The entire bed was covered with the cotton netting, and Amanda tucked in the edges so as not to leave even an inch of bedding vulnerable. Mosquitoes were tenacious creatures.

Amanda was thankful the book she'd grabbed was written in English, even if it was a copy of the Louisiana State Constitution. At the back, past the legal jargon, were descriptions of Louisiana cities and towns. Amanda passed the time reading about the early inhabitants of New Orleans, and how three nationalities had governed the city for more than one hundred years—the French, then the Spanish, then the French again briefly before selling it, along with the rest of the territory, to the United States for fifteen million dollars.

After a while, Amanda heard Colette sending the boys off to the attic. The roof reverberated with their activity for several minutes, then quieted down. Amanda could hear Colette singing them *C'est la Petite Poulé Caille,* a lullaby her French nanny used to sing. In English it was "The Little Spotted Hen." The soft, sleepy strains brought back waves of nostalgia for her home in New Orleans with her mother.

After Colette had entered her own room and shut the door, all Amanda could hear were the bullfrogs and crickets outside her window. Everything was startlingly foreign to her, even though the children and Colette had made her feel quite at home. Thoughts of all the people she had angered, the man she had nearly married, and the friend who had taken her in fought for possession of her mind. Many times she had to remind herself to breathe, to try to dispel the anxiety choking her at every turn.

One thought managed to break through, however, like a ray of sunshine during a violent Louisiana summer thunderstorm. Could it be possible that René had feelings for her?

Nonsense, she answered herself, remembering the casual talks they'd shared at the fence every morning during the past two weeks. Conversations between acquaintances. When he had proposed on that horrible evening in Port Cocodrie, he had reminded her they were friends. *Friends.* Not lovers.

As clearly as if she stood once again in her father's garden, she could picture René strolling down her street, his unusual wide-brimmed hat framing his smiling face. Every morning the same reaction had occurred within her. René literally took her breath away.

Why was that? she wondered. Why did he have such an effect on her? Was that what friendship was all about, or was she too naive to realize he had feelings for her and had been flirting all this time?

Just as she was about to let the nighttime sounds lull her to sleep, a knock came at the door. She instantly sat up, clutching the hand-woven cotton sheet to her bosom. "Who is it?" she whispered.

"It's me. René. I wanted to know how you are."

"Yes, of course," she answered, her heart beating faster at the sound of his accented voice. "Please, come in."

René entered the room, gingerly making his way to the bed. All was pitch black except for the bedside light. When he made it to Amanda's side, it was clear what kind of a night he had had. His shirt was torn and his face smeared with dirt and sweat.

"I'm sorry about dinner," René began. "I wanted to be

here, to be with you on your first night in my house. Was everything well? Did Colette show you where everything is?''

"I'm fine. Colette was wonderful.''

René brightened. "I was hoping she would be. Colette has been known to give a butcher some words, but she is a great one for hospitality.''

"She has been very sweet, but I do wish you would talk to her and convince her to let me help out with the household chores.''

René laughed, and he slapped a mosquito away from his cheek. "That would be like convincing the British to apologize. Colette came to live with us after her husband, Emile, died. We were glad to take her in, but she insists on not being labeled a burden. She refuses to let us do anything around here. As you can see, the house is always meticulous. That is the right English word, meticulous?''

"Yes,'' Amanda answered, "like the French word.''

René gave Amanda a curious look, then glanced over to the side table. "Do you mind if I clean up with your water? My meticulous cousin forgot to leave me some.''

"Of course.''

It was difficult to make him out after René left the light of the bedside, but Amanda could hear water being poured from a pitcher and a bureau drawer opening and closing. After what sounded like a piece of clothing hitting the floor, Amanda heard René splash water on his face, then sigh.

"You must be tired,'' she said, trying to imagine what a man would look like at his toilette. The image, she discovered with amazement, both scared and enticed her.

What if he wants to bed me? she thought. *Is that why he's here, alone with me in his room?*

"These mosquitoes are unbearable tonight,'' René said through the darkness.

"I'm sorry," Amanda said. "I would have shut the windows but it is so insufferably hot in here."

"*Merde,*" René said after Amanda heard a hard slap.

"You better get under a mosquito net," Amanda said, hoping he would get the hint and retire to his own bedroom. *But this is his bedroom,* she reminded herself.

Without warning, René lifted the netting and quickly crawled onto the bed. Amanda gazed up to find her tall husband sitting across from her bare-chested. In his hands was a clean nightshirt, but her eyes rested instead on the soft brown hair gracing the wide expanse of muscled chest and the broad, damp shoulders gleaming in the lantern's candlelight. She had never seen a man half naked before, and René Comeaux was quite a sight. To Amanda's horror, she felt her jaw drop against her will.

René must have realized his mistake, for he instantly pulled on the shirt. Amanda sought to regain her composure, but she felt like a fool. If only her mother had been around to tell her what to do on her wedding night. She hadn't the slightest idea.

"I'm sorry," René said. "I should let you sleep. I only wanted to talk to you about something."

Amanda attempted to meet René's eyes, but got only as far as the opening of his nightshirt. Brown hair peeked through his collar, and Amanda was shocked to discover she longed to run her fingers through it.

"I wanted to talk to you too," she said, amazed at her boldness. She had convinced herself earlier she would not talk about the subject unless René brought it up first. "I fear I have inconvenienced you," she began.

René stared at her curiously. As much as Amanda longed to gaze into those trusting eyes, she chose to stare at her hands instead.

"Inconvenienced me?" he asked. "In what way?"

"This is your bedroom, is it not?" Amanda answered softly. "And is this not your bed that you must share with your wife?"

René seemed to grasp her meaning, leaning back slowly onto one elbow. "I told you before, *chèrie,* I will not expect anything from you until you are ready. You are in a new house, a new situation. You must get accustomed to all this." Quietly, he added, "And to me."

This time, Amanda looked up. "But it is my duty as a wife," she practically whispered.

René sat up abruptly and took both her hands in his. He was so close Amanda could smell the scent of soap about him. "I don't want your love unless you give it to me freely and honestly," he said, staring intently into her eyes. "I don't want you to make love to me because you feel it is your duty or out of gratitude. Do you understand?"

Amanda simply nodded, and René read the relief that spread across her face. "But I thought husbands went crazy if they didn't sleep with their wives," she said softly, as if ashamed to be speaking of such intimate thoughts.

René laughed at her naiveté. "I promise I won't go crazy," he said, inwardly doubting his words. Ever since he had entered the room and seen Amanda's body moist with perspiration underneath a thin, cotton nightgown, his pulse had indeed gone mad. Holding her hands and gazing down upon her head of delicate blond curls was torture. How many nights had he dreamed of her lying in his bed? Yet here she was, ready and willing, and he had to be the gentleman of restraint.

Suddenly, René felt extremely tired. The lack of sleep and the extra work at the racetrack were getting the best of him. Sighing, he released Amanda's hands and leaned down toward the pillows. He would rest his head for a moment, tell her his thoughts and be on his way.

"I have an idea," he began, slowly stretching his legs the length of the bed. "I think I know a way you can smooth things over with your father."

Amanda still clutched the sheet to her chest, but relaxed and fell back against her pillows. They were now eye to eye, and René could smell the lilac water she used to wash her face. He looked away and forced himself to concentrate on the plan he had envisioned during the afternoon break in the races. "Is there a time of day that you and your father always spend together?" he asked.

"We always had lunch together," Amanda answered, slipping even further into her pillow.

"I think you should continue. Go to your house every day for lunch, as if nothing has happened."

"But my father is furious. I don't think he wants to see me right now."

René turned and gazed into her azure eyes, which were now so irresistibly close. "But that's the point. He may be furious, but he will slowly get used to the fact that nothing has changed. You're still his daughter, despite who you married, and you will still spend lunches and special occasions with him like before. After a while, it will seem that nothing has happened between you. Perhaps then he will be calm enough to talk to."

Amanda appeared lost in thought, her eyes reflecting the subdued candlelight. The nearness of her beauty overwhelmed him, and René shut his eyes to ease the pain of his wanting. Within seconds, he was fast asleep.

Chapter Five

No matter how little sleep he managed the night before, René awoke every morning shortly before sunrise. His mother had labeled him *le guime,* or the rooster, as a child. Ever since he was old enough to walk he would leap out of bed, ready to take on the world.

As usual, René's internal clock nudged him awake before the early rays of sunlight edged over the eastern horizon. This morning, however, after two days of nonstop activity, his tired, aching muscles gave him reason to wish the world would wait.

Since he had lost a full day of work traveling back from Port Cocodrie with his new wife, then spending the afternoon riding to the Richardson's house for a dose of verbal torture from the Judge, René had missed most of his daily chores at the racetrack. T-Emile had been good enough to exercise the horses and feed them, but several of his clients were unhappy they had missed a day of racing. They were literally lined up the next day ready to make use of the track when René arrived at daybreak, and some were still waiting to race their horses when dusk fell. Then, the LeBlanc horse had been spooked by a king snake and knocked down a wall and damaged two stalls in his fright. The men had worked consistently from sunset till nine o'clock repairing the damage.

And he never found time to speak to Alcée about his trip to town to obtain news of Henry Tanner.

René moved to rise when he heard a soft moan at his side. Glancing over, he suddenly remembered talking to Amanda the night before. Had he fallen asleep in the bed with her? He did recall feeling incredibly tired, as if a wave of exhaustion had instantly overtaken him.

Amanda stretched across half of the bed, her arm lying non-chalantly over her forehead, a slight smile on her lips. René settled back down and snaked an arm around her shoulders. She sighed with pleasure and nestled her face into the crook of his arm. René moved his free hand to her face, brushing the yellow curls from her forehead.

How incredibly right she felt in his arms, fitting into his embrace as if she was born to do so.

He remembered the day his father had taken him into the woods in search of a cypress log for a new pirogue, a canoe they would use in fishing. "You must search for the perfect log," his father said. "One that will allow you to completely transform it into a pirogue. If you look closely, you will see the boat existing within the tree trunk. Listen, and the log will whisper to you if it is the right one. Pick the wrong log, relying simply on what it looks like on the outside, and it will not allow you to carve it."

René's easy-natured father had then laughed. "It's kind of like choosing a wife. If men would use the same logic in picking a wife as they do pirogue building, they would live happier lives. Instead, they rely too much on beauty, and not enough

on what their hearts tell them and what's inside the hearts of
their women.''

When René had first walked down Main Street and encountered the blue eyes of his angel, he knew Amanda would fill
the empty parts of his life. His heart agreed when her smile
whispered of a happy, married life together.

Perhaps he was fooling himself. Alcée insisted he was. Still,
lying next to Amanda felt natural, like coming home.

René caressed the warm, satiny skin of her arm, while inhaling the feminine scent of her wavy blond hair. He kissed her
closed eyelids while his hand explored the gentle curve of her
back, pressing her tightly against him. Amanda murmured and
sighed, and bent her knee to allow them closer proximity.
René's heart raced with desire as he slipped his own knee
between her thighs.

Amanda sighed again, and René gently tilted her head back,
rubbed her generous lips with his thumb, then softly touched
her lips with his. His kiss was much like the one he'd offered
at the altar, a courting kiss one gave one's amour that spoke
of passion, but didn't give in to desire. Amanda reacted slightly,
neither pulling away nor awakening. Instead, she wrapped her
arm around René's back, emitting a soft moan as she caressed
the broad expanse of muscles there.

The temptation became too great. René deepened his kiss,
pressing Amanda closer with his hand at the small of her back
and urging his knee inward. She was so warm, so soft, so
incredibly near. He wanted her with all his soul, his mind bent
on only one objective: to love this blond angel, the passion of
his life.

Pulling Amanda closer still, René moaned. It was then
Amanda awoke, her eyes wild with accusations, her arms vehemently pushing René away, desperately trying to break from
his embrace. When she finally realized he had let go, she
grabbed the sheet, pulled it tightly against her chest and

retreated hastily to the far side of the bed. She sat trembling, staring at René as if she had just been attacked by a hungry alligator.

"I'm sorry. I was only trying to awaken you with a kiss," René said, knowing that only half of that was true. "Please, I never meant to hurt you."

As if she suddenly recognized him, Amanda let out a deep breath and began to relax. "No, I am sorry," she began. "I thought you were . . ." Amanda stared down at her free hand, which was busy twisting the sheet fabric into a tight knot. "I must have been dreaming."

René moved closer and brought her chin up with his finger so their eyes met. "Amanda, I asked you this once before, but I will ask you again. Did Henry Tanner hurt you?"

Amanda stared deeply into his eyes and shook her head slightly.

"Did he *try* to hurt you?"

At this question, she gazed back down at her lap. "Yes," she said quietly.

René slipped his hand gently around her cheek and kissed her forehead. His heart still beat wildly from their earlier embrace, and he inhaled her sweet aroma one last time before moving away.

"It was all my fault," Amanda said, almost to herself. "I am such a stupid girl."

"Don't say that, *cher.* You did not ask to be carried away to a drunkard's port in the middle of the night."

Amanda shook her head. "I did," she said, causing René's heart to skip a beat at the admittance. "I practically asked him to. I got exactly what I deserved."

Her last words were more sobering than if René had plunged his head into the Bayou Teche. So this was her story. Amanda had thrown herself at the town's rogue, and now the poor rich

American was forced to spend the rest of her days married to an Acadian.

"How devastating for you," he said sarcastically, "to end up having to marry someone like me."

Amanda's eyes instantly met his. "I never meant," she earnestly began. "René, you know I didn't mean it that way."

"Didn't you?" he asked as he pulled the mosquito netting free and headed for the door.

Before Amanda could answer, René had slammed the door shut between them.

What just happened? Amanda wondered. One minute she was dreaming pleasantly of René making love to her, and the next thing she knew she had offended him again. In between it all, Henry Tanner had made his horrid presence known, invading her sleep like a devil.

Amanda pulled her fingers through her hair in exasperation, trying to brush the curls out of her eyes. She could still sense René's gentle fingers on her cheeks, his lips softly kissing her forehead.

Next door, René was stomping through his room, and Amanda quickly realized he was dressing and heading for the racetrack. In a few minutes, he would be gone. She couldn't let him leave angry, offended by words she didn't mean.

Amanda threw back the sheet and netting and hurried to dress. She had to stop him, to explain her seemingly hurtful words. More than anything, she realized, she had to see him again. She couldn't spend another day and night without talking to René, without being near him.

Her fingers froze on her chemise's buttons. *She cared for René.* And it was more than simple gratitude. It always had been. From the moment she awoke in the morning in her father's dreary, dark house, she couldn't wait to see René's smiling, beaming face heading her way down the street.

Slowly and carefully Amanda peered up at the portrait, afraid of what secrets it would reveal. René's smile washed down upon her like a welcome rain. She wondered if their children would be tall like René, or resemble the Germanic and English paternal side of her family. Perhaps they'd have the dark eyes of his mother and Alcée. Amanda glanced back down at her bare arms and undergarments. Had it been a dream or did René touch her the way she imagined he did?

The butterflies resumed their wild activities inside her stomach and Amanda smiled. *Yes, she was certain. She cared for this man.*

René stormed down the stairs taking two steps at a time, his anger quickening his pulse. He was always so good at staying calm, always so diplomatic. His father used to say he could sell fish to a fisherman.

But women were another story. Amanda was right, he thought with a laugh. They were married two days and already she was slowly making him insane.

"Where are you headed in such a huff?"

René spun around to find Alcée returning to the house from the nearby fields with two ripe, plump watermelons under each arm. "Aren't they beautiful?" he asked René. "Always taste better when you pick them before sunrise."

"What did you find out in town?" René asked gruffly.

Alcée gently placed the melons in a covered spot on the back gallery. "Nice to see you too, nephew."

René ignored the comment, inhaling deeply to try to release his anger. "I'm sorry, Alcée. It's just that we haven't had a chance to speak about it yet."

Alcée waved his hand to let René know there were no hard feelings. "Women will do that to you."

René thrust his hands into his pants pockets and placed a foot on a nearby bench. Amanda's stinging words reverberated through his head. Still, it was his job as her husband to protect her, and he needed to make sure Tanner was no longer a threat.

"He's back," Alcée began. "He returned to the plantation yesterday. I don't know how he found out, but he knew you married Miss Richardson before he came back to Franklin. My source said he rode in straight from the coast to the plantation, skipping town altogether."

"I suspect he went from Berwick to Port Cocodrie and found Amanda gone," René explained, pulling on the leather boots he left there the night before. "I informed the innkeeper, so he would have passed on the information to Tanner."

"Then Tanner knew that you had left Port Cocodrie with Amanda with the intention of marrying her?" Alcée asked.

"Yes."

Alcée pulled his fingers through his hair nervously. "I don't like this, René. You have taken his woman from underneath his nose. He's not going to stand for this."

"He won't challenge me," René said, pounding his feet to shake the boots into place. "Any action he takes against me will only attract attention to himself. Tanner will not want Judge Richardson to know of his actions, I am sure."

"Tanner is a sly one," Alcée warned. "He may not attack you openly, but he will seek revenge."

"He works for the Judge, and Amanda is still the Judge's daughter. He won't take the chance."

Uncle and nephew stared at each other contemplatingly until Alcée broke the silence. "About the Judge's daughter. There's something I have to tell you about her."

Before he could explain, the upstairs door opened and Amanda hurried down the stairs.

"Thank God you are still here," she said breathlessly. René noticed her hair was not pinned up in its usual bun, but casually tied in the back with a ribbon as if she had been in a hurry, the blond curls cascading down her back. Underneath her skirt and layers of petticoats, René could have sworn he had seen two bare feet.

"I'll fix you breakfast," she started. "You mustn't leave."

"Non, merci," René answered back sternly, still reeling from her earlier words. "I don't eat breakfast."

"But you must. It's important to have a good breakfast before you start the day."

Alcée laughed at her last remark. "You've been married less than two days and already she's telling you what to do," he joked to his nephew in French. Amanda glared at Alcée. For a moment, René imagined she understood what he'd said.

"I have to go," René said, grabbing his hat. "Sunrise is minutes away. Colette brings food and coffee to us at midmorning, so you needn't worry about me starving."

"But . . ."

When René saw Amanda stumble for words, he knew she was searching for the right way to apologize. Damn, but women were complicated creatures. Suddenly, a wicked thought came to him. "I'd ask you to come with Colette, but I wouldn't dream of asking the daughter of Judge Richardson to be seen at a horse track."

Amanda's eyes flew open and her hands slowly found a defensive spot at her hips. René knew she wanted to object, but she wouldn't dream of upsetting her father and his Puritan views on horse racing and gambling. It was common knowledge in the parish that the Judge did not condone games of chance in any shape or form. But her following words surprised him more than her lack of shoes.

"I'm not married to my father," Amanda said as if doubting her words. Gathering up more courage, she added, "I'll be there at midmorning."

For a brief moment, René believed she was sincere in her attempt at an apology. Before logic could replace the pleasant thought, René imagined Amanda honestly did not mean what she had said before in his bedroom.

He gazed over at Alcée, who stood staring at his blond wife with curiosity. Then Alcée smiled, and again René hoped his wife would care for him. Before his recurrent doubts could make their presence known, René placed his hat on his head and headed for the racetrack, a smile lingering on his lips.

On a sugarcane plantation, sunrise in summer meant one thing and one thing only—another sticky, humid day of relentless, backbreaking work. Tanner despised everything about his job as slave overseer. He hated the insufferable weather, the demanding hours in the inescapable sun and semitropical thunderstorms, and abhorred the meager house that was completely inadequate for his needs and wants.

The most despicable aspect of the job was the pitiful eyes of the dark men he supervised. They stared at him accusingly, as if silently blaming him for their predicament in life. Hell, he didn't invent the institution; he wasn't personally responsible for shipping them to Louisiana. They were ignorant, primitive savages. They were lucky to have the work and a roof over their heads. And the next time one gave him so much as a glance, he would have him severely flogged.

Tanner angrily rubbed at his temples, but the throbbing pain would not abate. After a night and a day of one frustration after another, he had ridden back to the plantation and quickly sought refuge in every drop of rum he could find in the house. But all the grog in the world would not erase the fact that he owed William McDuff three thousand dollars—a sum he had held in the palm of his hand while Amanda Rose Richardson sat across from him in his carriage.

Why did he have to leave her at Port Cocodrie? he chided himself for the hundredth time. He could have taken her with him to Berwick, then back to town when he realized Judge Richardson had gone to Charenton instead. But what would the Judge have said to his shivering, frightened daughter standing before him like a kidnapped child? The Judge would have hanged him for sure.

Instead, the bitch married the Cajun horse track owner, for what possible reason he could not imagine. He'd presented the spoiled brat the best offer she would ever get. The Baldwin girl had said no one would marry her on account of her being Catholic. Why would she choose a Cajun when Tanner was ready and willing?

Maybe she'd been spooked when he'd tried to kiss her. He'd thought that was what she wanted. "Teasing bitch," he said aloud. *One minute she asks for it; the next minute she's bolting like a frightened filly.*

But the Cajun man? That was a puzzle. Even the Judge had been destroyed by the news. Who would have thought amiable René Comeaux would have had it in him. He was so demure, so businesslike and personable with the Americans. *He fooled us all,* Tanner thought, gritting his teeth with disdain, *sneaking behind our backs and stealing our women.*

The sun rose higher and men began to stir throughout the slave quarters. The pounding in Tanner's skull continued. McDuff had made his choice clear: three thousand by next Monday or someone's dapper body would be found floating in Bayou Teche. Tanner still had a week to raise the money. Horse track owners and pretty blond daughters of sugarcane-producing judges were prime sources of wealth. One way or another he would escape this trap.

As the men lined up for the morning's duties, Tanner dared them to even give him so much as a glance. It wasn't his fault they were slaves and he was stuck in this godforsaken place as their overseer. If he hadn't been swindled out of his inheritance by that con-man gambler from St. Louis, he would be in

New Orleans now enjoying his life as a gentleman, a voluptuous woman on each knee.

Come Monday, Tanner thought, someone might be floating in the bayou, but it sure as hell wasn't going to be him. One less Cajun in the world wasn't going to bother anyone.

Amanda tried hard to keep up with Colette and the boys, but maintaining raised skirts, watching the ground for crawfish holes or, God forbid, snakes, plus carrying a large sack of bread in one arm kept forcing her to lag behind. Just when she had a good grip on her skirt, forcing it high enough to avoid the mud but keeping it discreet enough to meet the top of her boots, the sack would slip beneath her left arm and she would have to stop and reassemble.

After a half-dozen times, Amanda admitted defeat. She was about to call out for Colette to stop when they entered a clearing. The large meadow contained tall grasses and weeds, but its center was laid out flat and bare before them. A long road with a low wooden fence on either side stretched from one end of the meadow to the other. At one end were a series of stables, plus a collection of wooden chairs underneath an expansive oak. At the other, about four arpents away, stood René, T-Emile and two men on horseback.

Colette waved to the group, then headed toward the stables with her children and coffee in tow. René immediately sent T-Emile to Amanda's aid, and the young boy grabbed her package, shyly smiled and moved to follow Colette.

Amanda stood alone in the middle of the field, uncertain of which direction to take. She could feel René's eyes burning into her, clearly surprised she had come. She remembered his earlier astonished stare when she had mentioned visiting the racetrack. This time, he was smiling.

René waved for her to join them. When she moved within

earshot, she realized the other two men were also Acadian. They had dismounted and stood about asking René a series of questions in French about why Judge Richardson's daughter was at the Comeaux/Dugas racetrack. René didn't answer, but continued staring at Amanda as if contemplating his next course of action. She knew he was calculating how he was going to tell the world he had married the American judge's daughter.

Finally, René turned toward the duo. "She's my wife," he said.

At first, neither one spoke. Then they both broke into laughter, slapping him on the back and saying in French what Amanda thought was, "Perhaps you are dreaming." René began to darken as the laughing and joking continued unabated.

"Bonjour," Amanda announced to the men, who immediately stopped laughing and stared at her. "Let me introduce myself," she continued in her best French. "I am Amanda Comeaux."

An awkward silence fell over the group. Amanda felt a soft breeze cool the perspiration gathering at her neck, and she shivered. Neither man moved to acknowledge her, and René stared equally as hard.

When she extended her hand, the plump, balding one who stood the closest accepted it gingerly.

"Amanda," René began, coming to life. "This is Eraste Boudreaux."

When the second, lean man offered his hand, René added, "And this is Cyprien Thibodeaux."

"It's a pleasure to meet you," Amanda answered, hoping they wouldn't mistake her meager French for fluency and start a lengthy conversation.

Before they could answer, René grabbed her elbow and led her down the track toward the stables. Looking over his shoulder, he barked out commands to the two men, who still stood staring.

"They're friends," he said to Amanda as they continued in the opposite direction. "We let them use the track when it's empty."

"I see," Amanda said, glad to be back in a more familiar language. "That's very kind of you. Are they old friends?"

René stopped suddenly, and appeared as if he didn't fancy small talk at the moment. "You speak French?" he asked sternly.

"I . . ."

Suddenly, Colette called her name, and she saw Pierre covered in Spanish moss, walking hunched over and baring all his teeth as if he would eat anyone in his path. Amanda laughed.

"He's the *loup garou,*" she told René. "Yesterday was my day to be werewolf. Today, it's his turn."

"Werewolf?" René asked. "In Louisiana, the *loup garou* is more of a swamp monster. He comes out of the swamps at night during the full moon and eats little children."

René laughed at his cousin falling backwards when the moss became tangled on a cypress knee. "Only bad little children, of course, which means my cousins have a lot to be worried about."

"We shouldn't scare them with such nonsense," Amanda admonished him. "They won't be able to sleep at night."

"Nothing will keep those scoundrels from a good night's rest, I assure you," René said with a smile.

"They're really quite sweet," Amanda said. "Yesterday, they taught me some wonderful French expressions and how to catch crawfish out of a mud hole."

René seemed to accept her explanation. As long as René spoke French before her, Amanda figured she might learn of his true feelings for her, words he might not utter in her presence if he knew she understood.

Colette had spread a large quilt next to the chairs and assembled several cups of coffee, fresh-baked bread and apples. She also added a large jar of preserves and a small container of water for the boys, who had no problem satisfying their hunger.

T-Emile busily ate several helpings of bread and two apples before Alcée arrived and shooed him away. Some Americans were expected, hoping for a late-morning race before the sun became too unbearably hot, and the track needed to be freshened. René rose to leave as well, heading for the stables.

"There's no need for you to go too," Alcée said to René with irritation, as if he had said those words many times before.

"I have to attend to the Baldwin horse," René answered, equally strained. A tension fell between the two that Amanda had not noticed before. She wondered if it was because of her intrusion into their house and lives.

"I will only be a minute," René said to Amanda, before leaving.

Alcée and Colette began their own argument, too quick for Amanda to follow. She decided to pursue René and tour the stables. When she entered the barnlike building, an enclosed set of horse stalls, Amanda almost collided with Wayne Baldwin.

"Miss Richardson?" he exclaimed.

Wayne Baldwin could have been the identical twin brother of his sister Sally, Amanda's best friend and confidante. The reddish-blond hair curled up just behind his ears as it did on Sally, and both were blessed with small waists and broad shoulders. Neither one was exceptionally tall, but their beauty and gregarious natures made one feel small in their presence.

"What in the world are you doing here?" Wayne stood before Amanda clutching the reins of a chestnut horse and blushing a deep shade of red. "Did Sally set you up to this? Did she have me followed? I swear I don't do this on a regular basis. Ask anyone. This is my first time. You won't tell your father, will you?"

Amanda feared the poor boy would have continued forever

if she hadn't stopped him. "Mr. Baldwin, I wouldn't dream of telling anyone. What you do is your business."

Wayne appeared somewhat relieved. "I only come out here every once in a while, and it's usually because someone forces me into a bet. Please don't tell my sister. Nothing escapes those lips and my father will have me hog-whipped for sure."

"I won't tell a soul, I promise," Amanda agreed. "Not even Sally."

"It's a well-respected track," Wayne continued. "It's not like it's really gambling or anything."

Amanda felt a surge of pride run through her. She had always heard that most of Franklin's prominent men and women patronized the racetrack, even if her father refused to do so. She knew René worked hard building the business.

"The two men that own and run this track are reputable men," Wayne added, then leaned in close to Amanda and whispered, "Even if they are Cajuns."

For a brief moment, Amanda heard and sensed nothing else, his prejudicial words echoing inside her head. As the world seemed to stop moving around her, Amanda realized the force behind those words. An American's words. She felt both ashamed and angry—ashamed that she belonged to a group of people who could judge a culture and people so easily, and angry because she felt inescapably a part of that culture. Wayne had become a mirror, and Amanda didn't like what she saw. The reality lurked under her seemingly unbiased surface. As much as she always enjoyed René's presence at the front gate, it never occurred to her to think of him in any way but as a friend. Alcée was right. Acadians were never allowed within the Richardson house, and Amanda never thought to fight that unspoken rule. She never would have married René otherwise.

"There you are. For a moment I thought you weren't coming." Amanda heard René approach them, but she couldn't bear meeting his eyes.

"I was just telling Miss Richardson that I don't usually come to the racetrack," Wayne said beseechingly.

"Of course you don't," René answered with a smile. "If I'm not mistaken, this is your first time, no?"

The two men gazed over at Amanda to see if she was buying their story, but she stood quietly staring at her feet. When the silence lingered, Amanda raised her eyes, first to René, then to Wayne. "Mr. Baldwin," she began softly. "I'd like you to meet my husband, René Comeaux."

Chapter Six

"René Comeaux?" Sally Baldwin shouted. "The Cajun racetrack owner?"

Wayne only nodded, as if afraid to divulge too much.

"Are you sure?"

"I saw them this morning," he said carefully. "I went to help a friend who has a horse at the stables and she was there. Amanda clearly told me she had married him, and Comeaux didn't refute it."

"A friend?" the older sister asked. "I know you've been racing for years."

Wayne's eyes grew enormous, as if they would burst.

"Don't worry," Sally said. "I won't tell Father."

Leaning against the front parlor window and moving a drape aside with her forefinger, Sally thoughtfully gazed out onto the busy street in Franklin. Well-dressed men and women were slowly strolling along the thoroughfare, careful not to exert themselves in the hot sun. Noon was only an hour away and already the heat had become unbearable. Sally wiped away a drop of perspiration that had dribbled down her cheek, and unconsciously combed the wet curls behind her ear.

"I don't understand," she almost whispered. "She tells me everything. How could she have eloped with René Comeaux? I knew something was amiss when she didn't arrive at the ball Saturday night, but I assumed she had changed her mind. She never was fully convinced."

"Sally, what are you talking about?" Wayne asked.

A thought planted itself in Sally's mind and began to take root. Amanda could have used Sally to set up a rendezvous with Tanner while she planned an elopement with the Comeaux man. Sally tossed her head to shake off such traitorous ideas. "Comeaux's practically a stranger."

"It doesn't make much sense to me either," Wayne answered. "Maybe it's on account of her being Catholic."

Sally turned and shot him a scrutinizing glance. Most of the Americans Amanda associated with knew the differences in their religions, but never spoke of it for fear of being rude.

"What did I say?" Wayne asked.

"Did you win?"

A childish grin stole across his face. "Of course I did. Mary's Blessing's the fastest horse in the parish."

Sally headed for the door, grabbing her parasol. "Next time you go," she said to her brother over her shoulder, "let me know what you see."

Judge Richardson was probably one of the ten richest men in Franklin, Sally figured, but his house clearly kept that fact a secret. While other Americans were building grand mansions as a testament to their lucrative sugarcane earnings, Judge Richardson preferred his older, more subtle dwelling.

The house mirrored the other Greek Revival homes of Franklin, but only utilized four medium-sized rooms on each floor, a central hallway containing an average staircase and a narrow porch in front. The early clay and cypress house would have been dwarfed by the newly emerging estates in town had it not been for Richardson's extensive English garden and delicate white picket fence that met the street. In almost every month of the year, flowers bloomed in the shrubberies and trellises, providing Franklin with a vibrant block-long stretch of beauty.

The exquisite garden almost made up for the lack of ballroom space inside the house. Almost. Sally knew the Judge preferred a more sedate, reclusive lifestyle, keeping the drapes tightly shut at all hours of the day and every season of the year. The flowers had been a concession to Amanda, who despised the darkness of her home. At every chance, Amanda cut flowers, mostly roses, to fill the somber interior with splashes of color. But never, ever, did the Richardsons offer balls or dances to other American families in town.

Sally knocked cautiously at the front door. She wasn't sure how to approach the Judge on this matter, but she had to know. She had to be sure.

Virginia appeared at the door, her face clearly troubled. She seemed to brighten at Sally's presence. "Sally, what a pleasure. Do come in."

Sally entered the narrow hallway cautiously, gazing around for signs of her best friend.

"Are you looking for Amanda?" Virginia asked.

Sally spun around, relieved. "Is she here?"

Virginia began to explain when the doors of the study swung open. The Judge stared at Sally expectantly, then gasped a deep breath of disappointment.

"No, sir," Virginia said. "It's Sally Baldwin looking for Amanda."

The look of despair that followed confirmed Sally's fear. It was true after all. "How could she?" she asked him, her heart breaking.

"Didn't you know?" the Judge asked.

Sally could only shake her head, amazed at Amanda's elopement as much as he. "It can't be true. It wasn't supposed to be René Comeaux."

Suddenly, Judge Richardson opened the parlor door wider. "Miss Baldwin, I think we need to talk. If you don't mind."

Sally followed the older man into the parlor that was twice as dismal as the rest of the house. Amanda said he spent most of his time at the house reviewing court cases and writing correspondence in the parlor. How could he see properly in this light? Sally wondered.

"Please," the Judge said, motioning to a chair, "sit down."

Descending gingerly in the stiff chair, Sally felt a sudden urge to cry. What if something terrible had happened on account of her secretive arrangements with Henry Tanner? Had Amanda met Tanner and experienced some cruel fate, or had she been plotting to elope with Comeaux and been lying all this time? If the latter was true, Sally was made the biggest fool of the parish.

"What do you mean, it wasn't supposed to be René Comeaux?" the Judge asked sternly.

Suddenly, Sally wanted to bolt. What could she tell Amanda's father, that she had arranged a secret meeting between Amanda and his overseer so that Amanda could receive a kiss in the moonlight before she turned into an old maid? Or that because of this illicit rendezvous, Amanda had done something crazy like marry the Cajun racetrack owner? If Amanda had purposely eloped with Comeaux, what good would it be revealing her secret meeting with Tanner or that she had failed to show up at a ball her father had forbidden her to attend?

"I know nothing of this," Sally finally said. "Amanda told me nothing. I'm as surprised as you."

"Were they ever together?" the Judge prodded, the anxiety obvious in his voice. "Did you ever see them meeting besides at the front gate?"

She did remember something, right before the ball.

"Yes," Sally said, recounting that afternoon in the steamy, crowded market. "She had met Comeaux at the market the afternoon before the ball. He had gotten her a glass of water, I believe."

And she had touched his arm and was looking lovingly into his eyes.

"What were they talking about?" the Judge urged.

At first Sally hadn't heard him. She was too busy thinking of how close they had stood, how friendly their actions had seemed. *So, she eloped after all,* Sally surmised. *Right behind my stupid, naive back.*

"I don't know, sir," Sally said, this time the tears breaking free. "I have no idea what has happened."

Virginia stood at the front threshold and watched Sally disappear around the corner, the young girl still wiping the tears from her cheeks. Like Judge Richardson, Virginia had sensed that Sally held a clue to this elopement puzzle and was just as disappointed when Sally revealed nothing.

"She's hiding something," Virginia heard the Judge say behind her. He was standing so close, Virginia could feel his warm breath on her neck. She swallowed hard, forcing away the thoughts that persisted whenever she was in his presence.

Virginia had fallen hopelessly in love with James Richardson the first week of her employment. Knowing how dangerous such feelings could be toward an employer, she had vowed to leave as soon as the Judge recovered from his broken heart and Amanda adjusted to the devastating news of losing her mother.

Ten years passed, and both still suffered from Genevieve Richardson's scandalous affair. Virginia hadn't the heart—or the strength—to leave now. She adored Amanda, who became the daughter she never could conceive with her late husband, and her love for James Richardson only grew stronger with the years.

Since Genevieve's death two years before, James had relied on Virginia not only to run his household and guide his daughter—Amanda had grown too old for a nanny—but to lean on in business matters. Virginia had even worked in the administration of his last campaign.

Virginia doubted James loved her in return, but she knew she was one of the few good friends the Judge had made over the years. He made that clear when he named her a beneficiary in his will, an action that both stunned her and offered her hope.

If only he could love me a little, she thought as the Judge's arm brushed her shoulder while he moved to close the front door. Like so many times before, the Judge casually made physical contact, treating her more like a relative than an employee. Virginia had been grateful for the gestures, but the desire that lingered in her bosom ached to be set free. She wanted more, that she could never deny. She closed her eyes briefly and took a deep breath, one she hoped would send the unwelcome thoughts away.

Instead, she opened her eyes to find the Judge's arm draped paternally over her shoulders, the door left open so they could view the street. For a moment, she imagined being his wife, standing in the front foyer wondering what to do about their rebellious daughter who had scandalously disappeared with a strange man.

Which was exactly what had happened. Amanda had become a daughter of sorts, and Virginia like a wife to this man. Perhaps the Judge needed what most men do when their daughters leave the nest—comfort and understanding. Without much fore-thought, she slipped her arm around his waist, her left hand resting on his hip.

Neither one said a word, and Virginia feared she had finally overstepped her boundaries. To accept an employer's friendly hand on your arm was one thing, but to return such an advance was unthinkable. "Never give in to temptation," her mother had carefully instructed her when she reached adolescence, "and choose the safer path." Virginia had heeded those words only once. She'd married Jess O'Neil, God rest his soul, a good provider and a steady worker. Jess never lifted a hand against her; for that she was eternally grateful. But she'd never loved him a day in her life. Before the dirt had settled on his grave, Virginia was halfway to America.

The Judge refused to move or speak, yet Virginia could not remove her hand. It had taken her ten years to put it there, and if she had just written her walking papers, then she would at least enjoy the ride.

"Will she ever come back?" James asked, hoping to dispel the disconcerting silence that lingered between them. He couldn't fathom what logic had made him wrap his arm about Virginia; it had just felt normal to do so. He quickly assessed his inappropriate behavior, and was going to remove his arm when she had placed her own about his waist, sending shock waves of emotion through him.

James couldn't decide on his next move. He knew what he wanted to do. He wanted to lift this redheaded woman with a complexion the color of buttermilk and make continuous, passionate love to her. Those wanton thoughts, so unbridled and exposed, had frozen him to the spot.

"Of course she will," he heard Virginia say, noting the slight nervousness in her voice.

Move your damn arm! he instructed himself, but still it remained firmly planted.

At least close the door before someone sees you. Logic
returned, and James released his embrace to shut the front
foyer door. Virginia relaxed her arm, then folded both arms
protectively across her chest. When he turned back towards the
parlor, she avoided his eyes.

What was I thinking of touching this woman in that manner?
he berated himself. *She is in my employ.*

As if sensing his thoughts, Virginia gazed up to meet his
stare. If James wasn't mistaken, desire lurked behind those
dazzling, beautiful green eyes he always had trouble avoiding.
She was daring him, inviting him.

Before he could comprehend his actions, James leaned forward and lightly kissed her lips. He didn't know what caused
him to do such a thing, but her response was more surprising
than his actions. Virginia emitted a soft moan and returned his
kiss, stretching her arms around his neck and pulling him in
closer. James deepened the kiss, savoring the sweet sensations
awakening within him, while Virginia's hands poured through
his gray-streaked blond hair.

God, she tasted sweet, James thought, just before a carriage
was heard arriving at the front of the house. James paused,
resting his forehead against Virginia's and closing his eyes to
try to resume a steady breath.

"We must . . ." he began.

Virginia instantly released herself from his hold and stood
back avoiding his eyes. She held the back of her hand to her
mouth as if shocked at her actions.

"I'm entirely to blame," James said, trying to calm the
awkwardness. "I don't know what came over me."

Virginia said nothing, but shook her head. "I shall leave
first thing."

The thought of losing his trusted Virginia flooded James's
mind. It was unthinkable. He couldn't live without her. He was

about to tell her so when the door quietly opened and Amanda appeared, the bright afternoon sunlight blinding them all.

"Have I interrupted something?" she asked.

All the way into town Amanda had fretted over the lunchtime meeting with her father and Gin. Her stomach became so knotted with anxiety, she couldn't imagine holding down any food. She even prepared a speech for when she entered the foyer and addressed her father for the first time since their meeting that fateful afternoon. But when she opened the door, her father and Gin appeared more guilty than she.

"Of course not," her father bellowed, blushing a deep rouge that matched Virginia's. "We were just discussing you."

What reprieve she experienced from her previous anxiety was short-lived. Amanda felt once again like Daniel in the Lion's Den. Still, something had happened. Amanda wondered if Gin had finally announced her feelings for her father. Gin never expressed them to Amanda, but it was obvious she painfully pined for the man in silence.

"I'll see to lunch," Virginia said, and quickly hurried away while James's gaze followed her out of the room.

Amanda decided to seize on the opportunity. "That's not like Gin. I expected fifty questions by now. Is something wrong?"

James spun around heatedly, literally forcing Amanda back a step. "Something wrong?" he shouted. "The child she loved and cared for for the past ten years disappears in the middle of the night after informing her she was going to bed, then runs off with the town's racetrack owner, and you ask is something wrong?"

"I . . ." Amanda began, jumping back another step.

"What are you doing here, Amanda?" he continued heatedly. "Have you finally come to your senses and left him?"

The idea that her father would think she was returning home

for good hadn't occurred to Amanda. "I've come home for lunch," she said meekly. "I want us to go on as before."

"We will never go on as before," James said between gritted teeth. "You have destroyed this family."

Tears Amanda had not expected welled in her eyes. "I didn't mean to hurt you."

"Waltzing out of here in the middle of the night like a wanton woman and eloping with a man you know nothing about, a man I never would have approved of?" the Judge shouted. "How could you, Amanda?"

The sobs reached her chest, and Amanda knew conversation was impossible. She covered her mouth to keep from sobbing out loud.

"Tell me you don't love him," James said softly. "Tell me this was all a big mistake. We'll have it annulled in no time. Marriages like this can be fixed. Tell me that's what you want."

When Amanda said nothing, still crying painfully into her handkerchief, James grabbed his daughter by her shoulders. "It's simple, Amanda. Tell me that's what you want."

Through her tear-blurred vision, Amanda could see the determination in her father's eyes. Anger over what she had done was expected, but where was the paternal concern? Why wasn't his heart breaking because she'd left him, and not because she'd married poorly?

Amanda had lost her mother when she was twelve years old. Two years ago, when they received news of her mother's death, she'd lost her father as well. At times she doubted he still loved her.

"No," she whispered, looking away to escape his furious stare.

James released her and stepped back, still staring at her intently. "Then tell your French husband that I will be more than generous if he agrees to an annulment. I'm sure he will not turn down such an offer. Tell him to name his price."

Thoughts of Tanner and his vow to make her father pay for the privilege of marrying his daughter came back all too clearly. "Is that what I am to you," Amanda asked, "a product to be bought or sold?"

"No, that's what you are to your fortune-hunting husband," James retorted.

"You're wrong, Father," Amanda said, meeting his eyes bravely. "René is a good man."

"René has his price. Tell him my offer and see for yourself."

"Lunch is ready," Virginia announced quietly from the back of the foyer.

While Amanda breathed a quick sigh of relief at the interruption, James grabbed his hat and headed for the door. "Tell him, Amanda," he instructed her as he opened the door. "You'll be surprised what the French want after all."

The horse beat out a steady rhythm along the bayou road as T-Emile drove the carriage home. Amanda was thankful for his shyness, for she wasn't in the mood for conversation, especially dialogue that had to be translated inside her head. Her thoughts remained in English, her father's angry words reverberating throughout her mind.

She must ask René about an annulment. It was wrong of her to think he wouldn't want a chance out of the marriage if one was available. He married her to protect her reputation, but would he remain married to her given an option?

Still, if she asked and insulted him, she would never forgive herself. He had been so kind, so generous. She couldn't bear the thought of hurting him once again as she had that morning.

As hard as she wished them away, doubts continued to creep into her thoughts. Why did René marry her? Was he really being noble or did he have other intentions?

It wouldn't hurt to mention the money. If René wasn't interested in her inheritance, he'd say so. If he wanted the money and the opportunity to rid himself of his wife, then best to know now and avoid a lifetime of an unloving marriage.

Tears pressed upon her eyes, and Amanda fought hard to keep them at bay. She didn't know which hurt worse, her father's angry shouting or the fact that René might not care in the least to be her husband.

As the house slowly came into view, Amanda knew what she had to do. She would give René his options and let him decide. After all, his life had been disrupted as much as hers. Perhaps he was secretly longing to return to normalcy.

"The daughter of a French aristocrat?" René asked his uncle as the two entered the house. Alcée had mentioned he wanted to have a tête-à-tête with him on the way back from the horse track, but René was beginning to doubt his motives. Alcée had tried several times to talk him out of loving Amanda, but this new trick was a bit far-fetched.

"She told me so herself," Alcée said earnestly.

"What are you talking about?" René said. "She's the daughter of Judge Richardson. The man who hates the French, remember?"

Alcée removed his hat and beat the dust from it before crossing the threshold of the workroom. "Her mother was Genevieve Vanier, the famous opera singer."

Now, this sounded familiar, René thought. "The French singer who came to St. Martinville?" he asked with a devilish grin. "The one you were in love with when you were sixteen?"

"René," Alcée said sternly. "Vanier was her mother. She left Amanda and Judge Richardson ten years ago for France and the opera stage. Some say she left with another man, a Frenchman. Judge Richardson despises anything French because he can't stand being reminded of her."

René searched his uncle's eyes for signs of dishonesty, but
found none. "You're telling a joke, no?"

"No," Alcée answered, unsmiling.

"Vanier, the opera singer?"

Alcée nodded, then added, "Vanier, whose family were
friends of kings."

René brushed his hands anxiously through his fine brown
hair. Marrying the daughter of a rich, prominent American
family was one mountain to climb, but the daughter of French
aristocracy? What could a simple Acadian offer such a woman?

"Don't be surprised if she leaves," Alcée said softly, offering
a friendly hand on René's shoulder. "She's not one of us, René.
How could a woman of her upbringing possibly be happy here?
She's bound to go home sooner or later."

René heard the advice being given by Alcée, but his thoughts
remained on the bright, smiling face of the woman he so dearly
loved. With a heavy heart he left the house, silently moving
into the diffused light of the oncoming sunset, staring down at
the slow-moving bayou.

It all seemed so easy—marry Amanda and let the world be
damned. He hadn't considered she might want the marriage
annulled. He hadn't realized how far apart they were socially.
They seemed like equals talking amiably at her fence.

Colette began to call Alexandre and Pierre into the house.
Dinnertime was approaching and Amanda hadn't returned. In
all likelihood, René thought, she had probably sent T-Emile
home with a letter stating she would remain in town, safe at
home with her father. While René's heart struggled with the
weight of that image, he couldn't help but hope she would
appear at his door.

As Pierre rushed by on the way to the house, René effortlessly
scooped him up and held him tight, the young boy reciprocating
the affection by wrapping his arms around his beloved cousin.
Wondering if he would ever hold children of his own—ones

with blond curls and eyes the color of a summer sky—René hugged the boy tightly.

Amanda stood staring, transfixed, at her tall husband lovingly hugging his cousin, whose six-year-old legs dangled to René's knees. The sun was setting behind the house, casting an orange glow on the bayou and reflecting on the soft brown hues of René's hair.

A woman couldn't ask for a more loving husband, she thought. Father had to be wrong. René couldn't have married her for the money. Still, she had resolved to give René the option, and now was as good a time as any.

She walked up silently beside him, just as he released Pierre from his hold and the boy bolted off toward the house. When René looked up again, his piercing brown eyes caught hers and the familiar knots tightened inside her. For three days now, she had hardly been able to breathe.

"How did it go with your father?" he asked quietly.

Amanda stared into his deep chestnut eyes, glistening in the setting sun, and his kindly words turned the knots into butterflies. "Fine," was all she could manage.

For a moment, René brightened. Then he turned toward the house, offering his arm to Amanda. "It's time for dinner," he said, almost as if it were a question.

As she placed her hand on his forearm, Amanda drew closer, reveling in the safeness she felt in his presence, breathing in deeply his scent of manliness and a hint of store-bought tonic. She would ask him later.

At dinner, few words were spoken, except by the boys, who could hardly contain themselves from speaking on every subject imaginable. Amanda was thankful for their nonstop chattering; it kept her thoughts from René.

Colette allowed Amanda to clear the table, but steadfastly refused to let her clean and dry the dishes. Since the boys seemed preoccupied with the game of *cache et fait,* a Louisiana version of hide-and-seek, and T-Emile had returned to some chores at the stables, Amanda joined Alcée and René in the living room. René sat absorbed at his desk, jotting down notes and numbers in a series of books. Alcée sat by the fireplace, polishing his boots.

"Can I help in any way?" Amanda asked.

Both men looked up and frowned in unison as if the question was absurd. Amanda couldn't understand why she wasn't allowed to participate in the household chores. Did they think she was incapable simply because she came from a wealthy American family?

"I'm skilled in many areas," she began. "I spent three years at a ladies' finishing school in Virginia." What she hoped would make an impression brought another round of frowns. Perhaps it was the language barrier.

"I must help out," she insisted. "Is there nothing I can do around here?"

Alcée brushed the boots aside and held out a chair. "You may be my harshest critic," he said with a dashing smile and a bow.

Before Amanda could question his statement, Alcée removed one of the violins off the shelf and began tuning the instrument.

"Alcée will perform at the drop of a hat," René said to her from across the room. "Don't encourage him too much or you'll never get to sleep."

Amanda smiled broadly now that she was finally feeling like part of the family. "Whose violin is the other one?" she asked.

Alcée laughed as he pulled the bow over the strings, testing several notes. "It's René's, but the man will never be a good musician until he understands that work stops at sunset."

"It has to be done," René grumbled without looking up.

"Only if you insist on making more money than we need," Alcée countered.

"We can always use more money."

"We have more than enough."

"Not to me," René added, his tone getting harsher.

Alcée sighed. "So, don't listen to me. Listen to your father," he instructed René, then turned the conversation to Amanda. "My brother-in-law, René's father, always taught us to be content with what sustains us. But Monsieur Businessman over there doesn't know when to stop and play the music."

"If you would have worked harder and played less, perhaps Marguerite wouldn't have married François," René retorted without looking up from his work.

René's words appeared to have pierced Alcée's heart. He stood staring accusingly at his nephew, visibly affected. René suddenly realized what he had said and looked up. "I'm sorry, Alcée," René began in a softer, apologetic tone. "I didn't mean . . ."

"Forget it," Alcée retorted abruptly, concentrating on his violin.

A heaviness instantly settled over the room. Amanda watched as René anxiously pulled his fingers through his hair. She wondered why his uncle worried about his working so hard, and wondered about the mysterious woman named Marguerite. When René continued the conversation, his tone turned quiet, almost pleading.

"I play second fiddle to my accomplished uncle," he said to Amanda. "It would be hopeless of me to even dream of being as good as him, so I stick to what I know, even if it takes me all night to do it."

Alcée digested his words thoughtfully. Finally, he said, "Some of us are meant to play music. Others are meant to be outstanding men of business."

René glanced up and smiled slightly at his uncle. Despite any misunderstanding they might have, Amanda sensed they would always be great friends.

"Now, madame," Alcée asked Amanda, "any requests?"

A list of songs rolled through Amanda's brain, but before she could utter a word, Alcée began the traditional French folk song *Le Pont de Nantes,* a song Amanda recognized from her childhood. The words were slightly different, but their description of a bridge in Brittany and the memory of her mother singing them came flooding back.

Alcée glanced over when the tears welled up in Amanda's eyes. He instantly charged into a song she did not recognize, a rousing song that sounded like it involved a lot of drinking and toasting. When René looked up and cast a warning look in Alcée's direction, Amanda assumed she was right. Alcée finished the short ditty and grinned.

"Perhaps something softer," he said.

Alcée closed his eyes to concentrate on a soft waltz, his bow moving effortlessly across the violin as if the movements were as natural to him as breathing. The violin sang eagerly in response, the notes of the song beseeching Amanda to listen, saying that here was a song of heartbreak, of undying love.

While the perspiration slithered down the backs of her knees and she fanned the stagnant, hot night air with her handkerchief, Amanda settled back in her chair and let the passionate music infuse her. Her heart seemed to stop pumping, replaced instead by a three-beat rhythm.

Alcée then began to sing a song of a man pining for his blond love, a man devastated that she has left him. He begs her to reconsider, not to listen to others and return to her family. He announces his complete love for her, adding that death would be welcome if she is not his.

For a moment Amanda imagined he was singing the song for her benefit. When he mentioned blond for the third time, she glanced over at René, who sat staring off thoughtfully. Surely, it was a coincidence.

When Alcée finished the song, Amanda applauded enthusiastically. Alcée responded with a slight bow. *"Merci,"* he said.

"Perhaps it's time you went to bed," René said, suddenly at Amanda's side and gently pulling her out of the chair. "It's late."

"I'm not tired," Amanda answered, hoping for more of the sad, yet romantic music and Alcée's intoxicating violin playing. She wondered how Alcée could have stayed a bachelor so long with such a remarkable talent.

"You should go to bed," Alcée echoed. "I'll play some more for you tomorrow."

"Please do," Amanda said, then immediately wondered if there would be a tomorrow. She looked up at René and her stomach tightened. She had to ask him.

The two walked up the stairs in silence, pausing only inside Alcée's bedroom door, the room now being used by René. Once she was inside the threshold to René's former room, a wall would separate them. "Well, good night," René said quietly, handing her the lamp.

"Good night," Amanda answered, feeling amazingly disappointed. What had she expected, a kiss good night?

Yes, her heart responded, which might prove he didn't wish for an annulment after all.

Amanda entered her bedroom, closing the door behind her. As she moved to undress, she could hear René doing the same next door. She sat down on the bed, chastising herself for being both a coward and a hopeless romantic. *If I'm not mistaken, Amanda Rose,* she scolded herself, *wishing for kisses in the moonlight is what got you into this mess.*

"Shut up," she said aloud. The confusion, the guilt, the doubts, the anxiety she was causing others came crashing around her heart once more.

"Go away," she told her emotions, but they refused to budge. She placed her head inside her hands and took a deep breath. She had to tell him. She had to have an answer.

Suddenly, a knock came at the door, causing Amanda to nearly jump out of her stockings. "Yes?" she said.

René opened the door slowly as if afraid she might be indecent. "I don't understand it," he began. "Colette forgot to leave me some water. Did she leave you any?"

Glad to be doing anything besides listening to her inner demons, Amanda checked the water pitcher by the side of the bed. "Yes, I have water. Bring your pitcher and I'll give you some of mine."

René approached her, shaking his head. "I don't understand her. She does things like clockwork. This isn't like her."

"It's because of a bet she has with Alcée."

"What?" René asked.

What had she just done? Amanda thought with horror. Would she ever learn to think before talking or acting?

"Uh, nothing," she answered. "I thought I heard them say something about it, but it's nothing."

"If there's a reason why she stopped putting water in my room, I'd like to know it," René insisted.

Amanda had to say something. She was already halfway wet, she might as well dive in. "Alcée is betting that I'll go home to my father. Colette bet him otherwise. She has been giving me water instead of you so you'll come into my room every night, increasing her chances of winning the bet."

The blush spreading across her face burned like fire on paper. She wondered if René could see her scarlet face in the near darkness of the room.

"I see," he said solemnly, then moved to leave.

Oh, God, would she ever stop saying the wrong thing, she berated herself. But since she was plunging headfirst into the deep water, she might as well say it all.

"René," she said, causing him to pause inches away. "My father wanted me to tell you he would grant an annulment if that was what you wanted."

When René refused to move or speak, Amanda added, "He said he would be generous."

René stared at her intently, and Amanda instantly wished she could retract the words. She had insulted him, of that she was sure.

"Amanda," René quietly began, "if you wish to go home to your father, then you must do what you have to do." Leaning in closer, René continued between clenched teeth. "But your father can go to Hell."

It took only seconds for René to march from the room and angrily slam the door. It took much longer for Amanda's breathing to slowly return to normal. But as she sat on the edge of the massive bed, a bed she had shared only hours before, a satisfying smile stole across her face. Glancing up at a happier view of her husband, Amanda began to hope that life was about to get better.

"One more game," Tanner insisted, trying to keep the desperation from his voice. The familiar panic rose in his chest when McDuff entered the room. It could only mean one thing. His lack of payment on his mounting debts had worn out Tanner's welcome.

"McDuff," Tanner coaxed, placing a friendly hand on the burly man's shoulder, "a few more days and I'm loaded. I swear the money's practically sitting in your pocket. In the meantime, how about a few hands to let me win back some of my hard-earned coins."

McDuff moved ever so slightly, knocking Tanner's hand aside. Tanner recognized the look McDuff was sending; he was not a man to listen to balderdash, especially from a down-and-out gambler who hadn't received a decent hand in over a month. Never since Tanner lost the family estate had he been busted so long. His Tennessee-born father had an expression for his present condition: "catawamptiously chawed up."

But he could turn his luck around. He felt it in the air. He wasn't defeated yet.

"A few hands," Tanner asked again. "You'll see. I've got Ole Lady Luck rolling with me tonight."

"Good night, Henry," McDuff said unemotionally. "Monday is fast approaching. I'd suggest you go home and find a way to pony up with that three thousand."

"I told you, Bill, the money's . . ."

"Better be in my pocket or a certain dandy will have a couple of broken legs, right before I bust his head open. Do we understand each other?"

"I'll have it."

"See that you do," McDuff answered quickly, pushing Tanner toward the door.

"You're making a big mistake," Tanner argued as he walked backwards towards the front of the gaming room and further away from the poker table. Knowing he'd be refused a game brought the panic to his throat. "One game," he now pleaded. "Just one game."

McDuff gave him a final push across the threshold and slammed the door. Tanner pressed his hands and forehead against the cheap wood, aching like a suitor whose loved one's father had bodily thrown him out. His body yearned for the feel of the cards in his hand, the rush of the game.

Although Tanner despised the border ruffians who lived in shanties on the outskirts of town, he knew they always had a game of craps in progress. Dusting off his waistcoat and adjusting his sleeves, Tanner headed for the lower end of Franklin.

Before he left the glow of the fading street lamp, he noticed a dark-featured man standing at the corner, his black eyes staring. "What are you looking at?" Tanner asked brusquely.

"Are you 'Enry Tanner," the man said, his French accent apparent.

"What's it to you?"

"Nothing," the man answered, keeping in the shadows. "Except that word has it around Port Cocodrie you've been compromising innocent women."

Tanner leaned closer to get a better view, but the man's dark hair and complexion and the lack of adequate street lighting made it impossible for him to get a good look. *Who is this frog?* Tanner thought. He never associated with Frenchmen.

"Are you a friend of that bastard Comeaux?" Tanner demanded. "You tell that son of a bitch he's got a lot of nerve."

When the man didn't answer, Tanner grew uncomfortable. "Like I said, what's it to you?"

The mysterious Frenchman continued to stare, seemingly contemplating Tanner's answer. Then he tipped his hat. "Let's hope nothing," he said softly, but with iron in his tone. "For your sake."

Tanner was about to retort, but the man quickly moved down the street toward the center of town. It didn't take the unknown Frenchman long in the intensely black night to completely disappear.

"Shit," Tanner mumbled to himself, wondering if Lady Luck had deserted him for good. "For my sake, my ass," he shouted to the darkness. "No one threatens Henry Tanner."

He instantly forgot the craps game. He had more important things to consider. McDuff was right. He needed to plank up three thousand dollars, and he knew a certain blond heiress who would be of service.

Chapter Seven

The floorboards continued to creak in Virginia's room, and James thought he heard the opening and closing of a trunk. Pacing his upstairs bedroom, he knew he had to stop her, but every time he grabbed the copper doorknob, his courage faltered.

What the hell was he supposed to say? *I'm sorry I lost all control of my senses and violated the trust that existed between us. Please excuse my indelicate behavior; can we return to normal now?*

What if she wants to discuss it? James thought with horror. The last thing he needed at a time like this was a heart-to-heart discussion about his needs with a woman. James suffered emotionally over the loss of his wife, but he never denied his physical longings. There were always women in the other towns where he conducted business who were willing to share his bed, and he had always been receptive. At least until two years ago. Knowing his loss was permanent had driven away all desire. Not to mention his *raison d'être,* he thought grimly.

Until today, James had forgotten the fire of passion, the delectable taste of a woman's lips, the silky texture of a woman's skin. Virginia had brought it all back.

"Damn," he said aloud as a line of perspiration broke out on his brow. James marched from his room, slamming the door in his wake.

Virginia stared down at the half-filled trunk with disgust. She prided herself on efficiency, but tonight she began to wonder if old age wasn't slowing her down at last.

"I'm only thirty-five," she said, mentally reminding herself that her mother had given birth to her at the same age. After six other children, her inner demons added, and she'd died eight years later, a month behind her father.

Virginia closed her eyes tightly, hoping to dispel the painful memories clouding her thinking. She would berate herself later, after she left Franklin. She planned to make an early morning steamer to New Orleans, and there was half a room to pack.

With renewed energy, Virginia began unfolding and refolding the wool sweaters long hidden in the back of her cedar armoire. Before she placed them in her steamer trunk, Virginia inhaled their musky scent. They smelled of home, of a simpler time when keeping house for Jess at their meager farmhouse was her only concern.

If only she hadn't come to Franklin, then perhaps she would have married again. If only James loved her as much as she loved him.

"What if? What if?" Virginia grumbled to the four walls. "A person could die wondering."

Virginia felt like crying—she knew it would probably do her good—but she refused to give in to the weak emotion. She was tired of crying, fed up with heartache. Let the balladeers sing their mournful songs of lost love and their "bonnies" back in Ireland. Virginia would have none of it.

She should be happy, Virginia thought as she threw a sweater into the trunk, not caring whether the sweater was folded properly or not. Her departure had been inevitable, ever since she'd first recognized her painful symptoms of unrequited love. After ten years and one thousand attempts at leaving, Virginia was finally breaking free. At last she would be rid of watching and longing for James Richardson, and move ahead with her life.

Folding her arms protectively across her chest, Virginia straightened. John Teele had spent months sitting next to her at Mass until she'd made it clear she wasn't interested. Peter McArthur always brightened at her arrival in the market. Perhaps she would remarry. New Orleans was full of Irishmen fleeing the recent crop failures. She didn't need James Richardson with his strong broad shoulders, piercing blue eyes and wispy blond curls. She would forget him and the feel of his eager lips on hers and his large hands pulling their bodies closer. She would forget everything.

Virginia sighed and collapsed on her bed. Forget the ten best years of her life?

The conflict raging inside her quickly dissipated when Virginia heard the neighboring door slam. James's knock was anything but discreet.

"Virginia," he practically shouted. "May I have a word with you?"

Virginia nonchalantly opened the door, poised stubbornly to reject any lovesick emotions she might feel over the sight of him. But her best intentions were powerless against his handsome trim figure gracing her threshold.

James also appeared taken aback at their meeting. The force of his earlier words lessened as he repeated, "I must speak with you."

"Of course, sir," Virginia answered, averting the studious gaze of his azure eyes while her hands were planted resolutely on her hips.

"Damn it, Gin," James said, his fever returning, "stop calling me sir."

Virginia stood quietly in the doorway, while James took the opportunity to enter the room and examine the trunk. "Are you leaving us?" James's question sounded incredulous.

"I'm taking the *Carnaval* into New Orleans at sunrise tomorrow," she stated firmly.

When James looked up, his concern was evident. "You must not leave on account of my indiscretion."

"I am as much to blame as you . . ."

"Nonsense, this business with Amanda has strained our emotions."

For several moments, neither one spoke, and Virginia could hear the cicadas outside her window announcing the onset of darkness. "I must go," she finally said. "I have done my service to this family. Amanda is now grown and married and it's time I did the same."

James's eyes widened. "You married? To whom?"

Virginia instantly wished she could retract her words. They were, after all, just words. There was no one at the present time she could call an interested suitor. Any more discussion on the subject and she would only embarrass herself.

"There have been interests," was all she said, quickly adding, "If you don't mind, I'd appreciate a reference."

James stared transfixed. "Of course," he whispered. "But is there nothing I can do or say?"

"No, sir," Virginia replied, folding her arms against her chest. "I am determined to leave."

For the second time that week, James felt his once secure world slipping away beneath his feet. First Amanda and now Virginia. Tomorrow evening he would be dining alone in a room that once had been filled each night with the lilting laughter of two very precious women.

Feeling his chest tighten, James sat down on the edge of Virginia's bed. He recognized the familiar heartache—he had learned to live with the unrelenting pain for the past ten years. But he had survived, thanks to the constant nursing given by two attentive women. They had been his strength during the darkest times of his life, unselfishly abandoning their own needs for his. And within the past three days he had sent them both away.

"Perhaps you will grant me one wish," James said quietly.

Virginia unfolded her arms cautiously. "Yes?"

"Allow me a few weeks," he said. "I would prefer that you had a situation to go to in New Orleans, instead of entering that city blind. Plus, you would be doing me a favor by staying with me until I can straighten out my problems with Amanda."

Virginia sat down on the bed an arm's length away, a look of defeat on her face. James began to hope he could stall her. "I will write to my associates in New Orleans and inquire about work," he said. "You must let me help you, even if it is only to secure proper employment."

Virginia sat silent, staring blankly across the room as if incapable of saying no to him. She had always been like this, faithful and obedient to his every need, despite her stubborn arguments. God, how would he ever live without her?

Her ruddy pinkish complexion glowed softly as the rays of the setting sun painted her proud high cheekbones with its brilliance. As on so many other occasions, Virginia's simple, unaided beauty astonished James. Unlike his wife, whose exquisite countenance was breathtaking, Virginia's attractiveness moved him passionately. James had adored his wife; he could fervently love Virginia.

Without conscious thought, James moved a loose curl away from Virginia's face. As if instinctively, Virginia placed her hand on his and pressed it tightly against her cheek. Her skin felt warm and alive and incredibly accessible. His body responded in ways he hadn't thought possible after so many years. His mind reeled with the possibilities. If he could only kiss her one more time as they had that morning. If only he could feel her pressed against him.

James released his hand and bolted upright. "Then it's all settled," he announced, trying not to meet her eyes. "A few weeks?"

"Yes, James," Virginia answered, not looking up.

"Good. In the meantime I'll make the necessary arrangements." *And do my best to keep you from leaving.*

James hesitated at the threshold. "I must go out to the plantation tonight. Word has it that Henry's been beating a slave again."

This time Virginia looked up. "I've never trusted him."

"So you've always said," James answered, watching the sunset turn her emerald eyes various shades of green.

"There are rumors in town that he's gambled a small fortune away and there have been threats on his life," Virginia continued. "A desperate man is apt to do desperate things."

James nodded. He had heard the stories as well. Plus Tanner had asked for a sizable advance on his salary several days prior, one James had not approved. "After I deal with Amanda, I shall hire a new overseer," he said.

"Thank you," Virginia said softly. "I don't know why, but I really dislike that man."

Tanner checked his pocket watch for the third time, but Katharine Blanchard would not get the hint. He had wined and dined her, made love to the little princess, now why wouldn't she leave?

Tanner imagined he had seen the last of the Blanchard girl

after that wild carriage ride when he had stolen her innocence.
She had retreated sobbing to the side of the carriage on the
ride home, refusing to talk to him. Then she had appeared that
morning at his doorstep claiming to be in love.

Katharine had served a purpose, no matter what she had
come for. Tanner needed a release, a chance to clear his mind.
He knew as well as Katharine that nothing could come from
their relationship. She needed a marriage that offered compensa-
tion as much as he did.

The quick roll in the sheets proved a nice respite, but now
he needed her gone. If he had to listen to one more story
about the uncanny ability of her fiancé, Bernard Mann, to make
thousands from sugarcane, he would physically pitch her into
the mud.

"Bernard Mann is your fiancé?" Tanner asked, as a thought
raced through his head.

"Why, yes," Katharine answered, acting as if they were
sitting down to tea.

"He might be interested in knowing how you spend your
afternoons," Tanner said, slowly twisting a lock of her hair in
his fingers.

Katharine's eyes grew wide with fright. "You wouldn't
dare."

"Wouldn't I?"

Tears welled up instantly in her eyes. "But why would you
do that to me? You know how much I love you. I'll do anything
for you."

Which was precisely what Tanner had in mind. "I'll reconsider if you bring Amanda Richardson to me alone," he said
firmly.

"But I don't understand. What does Amanda have to do
with . . ."

Tanner ignored her, wrapping the lock tighter in his grip.
"She lives with the Cajun racetrack owner now. She visits

town frequently, but never alone. I need to speak to her, but it's important that no one else be around. Do you understand?''

''You're hurting me,'' Katharine said, tugging at the strand of hair.

''Do you understand?''

''Yes,'' Katharine acquiesced, breathing relief when Tanner released her hair.

''When?''

''Friday is Anne's baby christening,'' Katharine offered. ''I'll ask her to come with me to the church.''

Tanner began to pace. ''Too many people.''

''You could get her alone after the service. Or I could tell her there is someone to see her outside. I don't know, maybe on the way there?''

For several moments, Tanner said nothing. It could work. He would make it work. ''Then it's settled,'' he announced. ''Friday you pick her up in your carriage and the two of you drive to church alone.''

Grabbing his hat, he flung open the front door. ''You can leave now,'' he instructed Katharine before disappearing around the corner of the house.

''I'm seventeen,'' T-Emile quietly said.

After several minutes of small talk, to which the young man contributed nothing, Amanda finally resorted to asking him his age. Knowing he would drive the carriage in silence after he told her this information, Amanda continued her line of questions.

''What does the T in your name mean?''

''My father's name was Emile.''

The horse's steady plodding persisted, but T-Emile's explanation did not. ''I don't understand,'' Amanda finally said.

''I'm 'Tit Emile.''

Amanda sounded the words over and over again in her head

until they eventually made sense. "I see," she said with a bright smile. "That's short for Petit Emile, which becomes 'Tit Emile or T-Emile."

T-Emile seemed to follow her interpretation with a nonemotional stare. Amanda wondered if he understood the name's evolution, or if he just didn't care how the name had originated. From what she had witnessed the past few days, the young man didn't seem interested in much, although he dutifully performed his chores without complaint. Perhaps most boys in their teens acted this apathetically.

"Everyone has a *sobriquet*," T-Emile added.

Amanda was so surprised that he had finally spoken without being spoken to, she almost glanced around the carriage to see if someone else had joined them. She decided to act upon his burst of congeniality. "Everyone has a nickname?"

"If they're not named after a relative, it's usually a description of the person," T-Emile explained.

The idea was intriguing, Amanda thought. "What is René's T-name?" she asked.

T-Emile smiled, which shocked Amanda more than his speaking on his own. "I shouldn't tell," he said.

"Oh, please," Amanda insisted with a sly grin. "After all, I am his wife."

"Well, don't tell him you heard it from me," the boy said.

"I promise," Amanda agreed.

T-Emile searched the horizon as if the empty fields had grown ears. "It's Tête Rouge."

Even a child would have known that *tête rouge* meant redhead in French, but René's locks were golden brown. "I don't understand," Amanda said. "He doesn't have red hair."

"It's not about his hair," T-Emile explained with a dimpled smile, his brown Dugas eyes shining with mischief. "He went fishing with his father one day and forgot to wear a hat."

The thought of René receiving a nickname that poked fun at a bad sunburn tickled Amanda. "Does anyone call him that?"

"Only his father."

"Tête Rouge?"

"That's right."

Amanda made a mental note.

"What is Alcée's?" she asked.

It took T-Emile several moments before speaking. "Gros Tête."

During the few seconds it took Amanda to translate *gros tête* into "large head," no one spoke. As if on cue, both Amanda and T-Emile burst into laughter as soon as she realized its meaning.

"He had an enormous head as a child," T-Emile added, and the two erupted into another round of laughter.

For the rest of the journey into town, the two talked amiably. But when the Richardson house came into view, both watched in silence as the horse made its way up the semicircular drive.

"I won't be long," she told T-Emile as he helped her down from the carriage. "Same as yesterday."

T-Emile smiled slightly, and climbed back up into the carriage to escape the fierceness of the noonday sun. Amanda hated to see the boy suffer in such heat, but she couldn't ask him inside. Her father would be furious.

"I'll send Maddie out with some lemonade," she offered.

The words sounded so patronizing, like an American aristocrat speaking to a field hand at her back door. She remembered Alcée's accusing words about Acadians not being allowed inside the Richardson home.

Not knowing what else to do, Amanda entered the dismal house, which appeared darker than usual. She stood in the hallway waiting for her eyes to adjust to the dimness.

"So you're home again today, are you?" Amanda followed the sound of Virginia's voice to the dining room, where her former nanny was setting the table. It was the first time Virginia had spoken to her since that fateful night.

"Have you forgiven me?" Amanda asked meekly.

"No." Virginia's tone was stern.

"Please, Gin. I didn't mean to hurt you."

"Didn't you?"

"It had nothing to do with you."

Virginia dropped a plate onto the table. By its sound, Amanda feared it had broken.

"Defying your father, who has loved and cared for you in every possible way, was one thing, but to secretly leave this house under my nose is unforgivable. We had a trust, Amanda, and you betrayed me. 'He's only a friend,' " she mimicked Amanda. " 'We talk about the weather.' How could you have been so deceitful? Why on earth wouldn't you think of telling me about it?"

Amanda began to speak, but knew only the truth could explain such actions. She and Virginia had never had secrets from each other.

"I'm sorry," Amanda said, but Virginia had angrily left the room, exiting into the back parlor.

"Well?" James asked as he approached Amanda from behind. "Are you back for good?"

"No, Father, I am not," Amanda answered.

"Did you tell that fortune-hunting husband of yours . . ."

"Yes, Father," Amanda answered, beads of perspiration appearing on her brow. She suddenly felt like an ambushed animal.

"And?"

"He's not interested."

"What did he say?" James insisted.

"Father . . ."

"What did he say?" James's tone growing louder.

Amanda paused, wondering how much indiscreet language

her father wished to hear from his delicate, well-bred daughter. "He said you can go to Hell," she finally said.

James stared at his daughter as if *she* had sprouted red hair. Then he heatedly marched out of the room, slamming the door to his office in his wake.

"Lunches are getting shorter," Amanda said to herself, hoping a bit of humor would keep her from crying. "This isn't good."

Sitting down at the table, which was filled with cool drinks, a salad, some fruit and slices of ham, Amanda realized she didn't feel in the least bit like crying. She began to help herself to the enormous buffet set before her. "No use letting this go to waste," she said with a small nervous chuckle.

Through the front windows, the two Virginia had talked James into opening, Amanda caught sight of T-Emile sitting silently in the carriage. She grabbed a glass of lemonade and her plate full of food. Before she reached the front door, Alcée's words came back to haunt her.

Amanda turned and placed everything back on the table. Then she opened the door and called to T-Emile. At first the boy refused to budge. When Amanda continued to coerce him, he slowly made his way up the stairs to the house, cautiously studying every corner and crevice.

"Don't worry," Amanda reassured him. "My father won't bite. Besides, you're my family now and my family is welcome in my house."

T-Emile ate just as cautiously, watching the doors. Amanda tried to enjoy the lunch, but a gnawing feeling inside made her anxious and jittery as well. She couldn't quite place the emotion or get rid of it, so she did what she always did when her father caused her pain. She retreated to the piano.

At first, Amanda launched into a sonata by Chopin. Then she remembered the soft ballad Alcée had sung to her the night before. She began to pick out the melody with her right hand.

To her surprise, T-Emile sat down next to her on the bench, gently hitting the correct keys.

"Do you play?" Amanda asked.

T-Emile grinned and shook his head. "It's all up here," he said, pointing to his forehead. "Alcée is teaching me."

"Will you sing me the song?" she urged him.

"Jolie Blonde?"

The name confirmed Amanda's suspicions that the song was intentionally sung for her, so she pressed T-Emile to teach her the words. T-Emile shook his head. "Alcée would kill me," he said.

"Oh? Why?"

A look of guilt washed over the boy's face, and he said nothing.

"I suppose this is an original Alcée Dugas song written on my behalf," she said.

When T-Emile began to shift uncomfortably on the bench, Amanda changed the subject. "How about another song, then? *Le Pont de Nantes?* I vaguely remember that song from my youth."

T-Emile nodded, and starting singing the French folk song in an amazingly brilliant voice. Amanda had not been prepared for such exquisite singing from a boy who rarely spoke more than a handful of words at one time. She sat mesmerized beside him, absorbing the beauty of the song, forgetting her home and the conflict raging inside it.

James sat defeated at his massive oak desk, staring down at a court document, but comprehending nothing. If only he could reverse time, have his daughter back, he'd lock her in her room and never lose sight of her again. Her magnificent playing of Chopin brought back vivid memories of Amanda performing for him in the front parlor. Amanda had loved the attention, always glancing back to make sure he was listening intently to her every note. She was his precious baby, his *petite chou,* or "little cabbage," as the French affectionately call their loved ones.

The thought caused his stomach to tighten. How long had it been since he'd called her that? Had it been ten years? Plus, he couldn't remember the last time Amanda had played the piano and cared if he was listening. Most of the time he had been busy studying the newspapers or court cases, hearing the songs only as background music. Had she been falling in love with a Cajun opportunist while he surrounded himself with work to escape the endless grief of Genevieve's death?

James's stomach growled. He was hungry, but food was unthinkable. He couldn't fathom eating at a time like this. But Amanda was enjoying lunch in the next room, and he would attempt to talk to her again.

When James opened the door to the hallway, he recognized the lilting melody of *Le Pont de Nantes.* He stepped back in time, returning to New Orleans and the constant parties his wife threw in order to collect an audience. She performed at every gathering, singing everything from classic arias to simple French folk songs. James grew tired of the endless exhibitions, of her consistent need for attention. He preferred quiet evenings at home with Amanda. But when he complained to Genevieve, he always received the same answer.

"I gave up a great career for you," she said time and again. "You have no right to tell me I should hide the greatest gift God has given a mortal. I have sung before kings, men much more important than you'll ever be. You should be thankful I'm still here."

No one, including all of their treasured friends, imagined she would desert her family to return to the stage. She adored Amanda, even if she appeared to love singing more. Her intimations had been spoken in anger, James rationalized. It had to have been that Frenchman she was seen leaving with that afternoon. Genevieve may have fallen out of love with James, but she never would have left him for another man. She was coerced, threatened perhaps. *You can't trust the French,* James reminded himself. *They are deceitful bastards.*

As the realization hit James that a man was singing in French in his front parlor, the blood rushed to his temples. James slammed his office door and stormed into the front room. "What the hell is going on?" he shouted.

T-Emile rose and stiffened as if he stood before an oncoming hurricane, not knowing which way to run. Amanda moved quickly to stand between the two men.

"This is T-Emile," she began. "He's René's . . ."

"I don't care if he's the Marquis de Lafayette," James shouted. "I want that Frenchman out of my house."

T-Emile didn't need to understand English. He grasped the Judge's meaning and headed instantly for the door, leaving it wide open in his path, the sunshine pouring into the semi-darkness like an angel appearing suddenly from heaven. Amanda watched him exit, and turned back to her father, shocked at his actions.

"How dare you allow him into our home," her father continued to shout. "There is never to be French spoken here."

Amanda watched her father retreat back into his dismal office, heatedly slamming the front door in the process. She struggled to regain her composure, but the anger brewing inside her pushed her into action. She followed her father into his study, her face burning with rage.

"How dare I?" she shouted back. "How could you be so rude to a man I am related to?"

"You will not be related long," James answered without looking up. He picked up the neglected document, and pretended to examine it. "You will get an annulment today."

Amanda was tired of being ignored. Angry tirades, short

rebuffs, then her father always announcing that they had spoken enough of whatever subject she had brought up. *Not today,* she decided. Moving toward the windows, Amanda tightly grabbed a handful of drapery and flung the curtains open. The intense afternoon sunlight bore into the room, illuminating even the darkest corners.

"I have had enough of living in darkness," she began, her voice shaking with intensity. "Do you think you are the only one who has suffered these past ten years?"

Reaching over to the other window, Amanda drew open the draperies. The once-darkened room began to glow in the sunlight, the neglected dust glittering in the sun's rays.

"You may have lost a wife, Father, but I have lost my mother. Did you ever consider that? Within the past two years, I have lost a father as well."

When Amanda glanced back, her father stood staring at her, his eyes wide with shock. She had never talked to him this way before. Still, she was not going to back down now. "I'm sorry she left, Father, but she left," Amanda continued. "And she's not coming back. But I'm here. And I'm half French, and there's nothing you can do about it."

Amanda took a deep breath. "I'm not going to hide the fact that I'm French anymore, or allow you to belittle my family. I am married to René and that's that. I am Amanda Comeaux now. There will be no annulment."

As Amanda stormed out of her father's office, she caught a glimpse of Virginia's astonished face in the hallway. Remorse instantly showed its ugly head, but for the first time in her life Amanda refused its presence.

"Let's go," she said to T-Emile, who was eagerly awaiting the chance to be rid of the Richardson home. As soon as Amanda's feet touched the inside of the buggy, he whipped the horse into action.

Amanda could feel her heart throbbing in her chest. She tried to breathe, to regain her composure, but her skin tingled, her mind reeled.

"Please forgive me," T-Emile said. "I didn't mean to . . . I shouldn't have . . ."

"It's not your fault," Amanda said, trying to reassure him. "It's my father. He's an irrational, uncaring man."

Deep in her heart, Amanda didn't want to think of her father in such a negative way. But she was angry, and the fever wouldn't subside. He *was* irrational, labeling René a fortune hunter and insulting his shy, sweet cousin. If only her father knew how René had saved her from the degradation of Henry Tanner. But he never would know, because he was too busy finding every Frenchman guilty without a proper trial.

"The stables, T-Emile," whispered Amanda.

Her wild emotions were restricting her speech. She tried again to resume normal breathing patterns, but her forehead continued to pound from the rush of her blood through her veins. She needed René.

Before T-Emile could adequately stop the carriage, Amanda jumped to the ground. She entered the stables, quickly examining each stall. Instead, she spotted Alcée.

"Where is René?" she abruptly said to him in French.

"At the other end," Alcée answered, surprised at her tone and her use of his language. "What is wrong?" he added, following her.

Amanda spotted René brushing the coat of a Creole pony. René glanced up from his job, and Amanda instantly rushed into his arms, tightly burying her head in his chest. He wound his arms about her, his concern evident. "What is it, *mon amour?*" he asked.

"Please, just hold me," Amanda answered softly.

"Is it Tanner?" Alcée asked. "Was he at your house?"

Amanda couldn't decide which was more shocking, Alcée's brotherly concern for her welfare, or Alcée's admittance that

Tanner was back at his job at her father's plantation. She released her hold and turned toward Alcée. "Tanner's back?" she asked, as if the news would unravel her on the spot.

When neither man spoke, Amanda realized the horrible truth. She sank onto a nearby bench, burying her head in her hands. René joined her on one side, Alcée on the other.

"What has happened?" René asked.

Just then T-Emile appeared breathless at the stall. "It's all my fault," he announced to the group. "I didn't mean to do it. We were just singing a song. It was so hot outside."

Alcée shot up a hand to silence the usually silent young man. "What are you talking about?"

"It's not his fault," Amanda insisted, looking up at the group. "Tell him it's not his fault."

"What's not his fault?" René asked.

"That my father got so mad. Tell him it was me he was furious with, not T-Emile."

"Why was he so mad?" Alcée asked.

"We were singing a song and my father hates to hear French being spoken, especially in his house. He forbids it."

"You invited T-Emile into your house?" René inquired incredulously.

Amanda stared at her husband as if the question was absurd. "Of course I did. You don't think I'd let my family sit out in the hot Louisiana sun like a hired hand."

Chapter Eight

The men said nothing at her comment, but Amanda felt a shift occur in the tension that had surrounded them for the past few days. It reminded her of the aftermath of a thunderclap, when a lightning bolt released the friction tingling in the air. As if a storm had indeed blown over the group, they all immediately brightened. René wrapped an arm about Amanda's shoulders and gingerly pulled her close. "Why don't you tell us what happened," he said.

Amanda quickly related the course of events, then insisted they explain to T-Emile that it wasn't his fault. Alcée reassured T-Emile in French, then then reminded him to unhitch the carriage. T-Emile reluctantly moved away.

"He doesn't believe you," Amanda said. "If I have hurt that boy, I'll never forgive myself."

Alcée stood up and pensively rubbed his cheek. He turned back toward Amanda and casually placed a foot on the bench beside her. Leaning an elbow on his knee, he incredulously asked Amanda, "You asked T-Emile into your house?"

Amanda couldn't fathom what had occurred when he spoke the innocent question, but the two men started laughing uproariously. When Alcée glanced over at René, they began howling.

"What is so funny?" Amanda asked, amazed they could deem such a horrific afternoon as humorous.

René straightened a bit and cleared his throat. "I'm sorry, my dear," he said. "You're right, this isn't funny."

"Perhaps you should go over to the Richardson house," Alcée said to René, a smirk creasing the sides of his lips. "Give the Ole Judge a piece of your mind."

"Yes, of course," René answered. "I'll not stand for my family being kicked out of his home three times in one week. Twice is the Comeaux limit."

The two men began to laugh again, René leaning over and holding his sides as if his ribs were about to burst out. Amanda could only sit and stare.

"I can't believe you two," she began. "That poor boy was almost in tears. My father scared him half out of his wits."

René glanced up and shook his head knowingly. "Yes, I'm sure he did," he said, continuing to laugh.

Their humorous assessment of the situation lightened Amanda's mood, but she did not feel like laughing. She was still shaking from her earlier confrontation.

"Tell me," René asked Amanda with an affectionate touch to her chin. "Did all this happen in that cheerful office of his?"

Images of Amanda ripping the curtains open returned. She had never shown such rebelliousness toward her father. Her act of courage after years of unappreciated obedience made her smile slightly.

"*Bon,*" Alcée said with a slap to his knee. "You're beginning to relax. This is good."

"I still don't see the humor in all this," she said, returning to her previous glum state. "My father being extremely rude to you is not a funny matter."

"Everything can be a funny matter," Alcée said. "You have to laugh at life or life will laugh at you."

"Your father has a right to be mad at all of us," René added, still smiling. "He kicks me out of his house, then I return a few days later married to his only daughter. The next thing he knows, there are Frenchmen singing in his front parlor."

The men started up again, but Amanda instead focused on René's comment. "You had words with my father before Saturday?" she asked him.

René stopped smiling, rose and anxiously stared at first Amanda, then Alcée. If she wasn't mistaken, he appeared perplexed by something she said.

"How about some coffee?" Alcée suggested as if on his nephew's behalf. "After what I've seen the last few days, I'd say you'd welcome a nice cup of *café au lait*. Am I right, Amanda?"

Amanda thought of the market and René's mention of her father. René said her father had called him an immigrant. When a silence fell over the group, Amanda realized Alcée had asked her a question. She also noticed René refusing to meet her eyes. "What?"

"Coffee?" Alcée repeated.

"Yes, that would be nice," she answered.

"Good. Then let us go rescue Colette from her heathen children and have some refreshment near the bayou."

"There is work to be done," René said quietly. "You all go on ahead without me."

Although Alcée stood in René's shadow, he suddenly appeared to tower over his nephew. "Your wife just had a trying afternoon and you're going to work?" he angrily asked René in French.

"There's a race in twenty minutes," René shot back. "Who's going to run it, T-Emile?"

"I don't care if the governor himself wants to race this afternoon," Alcée bellowed. "You will come with us to the house."

René gritted his teeth. Amanda could tell they were debating an old, painful subject. "This is not about a race, Alcée. This is about a business. I can't be known around this town as a man who doesn't run a consistent . . ."

"To hell with being consistent," Alcée returned. "It's the peak of summer. We shouldn't be running horses in this heat anyway. Cancel the race and tend to your wife."

Amanda agreed with Alcée that René worked too hard. During the previous days, she had seen less of René than she had standing at the fence of her father's house. She sensed he felt compelled to prove himself worthy of entertaining his American wife in style.

At the same time, Amanda admired René's drive and ambition. René possessed a natural-born ability to deal effectively with people—all kinds. He spoke English effortlessly, and so was able to amiably converse with Americans. Most of the Acadians Amanda had seen at the track seemed equally impressed. René always greeted everyone with a smile and a handshake, and they, in turn, appeared mesmerized by the personable man, drawn to his sparkling personality like a moth to an oil lamp.

Amanda also noticed that René had acquired an uncanny inner sense about people. In conversations—particularly with men shorter than himself, which was the majority of the town—he would prop a boot against a nearby stump or bench and lean down slightly when speaking. People felt that René was talking to them on their level, and his closeness assured them he was listening intently to their every word. She recognized that secret from her years of working the campaign trail with her father.

René was a politician of sorts, Amanda thought. But the one thing that placed him head and shoulders above the rest was that he was sincere.

"Why don't René and I stay and help T-Emile with the race," Amanda suggested. "I'd feel better if I knew the boy was all right. Then, perhaps, you and Colette could bring us some coffee later or keep it warm until we arrive."

Alcée sighed. "You understand quite a bit, don't you, Miss Richardson?"

Amanda rose and snaked her arm through René's so it rested in the crook of his elbow. "The name's Comeaux, Monsieur Dugas, or haven't you heard that I scandalously eloped with the Cajun racetrack owner."

When the smile forced itself free on Amanda's face, the two men quickly joined her. René picked up her hand resting on his arm and gently kissed the long ivory fingers. The thunderclap had done its damage, Amanda surmised; now the sun had begun to shine.

"I'd like my cup with plenty of sugar and cream, *s'il vous plait,*" Amanda added with a sly grin.

Alcée bowed. "For you, Madame Comeaux, anything."

The afternoon seemed to rush by, for which Amanda was grateful; it meant less time to ponder the angry conversation she had earlier shared with her father. She knew she must consider her actions, but for now she wanted to revel in the playful mood prevailing over the track.

René seemed infinitely happier. He joked with his two friends who used the track, and teased Wayne Baldwin on his "perfect" horse when he arrived to race her. His lighthearted mood was infectious; even T-Emile began to smile again.

After Wayne raced Mary's Blessing against Tom Glenn's Blue Darling, and came out a clear winner, the two Acadians asked to make a quick run down the track. "Of course," René answered. "As long as Mr. Baldwin is finished."

"Sure," Wayne called back from atop his horse. "How much winning can a man do in one week?"

Boudreaux and Thibodeaux mounted their Creole ponies and approached the starting line. René handed Amanda the flag. "What am I supposed to do with this?" she asked.

René slipped his arm around her waist from behind, drawing her hand with the flag upward. "You wave it down, with a quick motion like this." René imitated the starting signal, then backed away. "Your turn."

Amanda swallowed, planted her feet firmly apart and raised her arm in the air. When she pulled the flag down, the horses jolted into action and headed down the long, narrow lane. René effortlessly pulled her back before they passed, landing her against his chest, his strong arms holding her close.

For those few moments while they watched the horses approach the distant finish line, Amanda settled back into René's embrace, enjoying the close comfort of her husband's arms. As the dust from the horses' hooves twirled around them, she felt as if she belonged there.

"Having fun?" René asked.

Amanda smiled and turned to look at him, his familiar sparkling eyes beaming from beneath his white planter's hat. "Yes, I am."

Suddenly, René's smile disappeared. While his hand softly stroked Amanda's flushed cheek, a pensive look crossed his face.

"What is it?" Amanda asked.

"I didn't expect to see you again," he said solemnly. "Not after what you spoke of last night."

"I'm sorry, René," Amanda replied softly. "I certainly

didn't mean to insult you. But I thought you had a right to leave the marriage if you wished. I just wanted you to know that an annulment was possible.''

''And that your father was happy to pay me to accept one,'' René said, his anger at the subject apparent.

The familiar guilt returned. After everything he had done for her, she shouldn't be questioning his motives for marrying her. Still, Amanda had a right to know what kind of a man she married.

''My father wants me home again,'' she said. ''He'll do anything to achieve that. You said it yourself, he has a right to be upset.''

René stared hard at Amanda, his humor gone. ''You were testing me, weren't you?''

''Can you blame me?'' Amanda said. ''I made a bad judgment with a man before.''

René thrust his hands upon his hips so suddenly, it caused Amanda to jump. ''If you are comparing me to Henry Tanner, then I think I would like an annulment.''

''Of course, I'm not comparing you to, to . . . him.'' Amanda closed her eyes to dispel the thought of Henry Tanner and that awful night. She couldn't bear remembering anything about the horrid man. ''Please, forgive me,'' she continued. ''I honestly only wanted to free you of me if you so wished it.''

''I don't wish it.''

The quickness with which René answered caused Amanda's heart to still. She eagerly searched his eyes for affection, hoping he did care after all. Why, she wondered, was she so worried he might want an annulment? Only days earlier she had longed to return to her old life, wishing she could turn back time.

Now, she anxiously awaited the hours when she would see him again, disappointed, as she had been that morning, when other responsibilities kept her from visiting him at the track. If it hadn't been for Widow Pitre's neighborly visit that morning, she would have brought René his breakfast and reassured him she had not returned to her father.

René continued staring unemotionally, making it impossible to read his thoughts. Amanda couldn't help wonder if pride was the reason he remained married, and nothing else. If only she could fathom why *she* wished to remain married to him.

"What do you want, Amanda?" René finally asked.

The afternoon hour positioned the sun directly in Amanda's line of vision. The harsh rays pierced her forehead and blinded her eyes, while perspiration gathered on her upper lip and trickled down the center of her bodice. "I wish for autumn to arrive soon," she said.

René thrust his fingers through his hair and inwardly prayed that God would end his agony soon. It would all be so simple if Amanda loved him in return, but life was never simple. He knew from the very beginning she was not in love with him. What did he expect, that she would fall in love within a few days' time? *It may never happen*, he commanded himself, *so get used to the idea*.

Leading her by the elbow toward the shelter of a nearby live oak tree, René sighed and asked, "Where is your bonnet?"

"I must have left it at my father's house," Amanda answered, leaning into the comfort of the tree's shadow.

"You should never be without a hat in this heat," René reprimanded her. "You could get . . ."

"Une tête rouge?"

René stared down at his wife, who coyly smiled up at him. She appeared so small and helpless, so petite and naive. Yet when she began to assert herself, she beamed with an inner strength. "You're making a joke, no?"

Amanda frowned. "Of course I am. I'm funny, no?"

René couldn't help but grin at her foolish attempt at humor. Amanda was a fountain of surprises. "Who told you about my sunburn?" he asked.

A look of feigned ignorance crossed Amanda's face. "I really don't know what you're talking about."

Laugh at life or life will laugh at you, René thought as he smiled down at his wife. Alcée had suffered the anguish of a broken heart and learned to smile again. René at least was married to the woman of his dreams. He had a lot to be thankful for.

So why did his heart continue to ache so?

"Come," he said, briefly closing his eyes to shut out the thought and the unrelenting pain. "Let's go home and have some *café au lait.*"

The two walked back through the palmetto thicket and field of maturing sugarcane in silence. When the small path opened into the larger cow pasture, René joined Amanda by her side.

"May I be honest with you?" Amanda asked.

"Of course."

"I honestly don't know what I want," she began. "I thought I knew exactly what I wanted last Saturday, but I was wrong. Now, I only know that I don't want to go back."

It wasn't the explanation René had hoped for, but she appeared willing to stay. It would have to do for now. "You are always welcome here," he said softly.

The two continued on without speaking until they came in sight of the house. Colette greeted them nervously on the back gallery. "Something has arrived," she announced, twisting her apron anxiously in her hands.

René and Amanda rushed into the living room where Alcée stood, coffee in hand, staring at a magnificent piano.

"Your father sent it over," Alcée explained. "The men who delivered it said your father insisted you not be without your music."

The piano was a bad omen, René assessed. Her father was indeed furious. He was expelling his daughter from his home and life.

"I'm sorry," René began, placing a comforting hand on Amanda's shoulders. Instead of being glum, however, Amanda grinned.

"He's relenting," she said.

Before René could find time to ask how she came to that conclusion, Amanda crossed the floor and sat down on the piano's bench. She first tested the keys, then began to play a soft sonata.

"Well," Alcée said with a sly grin. "It's nice to see I'm not the only gifted one in this house."

René sat next to Amanda on the bench and watched his wife's long agile fingers passionately beating out the classical piece on the keys. He had heard such music before in St. Martinville, but nothing he had witnessed before could match the exquisite mastery of his wife's playing. Her fingers moved along the keyboard effortlessly, as if a divine power had taken possession of them. The peaceful, entrancing music claimed his heart.

Once Amanda sensed her captive audience, she stopped playing, self-consciously placing her hands in her lap. René stared at her, amazed at the transformation. "Why did you stop?" he asked.

"It was beautiful," Alcée added.

Amanda nervously pushed her blond curls behind her ears. "It was adequate."

"Adequate indeed," Alcée grumbled. "You must stop comparing yourself to your mother."

René had never seen the vibrantly talented Genevieve Vanier, and he never felt sad at not doing so. With all her magnificent beauty and voice, Genevieve Vanier could not have possibly been able to perform with such grace as her daughter had just done, he was sure. René placed his hand over Amanda's and lovingly stroked it with his thumb.

It was then he noticed the absence of jewelry.

"I have forgotten to buy you a wedding ring," he said. Before Amanda could react, René added, "We must go into town tomorrow and purchase one."

"We?" Amanda asked. "You and me?"

René had neglected to consider the gossip that would occur when he and Amanda walked the streets of Franklin together. "I realize people will talk, but how else am I to buy my wife a ring?"

Amanda smiled broadly, startling René. His wife was indeed full of surprises. "I don't care if people gossip," she said. "I can't believe I'll have you all to myself."

René shot Alcée an angry look. Alcée excused himself to the dining room for another cup of coffee. "Despite my uncle's accusations, I don't work all the time," René said gruffly.

"I know," Amanda said. "But I sometimes feel we had more time together at my front fence than we do in your house."

"*Our* house," René corrected her.

Again, Amanda flashed a bright smile. "Our house."

"Then it's all settled. We'll leave after breakfast, visit the jeweler and stop for a soda water at the Variety Store."

"That should have all the tongues wagging," Amanda said with a frown.

"Perhaps the Variety Store's not a good idea?"

"Of course it is," Amanda said, grinning, exhibiting her coy side again. "It's about time Franklin met the Comeaux."

James began to pace the front parlor yet again that afternoon. Instinctively, he knew sending the piano over had been the right thing to do. He'd meant it as a peace offering, as a concession that his daughter was not going to return home. Amanda would realize that moving an instrument of such size and weight would not be easy or able to be quickly reversed.

Still, James couldn't help fearing that Amanda would believe she had been banished from her home. After their angry confrontation that afternoon, James was afraid Amanda might assume he had finally broken the ties.

The familiar pain pounded at his temple. Was he doing the right thing? What did he know about raising children? He had left home and the guidance of parents when he was sixteen to study in France. When he married and his wife had borne Amanda in New Orleans, his Virginia family was too far away to be of help. Geneviève's family lived in the nearby Vieux Carré, but they only offered assistance to their daughter; her American husband had been a Vanier family outcast from the moment they married. Amanda was the only Richardson, despite her American bloodline, allowed inside the Vanier family home.

Amanda still received letters on special occasions from her mother's family. But none of this served her well. The child needed family, people who cared enough to warn her against conniving opportunists carrying her off in the middle of the night. She needed someone else beside an overprotecting father who would rather die than watch his only daughter experience the same pain he had suffered.

He wanted to wrap his fingers tightly around René's throat and strangle him. He wanted to shake him mercilessly until the boy admitted defeat and begged helplessly at his feet. He wanted his daughter back.

But Amanda wasn't coming back. And it wasn't René Comeaux who'd persuaded her of that.

"It isn't your fault."

James quickly realized Virginia had come to announce dinner. How long had she been standing there? he wondered.

"She was right," James said, rubbing his forehead. "I have spent ten years dwelling on my wife's leaving and not one moment on my daughter's pain."

Virginia handed James a cool washcloth and a glass of water.

Without him speaking of it, Virginia always seemed to know what he needed.

"You have been a good father," Virginia answered. "Amanda knows that."

James shook his head. "I have been an absent father."

"Perhaps," Virginia said, inching closer. "Your wife's death was quite a shock. And the finality of death is not an easy thing to accept, particularly when you have other responsibilities. You want to carry on as before, to love others as you had before, but a darkness settles around your heart and keeps you from them."

"Yes, that's it exactly," James said, amazed that someone could put words to the emotions.

"People keep waiting for you to emerge from this darkness, as if mourning lasts exactly one year and a day," Virginia continued. "But the darkness has a mind of its own. And it will not lessen until it deems it is time."

"Yes."

Staring at Virginia's calm emerald eyes, James wondered how he had managed to rely on this woman for ten years, to leave on business convinced the household would survive with Virginia at the helm, without ever knowing the details of her marriage. He knew she was widowed; she'd said so at their first meeting. She had stood, pale and trembling, in the front parlor of his New Orleans Garden District home, her accent and dress indicative of those "fresh off the boat." He could have asked her then, or during the numerous opportunities since when they had been alone together. Had James been as completely ignorant of his most faithful servant's needs as he had been of his daughter's?

"You must have loved him very much," James said, venturing into emotional territory he usually avoided.

"No," Virginia answered. "I married him because he was

a good man and a good provider. Women don't always have the luxury of waiting for love.''

"I'm sorry." After years of kindness and sympathy from Virginia, James's words appeared hollow.

"Don't be," she continued, gently placing the cool cloth at his nape. "I mourned for myself. I was stuck in a new world without family and friends. I had no place to live. People made fun of the way I talked. I didn't even know how to find a job."

The image of Virginia pleading with James to give her a chance to be Amanda's nanny made him smile. "You did very well."

Virginia shook her head, grinning slightly under her usual mask of control. "I never could understand why you hired me, with my pitiful clothes and no references. The other applicants must have been horrid."

"You were the only one I saw."

Virginia's smile vanished, and James took the opportunity to seize her hands. He wanted to continue the connection they were establishing. He wanted to feel close to her, to ease the constant pain that had troubled him since Genevieve's disappearance, to relieve the burden of Amanda's elopement.

"I have always been a good judge of character," he said. "That's why I've been elected overwhelmingly to two terms. I knew immediately you were the perfect woman for me."

Virginia stiffened at his touch, and James discreetly released her hands.

"How do you judge René Comeaux's character?" she asked.

James took a long drink from the glass of water. When the refreshment failed to eliminate the drumming in his head, he began to rub his eyes with his thumb and forefinger.

"He's been here before, hasn't he?" she continued. "Maddie said he visited you the day before Amanda left with him."

James removed the cloth and leaned his head back to stretch the muscles in his neck, but the throbbing continued unabated.

"He came claiming he was in love with Amanda," he said. "He asked for permission to court her, which I, of course, denied him."

Virginia took the empty glass and cloth from James's hands and sat down across from him in Amanda's favorite arm chair. "Then there was something between them after all."

"No," James practically shouted. "I don't believe it for a moment. My daughter would have never defied my wishes."

"Your daughter eloped," she reminded him.

James shook his head fervently. "She was pressured. She was probably blackmailed."

"She was talking about René Comeaux the day she left. She said they were friends."

"Friends, Virginia," James repeated emphatically. "You don't elope with a friend."

Virginia leaned forward, staring hard into his eyes. "If René Comeaux was denied because he was French, then couldn't it be assumed she acted in defiance of you?"

"No," James insisted. "She never would have defied me. There's something else going on here."

"She was afraid of becoming an old maid."

"She never would have defied me," he repeated.

"Well, I certainly cannot win a term as judge," Virginia said, smiling slightly. As a woman, she wasn't even allowed to vote. "But I don't believe Mr. Comeaux is the guilty party. I don't know why, but I think there is more to this than Amanda has been telling us. I agree that she may not be in love with Mr. Comeaux, and the elopement was not her idea, but something else is at work here."

"What?" James asked.

Virginia shrugged. "I don't know."

The two stared at each other thoughtfully. After the truly exasperating day, James was thankful to have Virginia by his side. He couldn't possibly let her go.

"Miss O'Neil?" the cook called from the hallway.

"Yes, Maddie?"

"Did you not hear the door?"

"No, Maddie, I'm afraid we've been deep in conversation. Is someone here?"

"Yes, ma'am," the cook answered. "A gentleman by the name of Philip Vanier is here to see the Judge."

Ten years had had little effect on the dark, elegantly handsome man seated before him, James thought with a twinge of jealousy. The black Vanier eyes that had captured James's heart were not lost on Genevieve's younger brother. He too had inherited the Vanier thick silken hair, although Philip's was as black as a moonless night.

"You've done well in sugarcane, James," Philip said in his clipped Creole French as he examined James's elegant, book-laden office. "I suppose this might make up for your living in this godforsaken country."

James poured his brother-in-law a brandy and set it before the fashionably dressed man. "I don't speak French anymore, Philip, so if you wish to converse with me, you'll have to try English."

Philip grinned and emptied half the glass. "I heard rumors you had denounced your French ways," he answered in heavily accented English, "but I thought you might have come to your senses after all these years."

"I came to my senses ten years ago."

The two men glared at one another in silence. They had not spoken since the scandal broke, when Philip had insisted his sister left on her own accord.

"I am sorry for your pain," Philip finally said, and James believed he meant it. "With that spoken," Philip continued, raising his glass in a salute and returning to his normal haughty self, "I shall not say it again. I am here on business."

"And what business may that be that concerns me?"

Philip grinned and leaned back into his chair. "So eager to rid yourself of me, are you?"

"I have problems at the moment that need immediate attention," James said. "I do not wish to be rude, but . . ."

"But Vaniers are not particularly welcome in this house, no?"

James slammed his drink on to his desk and leaned so close to Philip he smelled his expensive Paris cologne. "I was never welcome in the Vanier house, or have you forgotten?"

Philip sat before him silently, his countenance never faltering. "And have you forgotten how that feels? To be married to a woman whose family despises you simply because of your nationality?"

James straightened at the reference. Surely Philip could not know Amanda had married an Acadian.

"I know all about it," Philip said as if reading his mind. "Although I must admit Amanda could have done much better in a choice for husband, I hope you don't make the same mistake my parents did with you."

When James refused to comment, Philip continued. "They spent years working Genevieve against you, convincing her she didn't love you, that she sacrificed her singing career needlessly for you and Amanda. My mother is the one who arranged for her trip back to France. There was no other man."

James attempted to interrupt, but Philip raised his hand. "Please, hear me out. What do I possibly gain in telling you this? My sister, your wife, is dead. So are my parents. There is nothing left between you and me but the truth."

James felt defeated from the myriad emotions flowing through him. "And Amanda?" he whispered.

"She loved Amanda," Philip continued. "She wrote many

times asking for her to join her in France, but you always returned the correspondence.''

''Genevieve made her choice,'' James said solemnly, fearing as he always did that his wife had died lonely of a broken heart. Philip remained silent, and James wondered if his thoughts mirrored his own. For the first time in ten years, James wished he had read the mountain of mail his wife had sent him over the years.

Philip reached over and filled James's brandy glass. ''I have been through this town several times on business, wishing to speak with you,'' he said. ''So many times I doubted you would see me. But when I heard that Amanda had eloped with a man—an Acadian, no doubt—I though you might finally agree to see me.''

''It happened Saturday evening,'' James said, amazingly thankful to have family to confide in. ''We are all in shock.''

''Perhaps I could take a trip to this racetrack,'' Philip offered. ''Gather an objective opinion of the man.''

For the second time that afternoon, James felt a weight being lifted from his shoulders. ''I'd appreciate that.''

''*Bon*,'' the Frenchman answered. ''Now let us speak of Genevieve.''

Chapter Nine

Everyone seemed so lighthearted after dinner, such a departure from the normal anxiety gripping the household. Alcée performed endlessly on the fiddle, while Amanda accompanied him on piano and occasionally danced around the room with the two children. T-Emile reluctantly agreed to sing again with Amanda, and after a few stanzas of *Sept Ans sur Mer,* an old French maritime song, he began to smile as well. René had his usual work to finish, but managed to dance to a couple of tunes before Amanda finally retired to bed.

While Amanda lay awake in her bed, the sheets flung from her body as if the hot cotton burned her flesh, she remembered the day's events, amazed that such a horrific afternoon could turn into such a pleasant, joyous evening. She had to hand it to her new family—they sure knew how to have a good time despite what life handed them. Although she couldn't forget her earlier confrontation with her father, the lively music and dancing made the memory bearable.

Amanda turned her pillow over, hoping the other side would be cooler. The late-night hour offered little respite from the stifling August heat. Even when Amanda lay still in her bed, her arms and legs lifeless at her sides, the perspiration continued. She imagined herself drowning by daybreak.

Sitting up and gathering her hair for the dozenth time that night, Amanda wished she could cut the blond mass off. Her curls were one of the few nice features she possessed, but in hot, humid August the mound of hair felt like suffocating Spanish moss clinging to the cypress trees.

Holding her hair up so it would spread out on her pillow and not her shoulders, Amanda released it and fell back against the bed to sleep. Instead, the memory of her husband's gentle grip on her waist and hands, holding her close as they turned round and round the living room floor, came to mind, and she stared wide-eyed at the intricate design on the bed's canopy. The way René had smiled down at her, had pulled her close when she smiled back, made her stomach tighten. Being close to René was like dancing in heaven, she thought.

It was there again, that old familiar feeling. Every morning René's appearance at the fence had caused the same reaction. Knowing him better and living under the same roof had only made it worse. Before, she was glad for his company every morning. Now, she longed for it day and night.

I'm falling in love with him, she thought. The startling revelation should have shocked her, should have sent her rational senses reeling, but it failed to evoke any emotion as she lay, serenaded by the frogs and crickets outside her bedroom window. Instead, Amanda felt at peace, as if she surrendered to something she had known all along.

As Amanda kicked the sheets further away and verbally prayed for a breeze, she heard voices in René's bedroom. If she wasn't mistaken, René was telling one of the boys a bedtime story.

Creeping to the door, she made out Pierre's young, high-pitched voice rambling on, with René interjecting that he was talking too loud. Amanda opened the door slowly and peered inside.

"Look," she heard René say. "You woke up Tante Amanda."

"I couldn't sleep," Amanda said in French, trying to both reassure Pierre and not appear intrusive. "Am I interrupting anything?"

"I was trying to get Pierre back to sleep," she heard René say. Without the aid of a candle, Amanda could barely see their faces. "Would you like to join us for a story?"

Amanda lifted the mosquito net and crawled next to Pierre, at the same time trying in vain to discreetly pull down her nightgown and cover her exposed shins.

"Why don't you sleep with René?" Pierre asked.

For a moment, Amanda was at a loss for words, but she remembered her father's advice about politicians being put on the spot. *Use humor,* he had said, *to diffuse the situation.*

"René snores," Amanda answered, straight-faced.

René sat up in bed, and Amanda could make out his beaming eyes in the darkness. "I do not snore," he said with a smile.

Amanda glanced down at Pierre and winked. "That's what they all say."

Pierre giggled heartily, and Amanda immediately read the concern on René's face. She didn't know much about children, having been an only child, but she did remember that you never—never—get a child in a laughing mood before bedtime or they will never go to sleep.

"I think it's time for that bedtime story," she said quickly.

Pierre stopped laughing and turned toward his cousin. "The one about the crawfish following our family?"

"All right," René said, "but I want you lying flat on the bed with your eyes closed. Agreed?"

The young boy nodded and settled down on his pillow. Amanda did the same, softly stroking Pierre's hair to calm him. René leaned on his elbow so the two could hear him well.

"The Louisiana crawfish was originally a lobster who lived in the cold waters of Canada," René began. "French people had settled the area and called this new home Acadie or Acadia. The lobster called these Acadians his friends and they all lived peacefully together."

Pierre nestled further into the pillow as he listened intently to his uncle's tale. Amanda too was intrigued by both the story and René's soft, entrancing voice.

"When the British and the French fought one another in Canada and in Europe, the Acadians tried to stay out of the conflict, asking only to plow their lands, fish the sea and hunt and trade. But the British took over the land from France, and insisted the Acadians swear allegiance to the British crown and the British church. The Acadians had all the good farmland in Acadia, or Nova Scotia as the British now call it. The British wanted that good land, and they wanted everyone to speak English and be Protestant.

"When the Acadians refused, although they still asked to be left alone, the British put them on ships and sent them away from Acadia. Families were separated, their farms burned, their livestock killed. Many died on the ships that were sent all over the world. Some Acadians went to the American colonies, some were sent to the Caribbean. Some suffered in English prisons before they were allowed to go back to France."

Amanda watched René's eyes grow dimmer as he paused at the thought of his ancestors experiencing such pain. She wondered how the Comeaux and Dugas families fared during *Le Grand Dérangement,* or expulsion from their homeland.

"The poor lobster was so sad," René continued. "He missed his friends and he didn't know where they were. He began a long search along the ocean bottom to find his friends, the Acadians."

Amanda glanced down at Pierre's flickering eyelashes, and knew the entrancing story was doing its job.

"Slowly, over many years, the Acadians heard about the French-speaking territory of Louisiana," René continued. "From all over, the Acadians traveled to Louisiana to make a new home for themselves.

"While the Acadians reunited along the bayous and prairies of their New Acadia, the lobster was right behind. But he had traveled long and hard and had lost a lot of weight. By the time he made it to the Bayou Teche, he was only a shadow of his former self.

"The lobster, now a crawfish, rejoiced when he finally saw the Acadians. Throwing his claws into the air, the crawfish sang and danced so hard he burrowed himself into the mud where he lives to this day."

René peered down at the boy, whose small body had suddenly turned lifeless. "He's asleep," he whispered to Amanda.

"That's quite a tale," Amanda answered, still enjoying the boy's fine hair through her fingers. "Considering that the Acadians are a crawfish's worst enemy."

Even in the darkness of the room, lighted only by a distant moon, Amanda could make out her husband's glistening eyes. She sat up to try to make out his face. "Or that New Orleanians were eating the crustacean before the Acadians arrived," she added.

"Go ahead and break his heart," René said with a smile. "Why don't you tell him Père Nöel isn't real as well?"

"Père Nöel isn't real?" Amanda asked, straight-faced.

Placing his hand over hers and wrapping his fingers around her soft skin, René gently raised her hand to his lips. Amanda's heart jumped as he brushed his lips across her knuckles.

Amanda had enlisted the aid of her best friend simply to

ask a man to escort her to a ball; she never would have so much as approached Henry Tanner to ask him for anything. And yet naive Amanda Rose Richardson Comeaux assertively moved her hand from René's grasp and placed it lovingly on her husband's cheek.

It was so dark. She had only wanted to locate him.

Fool, she thought, that wasn't it at all. She wanted to touch him, to feel the taut texture of his face, those broad high cheekbones, that round stubborn chin, the thick eyebrows that rose in defiance whenever René felt insulted. He was her husband and she wanted to feel close to him.

René quickly placed his hand over hers, passionately kissing the inside of her palm. Feeling herself melt in places she never considered before, Amanda actually leaned forward, wishing to be kissed.

Their kiss was more than Amanda had expected, excitedly more. René had met her lips with a force she had not experienced before, as if a passion had been building inside him since their awkward wedding in Father Breaux's living room. He placed his hands on her waist and drew her closer, sliding one hand along the thin cotton of her nightgown.

Their closeness was invigorating, and Amanda desired more. She slid her hand along René's cheek, feeling the soft fine hair lingering on his nape. The movement made René groan with pleasure, and his hand inched its way up her back.

What happens next? Amanda wondered. Gin had adequately explained to her the facts of life, but was saving the actual instructions for her wedding day. Since she had denied Gin that maternal lecture, Amanda literally stood in the dark as to what was expected of a wife and, to be more exact, what went where.

Unconsciously, Amanda's hand fell to René's chest, and she began to eagerly stroke the soft brown hair of his chest. Within seconds, the reality of her actions came crashing through her momentarily dormant logic. He was shirtless, she thought with horror. For all she knew, he was stark naked. And there she was, lying in his bed with nothing on but a light gown, with a six-year-old child between them.

Amanda audibly gasped, hastily retreated from the bed mumbling something about needing her sleep and rushed to the refuge of her room, being sure to close the door tightly between them. Because of the darkness, she had been saved from what must have been quite a startled look on her husband's face.

When morning arrived, René never mentioned the incident, nor appeared bothered by his wife's reluctance to act on her matrimonial duties. Amanda wished she could just as easily forget her foolish actions the previous evening in his bedroom, but the thoughts refused to leave. When the couple headed for town to purchase a wedding ring, Amanda tried desperately to concentrate on anything but what had transpired the night before. She focused her eyes on the horse's steady cadence, loosening the top two buttons on her blouse as if to release the steam pent up inside her. The morning had only just begun, and already the air was thick with a humid heat pulsating from the moist ground.

"What is that expression by that famous American of yours, 'A penny for your thoughts'?" René finally said.

Amanda wanted to say she was thinking it was time they considered sharing a bed, but the fear held her silent. Instead, she focused on his question. "What do you mean, that American of mine?" she asked back.

"Ben Franklin, am I right? They named the town after him."

"He's not *my* famous American, he's ours."

René turned and gave her a disconcerted stare. "You're saying I'm an American."

"Of course you are."

There it was again, that naive, innocent look Amanda exhibited at the most unusual times. René watched her features carefully as his wife stared up at him, honestly amazed he didn't share her views on American citizenry.

"When were you born?" she asked.

René grinned. He knew where this conversation was headed. "The year 1820, and yes, it was after Louisiana was granted statehood."

"Then you see," Amanda exclaimed, "you are just as much an American as I am."

The position of her delicate chin, the way her incredibly blue eyes sparkled when she became excited, all further endeared her to René. Still, Amanda had a lot to learn about life. That had been evident the night before. Thinking back to when she had discovered his bare chest and rushed from the room like a frightened rabbit made René smile. God, he loved his wife.

"I am an Acadian," he finally said, trying to think of something else beside the endless longing to be intimate with Amanda.

"You are also an American," she reminded him.

René shook his head. How could he explain to a woman whose father made the ground move whenever he felt the desire that *his* people were always the ones who were shaken? Like his parents and their parents before them, he didn't trust government, colonial or otherwise. Government seized what was valuable, and discounted the consequences to the people it injured. The Louisiana Indians were testament to that manifest destiny. If, in time, the Americans found the Louisiana swamp lands and southwestern prairies beneficial to their commerce, the Acadians would be exiled once again.

"You don't vote, do you?" Amanda asked.

When René didn't answer, she became indignant. "René, don't you understand that the United States was founded on a representative government, so that the people of America would never have to experience the tyrannical rule of Britain again?

This country is ruled by the people, not by a crown that forces people out of their homeland without due cause.''

"And what constitutes due cause, Amanda?'' René reiterated. "All it takes in this country is a piece of paper to force people from their land. Look at the Indians. How are they represented?''

"There are treaties,'' she argued.

René laughed. "We had a treaty when France ceded Acadia to the British in 1713. The English agreed to allow us to remain in Acadia and remain neutral in the wars. We kept our end of the bargain. They did not.''

"That was England, René,'' Amanda countered. "We're talking about America.''

"Americans are English,'' René retorted. "It's all the same.''

Amanda shot him such a hardened stare, René imagined her gaze burning his skin. *"Je suis français, aussi,"* she said with a fever he had not seen before. "And my father helped create a government representative of both French and Americans in New Orleans.''

René leaned back to gently brush the damp curls away from Amanda's face. "Little good it did. They split New Orleans into three municipalities to keep the warring nationalities apart from one another.''

"My father was against that move,'' Amanda answered softly. "It all started because a Creole was acquitted of killing an American during a duel. The Americans went crazy because the Creole got away with murder.''

"That's exactly my point, *ma chèrie,*'' René said. "People have killed each other in duels for centuries. But now that an American has been killed, it's different. If an Acadian had been killed, or a Negro, no one would have objected. The English belief that everyone is less important than they are permeates America. It's in their blood.''

Amanda shook her head vehemently. "All the more reason

to vote, *mon ami.* The more Acadians elected to office, the more people in power who represent your interests. If only Americans—or those of English descent as you erroneously believe we all are—vote and are elected, then only Anglo-Americans will dictate what happens in this country."

René moved his hand back to the reins. He had to admit his seemingly naive wife had a point.

René parked the buggy outside the jeweler's store and helped Amanda down. While he tied the reins to the outside post, Amanda entered the small building facing Main Street.

"Good morning, Mr. Levy," she said to the jeweler.

"Good morning, Miss Richardson," the elderly man answered.

Before Amanda could correct him, René entered offering his salutations.

"Good morning, Mr. Comeaux," the jeweler said. "What can I do for either of you this bright day?"

"We'd like a wedding ring," René announced.

The thick black and white eyebrows of the jeweler, which to Amanda resembled bristly Spanish moss when it had been hung out to dry in the sun for mattress stuffings, seemed to grow in size as he gazed first at René, then Amanda. René continued, ignoring the startled man's expression. "Something with diamonds, big ones," René said.

Amanda approached the counter to stand by René's side. "Something simple, a gold band, please, Mr. Levy."

"Nonsense," René continued. "You can have anything you like."

"And I'd like a gold band," she insisted.

René leaned close to her left ear so only Amanda could hear him. "I'm perfectly capable of buying my wife a proper wedding ring."

Amanda hadn't thought she might be insulting René, but she really preferred simple jewelry. Large jewels on her petite hands always appeared pretentious.

"It's not about money," she answered in French to avoid any further embarrassment. "I honestly want a gold ring."

At first, René appeared taken aback when she spoke French. But when he started grinding his back teeth, Amanda realized he was not pleased.

"You're trying to be nice, to save me money," René answered in French. "But it's not necessary. I am a man of means; I can buy you anything you desire."

"But you don't understand, René. I desire a simple ring."

"It's about your father, isn't it?" he continued. "You don't think I can compete with him so you're trying to save me the humiliation. Or is it because you don't believe Acadians can afford diamonds?"

"It is about my father," Amanda spat out, losing patience with him. "But it's not about my taste in jewelry. You want to place a large diamond on my finger to impress my father and every other American in this town."

The two glared at each other, until the jeweler caught their attention. "I think I have a solution to this problem," he said. From a back case, he withdrew a jeweler's box and placed it on the front counter. "Jewelry should complement a woman's personality or her features. I don't think diamonds are quite right for Miss Richard . . . uh, Mrs. Comeaux?"

Amanda smiled to reassure him that Comeaux was the correct name and to thank him for coming to her aid.

"However," the jeweler continued, "I don't think a gold band will do those lovely fingers justice either."

René huffed at the jeweler's last statement, grinning down at his wife in victory.

Mr. Levy opened the box filled with rings of different shapes and sizes, and picked a sapphire ring graced with small diamonds on either side. "Blue seems to be your color, Mrs. Comeaux," he said, and placed the elegant yet simple ring on her finger.

It was perfect. Amanda turned to René beaming.

"Bon," he acquiesced. "But you must let me make it up to you." As the couple made their way down Main Street, Amanda couldn't stop staring at the sparkling blue stone on her left hand. "It's really beautiful, René."

"I'm glad you like it," he mumbled, and Amanda knew he still bristled from their earlier conversation.

"If you want to spend money on me," she said with a grin, "I would love a cool glass of soda water."

"All in good time," he said.

"The Variety Store is in the other direction," she reminded him.

"I wanted to show you some rosebushes Mrs. Deshotels has for sale. I wanted it to be a surprise, but she began asking questions and I don't know the first thing about roses."

"Neither do I. What are the rosebushes for?"

Amanda nearly tripped when René stopped short. "What do you mean, you don't know anything about roses?"

He had to be the most exasperating man sometimes, Amanda thought as she watched her usually calm husband raise his hands to his hips in defiance. What had she said now? "I know nothing about roses, René. What's there to explain about that? I'm terrible with plants. Everything I touch seems to die."

René didn't move. He stood staring down at her with a stern, quizzical expression. "I know you must think Acadians are simple people, that we only make enough money to sustain ourselves. But not all Acadians are poor farmers, Amanda. I can afford a few rosebushes so my wife can start her own garden. You don't have to lie to save me money."

Why was she always insulting this man? She must be miscommunicating somehow. "Why would you think I like roses?" she asked, hoping to find the cause of his consternation.

"Are you going to deny that you worked every morning in your rose garden in front of your home?"

Suddenly, it all made sense. They had met every morning over the front fence, her garden utensils in her hand.

Now, how do I explain this one? Amanda asked herself. *How do I tell the man I love, who may not love me in return, that I pretended to prune rosebushes for weeks just for the opportunity to speak to him on the street?*

He might be flattered, she thought. *He might realize I care for him and exclaim his love in return.*

He also might think I'm a forward woman. After all, I did thrust my hand to him in front of God and the world without a proper introduction.

Amanda vividly remembered how René had walked down the street that first morning, tipping the white hat framing his smiling face. For some unknown reason, Amanda had leaned over the fence and offered her hand in greeting.

"What was I thinking?" she whispered audibly.

"What?" René asked.

"Of course I like roses," she said, gazing up at him with a bright smile. "But I'm honestly not good at gardening. My garden at home was tended by a man we hired. I only went out in the mornings to cut some for the tables."

Amanda abruptly turned and moved down the street in the opposite direction, hoping it would signal the end of the conversation. René instantly joined her, but remained silent until they entered the crowded Variety Store.

"There's a table in the back," he said, leading Amanda toward it, placing an order for two sodas at the counter along the way.

As the two took their seats, Amanda could hear the gossip spreading among the American merchants. Word must have gotten out around town that the Judge's daughter had eloped with the Cajun racetrack owner. She instantly felt remorse for putting her father in such a position. Because of Amanda, the Judge was enduring the second scandal of his life.

"As you said, all the tails are wagging," he said.

Looking up at the face of her sincere husband, who still seemed aggravated about her lie about roses, Amanda tried in vain to hide her mirth. "It's 'tongues wagging,' " she corrected him, while a smile fought to be released.

René finally smiled back. "In whatever words, they are talking about us."

Taking her hand in his, René added, "Let's really give them something to talk about." He gently raised her hand to his lips, grinning mischievously as he kissed her fingertips.

Hearing the women to her left gasp, Amanda felt the blood rush to her face. She quickly withdrew her hand from his, and covered it with her other hand as if to protect herself from further advances.

"I have embarrassed you," René said. "I am sorry."

"No, that is not it." Amanda could feel the blood pumping through her veins. "You said I should not give my love to you unless I do so honestly. I expect the same from you."

For several moments René said nothing. Amanda could hear the women whispering something about the brazenness of the French, but all she could focus on was her husband's intense, handsome face.

"You're right," he finally said. "You're absolutely right."

Picking up her hand once more, René lovingly raised it to his lips, this time closing his eyes as he passionately planted a kiss upon her knuckles.

James stared at the pile of letters gathered before him. The late-morning sunshine cascaded down upon his desk, sending a wave of dust about him, making it almost impossible to read the faded words. Through the humid haze he made out his wife's delicate handwriting: *I will always love you.*

Genevieve had written him faithfully through the years, sending them in care of her brother. But James had made it quite clear the many times Philip had asked to forward the letters to him that there was to be no communication between him and his wife. The day Genevieve walked out of his life was the last time he would ever speak or hear from her again. He wanted nothing more of the Vanier family.

James had had no idea of the pain she'd experienced leaving him and Amanda. Her letters were filled with longing and regret. There had been no other man, and her career was never fully resumed, although she consistently performed until her death. She would have remained famous had she stayed in New Orleans. The Creoles loved their diva and treated her like a queen. At the same time Genevieve would have enjoyed a loving home and family.

Genevieve Vanier had had it all. And she had cast it to the wind.

For the first time in ten years, James felt relieved.

As he read on, long nimble fingers quietly snaked their way down the front of his chest, one hand sporting a bright blue sapphire. James registered his daughter's arrival at the same time she pulled her arms close about his shoulders and hugged him tight, her head of plump blond curls soft on his right cheek.

"I'm sorry, Father," Amanda said softly.

James gently stroked the tender arms wound about him, raising a hand to lovingly pat his daughter's face. "It's all right, my love," he said. "I can read much better with the drapes open."

Amanda unlocked her grasp and gingerly knelt down at her father's side. James could tell she was examining him, possibly expecting another angry outburst. He cupped her satiny face in his hands. "I haven't been much of a father these last ten years, have I?"

Before Amanda could answer, he continued. "Don't deny it, Amanda. I have failed you."

Amanda shook her head. "You were suffering."

"That's no excuse. So were you."

When Amanda looked away, her eyes locked on the letters scattered about the desk.

"Your mother wrote us constantly," James said. "I never allowed your Uncle Philip to forward the letters until now. I felt it was time."

"She wrote me at school," Amanda said softly.

The news shocked him as much as Amanda flinging open his curtains. "Why didn't you tell me about them?" he asked.

"You never allowed me to speak of her."

James instantly wondered how much pain he could have avoided had he cleared the air with Amanda. Had she known all these years about Genevieve's grieving? "What did she say?" James asked.

Amanda sighed and wrapped an arm through his. "She said she loved us and missed us and hoped that someday you would forgive her."

For several minutes father and daughter enjoyed the welcome company of each other's embrace, quietly staring at the pile of letters before them. The pain was finally disappearing, and Amanda was there to walk with him into the light.

Despite their earlier resolution, lunch remained strained as the conversation drifted back to René and their elopement. When Virginia arrived with the meal, she immediately began an intensive inquisition into René's intentions. James continued to offer the possibility of an annulment, and Amanda adamantly refused. By the time two o'clock rolled around, Amanda felt they had returned to their previous stalemate.

"Can we talk about something else?" she pleaded as she turned the azure-colored ring round and round her finger.

"Is that what your husband calls a wedding ring?" James snapped.

"It's a beautiful ring," Amanda retorted, the questioning and insults getting the best of her.

"Amanda, dear," Gin began again, "we're only trying to piece this puzzle together. You must see how utterly confusing all this seems. The whole elopement is so unlike you."

Amanda instructed herself to breathe deeply and count to ten. *All will be resolved or forgotten in due time,* René had said.

Before she could answer, a knock came at the front door. Glancing over at the mantel clock, Amanda realized with horror that it was time for René to pick her up for the trip home.

"I'll get it," she said, abruptly rising and knocking over her water glass. As if James understood, he rose as well.

"Nonsense," he bellowed. "This is my house and I shall answer the door."

"Father, you never answer the door," Amanda argued nervously.

"You never disobeyed me before," he countered. "I shall see to the door myself."

Amanda watched with trepidation as her father moved down the hallway. James reached the threshold in a few easy steps, quickly flinging the door wide open. René stood before him, his hat held tightly in his hands. "Good day to you, Judge Richardson," René said.

If Amanda wasn't mistaken, René appeared as calm as a bayou at midnight, his eyes exhibiting neither cheer nor animosity.

"What is it you want?" James asked, looking down his nose at the younger man.

"I'm here to take Amanda home," he said.

The two glared at one another like bulls fighting over a cow, each one hoping the other would be the first to look away. Amanda was surprised to find a flicker of admiration in her father's eyes.

"I want to have a word with you, young man," James said sternly.

"Of course, sir."

"Tomorrow. Perhaps you will both come."

Amanda wanted to throw her arms around her father again, to rejoice that he was finally coming around, but like René, she remained calm, waiting for his next move.

"Tomorrow will be fine," René answered.

"Good," James said, quickly gazing back at his astonished daughter. "I've given the cook a few days off, so perhaps we'll meet for tea?"

"Tea?" René asked, a slight grin appearing underneath a pair of curious eyes. "I didn't know Americans drank tea."

James thrust his hands in his coat pockets. "You're right," he said brusquely. "What the hell is an American doing drinking tea? We'll meet for coffee then?"

"Coffee will be nice," René answered, still displaying a cool exterior.

"Good, this time tomorrow then," James said, ending the conversation.

Amanda wanted to continue staring at her changed father, the man who until this day had steadfastly refused to have anything French in their home, including coffee, but James seemed impatient to usher her out the door. Before she left the shadow of the hallway, she reached up and hugged him.

"I love you, Papa," she whispered.

James pulled his daughter close and kissed the top of her head. "I love you, too, *ma petite chou*."

If merely facing Judge Richardson wasn't enough to affect René, the Judge speaking French clearly was. René stared in astonishment. James noticed his glare and his face colored. "Haven't you ever heard anybody speak French before?" he said gruffly.

René never faltered, nor abandoned his composure, but his eyes glistened as if a smile was not far away. Placing his hat upon his head and tipping it politely to the Judge, he placed Amanda's hand in the crook of his arm and led her down to the waiting buggy.

Amanda stole one last glimpse at her father at the top of the steps, his hands defiantly anchored on his hips. She hadn't won him over yet. Still, Amanda couldn't resist the last word.

"A demain," she said with a grin, indicating they would meet again tomorrow.

Before she could study the aggravated look on her father's face, they were headed north toward the bayou and the farmhouse she now called home.

Chapter Ten

There was wild music coming from the left side of the house, a fiddle that sounded as if possessed by the devil, and a piano that pounded a fast tune too raucous for such a delicate instrument. Katharine cringed at the lively melody, tweaking her nose at such common frivolity. Surely, Amanda could not be living among such peasants.

When the familiar ring of Amanda's laughter rose above the music, Katharine finally stepped out of the buggy. The rumors were true after all. Amanda had left the comfort of affluent, educated American society and moved to the outskirts of town with gambling, uncivilized Cajuns!

Before she entered the light of the apparent living room, Katharine stood on the front gallery and stared at the people inside. There were two men near the fireplace, one aggressively wearing out the bow upon a crude violin, and a younger man playing second fiddle to his left. Amanda was perched at the piano near the window, intent on following their lead. Another man sat at an oak secretary at the back of the rustic room, busy studying a set of books while tapping his feet to the music.

Katharine detested folk-style music, although she had to admit the tunes did incite one to dance. But it was immigrant music, songs that betrayed one's status in America. Her family had achieved great wealth raising sugarcane along the banks of the Teche, enabling her to study at the finest schools and spend winters in New Orleans society. Yet all her father had to do was open his native Scottish mouth, or sing one of those ''Old World folk tunes,'' and her peasant heritage was evident for all the world to see.

The Cajuns, Katharine found, carried their social status around their necks like a chain. A few spoken words and you knew exactly what caste to assign them to. Katharine didn't understand much French, but she detected a distinct difference between the refined conversations of the Creole French in New Orleans and St. Martinville and the rough dialect of these bayou dwellers.

A slightly plump woman around Katharine's mother's age entered the room and spoke loudly to the group in French. When Amanda and the others finally heard her, they appeared to apologize and began disbanding for the evening. The woman smiled her thanks and left, moving up what Katharine assessed was a back staircase. The younger fiddler shyly put his fiddle away and left the room through the back entrance as well.

Katharine knew the hour was late, so she gathered up a deep breath and entered the room, pretending to knock on the open front door. ''Knock, knock,'' she said, offering up her best smile.

A silence followed, so overwhelming that Katharine stepped back a pace.

''Katharine?'' Amanda asked, as if her eyes were betraying her.

''Yes, it's me,'' Katharine answered. ''May I come in?''

"Of course," Amanda said, rising to greet her.

Within seconds of her crossing the threshold, the room came to life. The seated man rose and stood behind Amanda, the fiddle player offered her a chair and Amanda straightened her bodice and skirt as if caught with her finger in the pie.

"Katharine, this is René Comeaux, my husband, and Alcée Dugas, his uncle," Amanda explained.

Katharine had to admit that up close these Cajuns didn't appear that different, except both sported shirts of what was sure to be homespun and home-woven cotton. The vest of the fiddle player had to be one of the purest shades of sky blue Katharine had ever seen. She wondered how they dyed it that color.

"This is Katharine Blanchard, a friend of mine."

Amanda seemed genuinely shocked to see her, as well she should be, Katharine thought. Katharine had been absent from society the past week to be close to Henry, but she'd managed to obtain quite an earful of gossip when she and Becky Parkinson visited the Variety Store for a soda that afternoon.

"I don't mean to intrude upon your party," Katharine said, trying to hide her disdain, "but I must ask a favor of you, Amanda."

"Of course. What can I do?"

Katharine paused and glanced at the two men, who watched her intently. Hadn't they seen an American before?

Amanda seemed to grasp her insinuation, and led her toward the front gallery. "Excuse us for a moment," she said quietly.

"Girl talk," Katharine added over her shoulder with a smile.

When the two reached the sanctuary of the outside porch, Katharine began her prepared speech. "Are you planning on going to the christening tomorrow?"

"I was considering it," Amanda said.

"I'm so relieved," Katharine said, linking her arm in Amanda's. "I was hoping you would ride with me to the church.

My brother has plans and my father can't take time from his work. You know how men can be sometimes."

"You want me to ride with you?" Amanda asked, surprised.

"I really hate going out alone," Katharine added.

"What about Bernard?"

"Who?"

"Your fiancé."

Katharine shook off the brief spasm of guilt. "Oh, of course, Bernard. He's busy with the plantation."

"I certainly don't mind, Katharine," Amanda said, "but it doesn't make sense to drive all the way out here to have company to ride back into town."

"I know, Amanda. But company's company. We could catch up on everything."

Amanda's curious gaze suddenly shifted to a wary glance. She moved away from Katharine, folded her arms across her chest and looked down at her feet. "I see."

"No, you don't see." Katharine was beginning to lose patience. Why couldn't Henry love her without making her perform his little tasks? "I honestly don't care who you married, Amanda. I just want some company to the church."

"All right."

Amanda stared straight at Katharine, as if trying to read some hidden message. Katharine couldn't reason why, but she felt immensely guilty.

Because of what she offered to Henry on a daily basis, which should be saved for her marriage to Bernard, guilt consistently racked her being, but that had nothing to do with Amanda. It had been three weeks since Henry escorted her to the Talbots'. Surely, a woman wouldn't feel ill that soon. Besides, she reasoned, she couldn't possibly have gotten pregnant on the first time!

"Katharine, may I ask you something?" Amanda inquired.

"Certainly."

"You haven't seen Henry Tanner lately, have you?"

Bile rose in Katharine's throat yet again, and she had to briefly close her eyes to fight back the nauseous sensations. She feared there was something between Amanda and Henry after all. "Why?" she asked.

"Sally said he escorted you to the Talbots' ball," Amanda explained.

"Yes, so?"

"I've heard bad things about him, Katharine. I just wanted to warn you in case he asked you again."

The nausea finally relented, but Katharine felt as if her blood had been completely drained from her body. Her head throbbed, and the pungent, moldy odor of the damp ground, freshly sprinkled from a quick afternoon thunderstorm, invaded her nostrils. "There's a lot of rumors going around, Amanda. You of all people should know that people love to gossip in this town."

"Yes, but . . ."

"He's a fine gentleman from an upstanding New Orleans family. He lost almost everything—his land, fortune, status in society—when a cutthroat con man robbed him and forced him to work for a living."

Katharine grabbed the porch railing to steady herself. "He's been trying to raise the money to return home and protect his sister from further bankruptcy and scandal. He must come up with an enormous sum by next week or she will lose what little he has unselfishly managed to hold on to for her behalf. His whole purpose in life is to allow his sister to maintain her position in society, even if it means working at a job beneath him."

Why wasn't Amanda acting sympathetic? When Henry told her the story, Katharine was close to tears.

"What time will you be around in the morning?" Amanda asked unemotionally.

"Will nine o'clock suit you?"

"Yes," Amanda agreed.

"I'll see you then."

Amanda walked Katharine to her carriage and its waiting driver, gently shutting the door when she was safely inside. "Tomorrow at nine," Katharine uttered before pressing her handkerchief to her nose. Within seconds, the buggy lurched toward town.

Amanda watched the buggy leave her sight and the dust settle along the road in front of the house. Tomorrow she must discover why Katharine had chosen her, of all people, to be her "company."

And explain to Katharine that Henry Tanner had no family.

"The mosquitoes will eat you alive if you don't come in." Alcée rounded the side of the house, finishing the knot in his cravat and pulling on a waistcoat.

"Where are you going at this time of night?" Amanda asked.

"My dear, I am in search of refreshment," Alcée answered with his now-familiar bow.

"You're going drinking?" Amanda had heard that men succumbed to such an atrocious sin, but she'd never personally met one who did. She stared at her in-law, refusing to conceal her surprise and disapproval.

"We all have our faults," he answered with a shrug.

"Drink is the aid of the devil."

Alcée laughed heartily. "Then I shall embrace the devil for a few hours, and he shall be rewarded in the morning when I awake with a pounding headache."

"But why?"

A sadness filled Alcée's eyes, a darkness Amanda had not witnessed before. Looking into those expressive black eyes, Amanda could almost feel his pain.

"Your father isn't the only one who suffers from a broken heart, *ma chérie*. And tonight I suffer from an unusual bout of melancholy."

"But surely it can't be as bad as all that?" Amanda pointed to the living room. "Your playing?"

"I can escape any pain while I'm playing. But as you can see, the music has stopped."

"Who was she?"

Several minutes passed before Alcée spoke, and Amanda wished she knew the man better. She would have liked to offer comfort, but she dared not make physical contact. There was still so much uncertainty between them.

"Her name was Marguerite," he finally said. "We were going to be married."

Alcée sighed, and Amanda knew instantly she was treading on sensitive ground. "What happened?" she nevertheless asked.

Amanda doubted Alcée would explain; men were not prone to talk about such emotional subjects. Her father stood as a prime example. Surprisingly, Alcée continued.

"I was one of six children. Louisiana law states that parents must leave their land equally to all children. My family's farm could barely provide for one family, let alone six more. I left Loreauville to come here with René, hoping to make enough money to either buy my own *petite habitation* or enable my father to enlarge his farm. Marguerite married another in my absence."

"But why?"

"She was worried about becoming an old maid."

His words descended on her as the earlier thunderclap had done, startling her senses. Amanda backed up along the porch until her hands found the swing and she gingerly sat down. Hearts weren't broken because of her fear of becoming a spinster, but her whole world had been transformed anyway. Had this Marguerite experienced the same fear?

"Did she love you?" Amanda asked.

Alcée stared thoughtfully down at Amanda, at the same time

loosening his cravat. "I suppose," he answered softly while joining her on the swing.

"Didn't she ever declare her love to you?"

Alcée hesitated, then said, "Yes."

Two people torn apart simply because one feared growing old alone. Amanda understood such apprehensions, but seeing Alcée in such pain made her wonder how a woman could do such a thing.

"He was a good provider," Alcée said, as if reading her mind. "She was never sure that I would be. I was always playing my fiddle instead of worrying about finding us a good farm and a means to support ourselves. She was better off with him."

"Was?"

"He died last winter of influenza."

"She's a widow?" Suddenly, things sounded a lot more optimistic.

Alcée, however, didn't appear uplifted by such news. The darkness that had permeated his countenance at the beginning of their conversation returned.

"Where is she now?" Amanda asked.

"With his parents."

"Has she . . ."

"No."

Alcée abruptly stood, leaning on the front gallery railing, and stared off into the moonless night. The bright lamplight from the living room cast a glow on to his thick, black hair and subtly handsome face, allowing Amanda a rare chance to study his interesting profile. His equally black and quite bushy eyebrows popped from his forehead as if they had minds of their own. His cheeks were well-rounded and sun-kissed, and were it not for the classic shape of his elegant nose, would have made him appear like Père Nöel himself. His discreet lips and the laugh lines that appeared when he smiled gave him an aspect of authority.

In sum, Alcée resembled what Amanda envisioned as the perfect big brother. She found Alcée excitedly passionate at times, especially when recounting a favorite story or performing on his beloved violin. He was mostly playful and full of smiles, yet always concerned.

She wanted so very much to be a sister of sorts.

"She's in mourning," she offered. "If I were in her shoes, I would not have contacted you until a year and a day had passed."

Alcée sent her an appreciative smile. "It has been eleven months."

"Eleven months is one month shy."

"Perhaps."

For what seemed like an eternity, Alcée remained silent, until he finally changed the subject. "Have you ever been in love, Amanda?"

René rubbed his eyes, thankful that the last entry had been made. Alcée was right. It was too hot in August to race horses in Louisiana, and it was time he took a break. Tomorrow he'd announce the track closed until cooler weather.

Watching Amanda talking amiably with his uncle gave him hope. They seemed to agree with one another, even though Alcée still expected Amanda to bolt home to her father. Why she hadn't was still quite a mystery to René.

Sneaking into his room in the middle of the night, insisting that they only show love honestly—all signs that she cared. Yet at times, her actions proved otherwise.

If only Amanda would let him show her *his* feelings, he thought, trying to fight the tension in his trousers. Just the mention of her name or the thought of her delicate hand in his

sent blood rushing to places he couldn't control. He wanted
her so badly he felt as if he was slowly being consumed by a
blazing, internal fire. The perspiration he lost at an hourly rate
made him wonder if he would be half his weight by week's
end.

René grabbed the book and moved toward the bookcase at
the other end of the room. As he approached the front threshold,
he overheard his uncle asking if Amanda had ever been in love.

For the several moments that followed, René swore he could
hear his heart beating in his chest. Amanda hadn't answered,
but Alcée's next question made him realize she had shaken her
head.

"Never?" Alcée asked.

"No."

"I find that very hard to believe, a woman as pretty as
yourself," Alcée added.

"Pretty?" René heard his wife ask with a laugh. "Hardly
the daughter of *'formidable'* Genevieve Vanier."

"You must stop comparing yourself with your mother."

"But I'm not my mother, you see," Amanda said firmly.
"There were no suitors."

"None?"

Alcée turned to lean upon the railing, and caught René's eyes.
The two exchanged a knowing glance, but Alcée continued on
as if his nephew was still seated at the back of the room, well
out of earshot.

"I'm a Catholic," René heard Amanda say. "The American
families we associate with are Protestants, and they don't marry
Catholic girls. And the Catholic families are, well, mostly
French. I don't have to tell you how my father feels about
them."

"But surely there were suitors," Alcée prodded.

René assumed his wife was again shaking her head, for she

said nothing. Alcée, on the other hand, frowned in disbelief.
"None?" he asked again.

Even with a wall in between, René heard his wife sigh.
"None," she answered.

Was it likely Amanda knew nothing of his first meeting with
her father, René wondered, or was she cleverly pretending in
spite of everything that had happened since then?

"And there was no one who caught your eye?" Alcée
inquired further.

René instantly wished he had not intruded upon the conversation. He willed himself to walk away, to escape the torture his
wife was inflicting upon him, but his curiosity demanded he
stay. Perhaps he would learn the painful truth and be done with
it.

After several excruciating moments, he heard his wife giggle.
"There was one," she said, and René feared the worst. He
pictured the man, some dandy American who spoke proper
English, danced the latest steps and knew what wine to drink
with what course. And because René hadn't the nerve to leave
the damn bookshelf, he was forced to listen to every horrifying
detail.

"He was a tall, friendly man who used to shadow me with
his presence," Amanda began. "I looked forward to seeing
him every day because not only was he interesting to talk to,
but he blocked the hot sun from my face as well."

Amanda giggled again before she continued. She was
enjoying herself, remembering a man who meant more to her
than *he* ever would.

"He wore the most unusual hat, some kind of native plant,
I believe. I was so intrigued by it that I actually offered my
hand in greeting just for a chance at meeting him. Can you
believe I did something so bold? He must have thought I was
the most brazen woman."

Alcée shot René a sympathetic glance, but René's thoughts suddenly turned hopeful.

"I actually lied to my family because of this man," Amanda continued. "I had never done that before. I told them I was interested in learning how to garden, which I actually despise, just so I could be at the front fence every morning when he walked by. He used to come by my house every morning about ten o'clock."

Before René could adequately digest her words, his palmetto hat came slamming down upon his head. "What the . . ."

Turning, he found his normally shy cousin grinning from ear to ear. "Caught you," T-Emile whispered. "I can't believe you're eavesdropping on your wife."

Alcée heard him talking, and quickly remedied the situation. "Here's René now," he announced to alert Amanda to change the subject.

T-Emile followed René onto the front gallery, and for a brief time the men awkwardly stared at one another. Amanda, surprisingly, appeared at ease, and was smiling a heartfelt smile. She left the swing, rose up on her tiptoes and removed the hat in question from René's head.

"What is this thing made of anyway?" she asked, blushing profusely in the light pouring from the open door.

René knew Alcée finally understood who the man of her description was; he could almost feel his broad smile at his side. The object of René's complete attention, however, was the blue-eyed darling standing in front of him.

"Palmetto," he answered. "We learned it from the natives."

"Indians?" Amanda asked, looking both astonished and still happy to see him.

"Someone had to teach us how to live in the wilds of Louisiana," he explained. "Besides, it makes a great hat."

Until that evening, René had had doubts about that hat. He'd entertained thoughts about buying a cotton planter's hat, like the ones Americans wore. Dressing like the Americans might make his wife more comfortable, more likely to care for him, he believed.

After tonight, he was going to wear that hat every chance he could.

"I came to tell you, René, that there's a man in the stables," T-Emile interrupted. "I went over there to check on that sickly Vaughn horse, and this man arrives and says he wants to see you."

The light glistening in his wife's eyes suddenly grew dim. He couldn't leave her now, not after those touching words of endearment. René sighed and turned toward Alcée, who seemed genuinely puzzled he was glancing his way. "Alcée, do you mind?" René asked him.

Alcée smiled broadly once again and slapped his nephew on the shoulder. "Of course not. I'd be glad to."

René felt a thousand times relieved, until T-Emile stopped Alcée from reentering the house and grabbing his hat. "No, he asked for you, René," T-Emile said. "He asked for you by name."

There was nothing anybody could do. René built his business on a reputation that he was available to anyone day or night. *You reap what you sow,* his mother always said.

René felt the familiar burning of unrequited passion searing his flesh. Looking up at Amanda, he read disappointment in her eyes. *Why tonight?* he thought, wondering if God enjoyed a good joke once in a while at his expense.

Taking a deep breath to try to relieve the pounding in his head and loins, René turned and headed off into the dark night toward the stables.

Amanda couldn't believe her luck. A barrier had come crashing down tonight, she was sure of it. She felt it in the air between them, as if René had actually listened in on her declaration of love. The way he had stared down at her, the love that seemed to be sparkling in those rich brown eyes—he had to have feelings for her. But now his mistress, the racetrack, was luring him away, and Amanda could only sit and watch him walk off into her commanding arms.

Alcée too appeared disappointed that his nephew was again taken away by the demands of their business. He sent Amanda a sympathetic look.

Then suddenly, Alcée's eyes glistened. "Amanda," he said in a call to action, making her jump. "His hat. René needs his hat."

Amanda caught his meaning instantly, and bolted down the path leading away from the house. René hadn't gone far from the house's encompassing light, and Amanda found him quickly. "René," she called to him breathlessly.

When René turned, Amanda swallowed hard, hoping the action would slow down her fast-beating heart. "You forgot your hat."

While her heart raced like a thoroughbred, her husband's actions seemed to slowly unfold before her. He accepted the hat, staring at it as if it had suddenly turned back into a palmetto palm. Then René glanced up at Amanda, at the same time cupping her cheek with his left hand and wrapping his right hand around her waist. In seconds, his lips were on hers.

Amanda wasted no time pulling her own hands to his shoulders and wrapping them tightly around his neck. His lips were hot and demanding and so welcome. As Amanda threaded her fingers lovingly through his soft hair, signaling to René that she approved, René sent his tongue flickering inside her mouth, dancing to a tune Amanda had never dreamed of before. The action sent sensations coursing through her, awakening areas of her body that suddenly required she press closer.

She leaned into his embrace, tightening her hold around René's shoulders and allowing her tongue to discreetly meet his. René groaned and laid a flat palm against the curve of her back, pressing her into his arousal. Amanda remained ignorant of men, but she instantly recognized that her husband desired her intensely. To her amazement, the following moans of pleasure were hers.

René's lips left hers, leading a trail of sensuous kisses along her cheek to the tip of her jawline while his hand slipped up to her bodice and gently massaged her soft breast and nipple. His touch made Amanda gasp, and her knees weaken. *If this is lovemaking,* Amanda thought as she tilted her head back to allow René ample room at her neck, *then fear be damned.*

Amanda smiled at her use of profanity, even if it was only within her mind. Bringing her head level, she looked into René's eyes, placing a soft hand at his face. René sighed and drew her close, holding her tightly against him.

"I have to go," he whispered.

"I know," Amanda softly answered, but she refused to relinquish her hold on his neck.

Life was so ironic, Amanda thought during the brief moments they held each other. Only days before she had longed for a kiss from a man she despised, and only conversation from a man she adored. At the time, it made perfect sense. Now, it had all been made right.

René finally broke away, never taking his eyes from Amanda's face. He placed his hat firmly on his head, adjusting the angle and smiling grimly. He lovingly touched the tip of her chin, allowing his thumb the pleasure of caressing her cheek once more. Then, without a word, he was swallowed up into the darkness.

Even with the remnants of their interrupted lovemaking tugging at the seams of his trousers, René couldn't help but feel ten times happier. His wife cared for him, and obviously had done so for quite some time. The dark Louisiana night seemed a thousand times brighter.

Why she denied knowing he had asked her father for her hand was still unclear. Did her father lie about Amanda not accepting an Acadian's affections, or was Amanda trying to change history to suit her current situation?

Familiar doubts returned, but René willed them away. She could have left, had the marriage annulled at any time, he reminded himself. Amanda had offered herself to him tonight, and that wasn't the action of a woman waiting to return home to her father.

Whistling happily, René entered the quiet stables, lighted only by a sole lamp in the small corner the men called an office. As he approached the area, René could make out a medium-sized man with dark, wavy hair exquisitely kept in the latest style. He stood poised by a wall, his arm delicately draped on the sill of the makeshift window, as if afraid the stable dust might infiltrate his clothes. His dress and manner were equally impressive, exuding wealth and good breeding. René wondered what the dapper man could possibly want from him.

"Bon soir," René said, instinctively believing the man to be French. "I am René Comeaux."

The man turned, said nothing and refused to accept René's outstretched hand. Instead, he grinned slyly as he took in René's attire, starting with the crude palmetto hat and ending with his dirty, work-worn leather boots.

"You're an Acadian," he said with a patronizing smirk.

Ever since he was a boy, French Creoles had always incited two reactions from René, depending on the severity of their scorn. If he wanted their company or saw an opportunity by mixing with the upper-class French descendants, he adopted their mannerisms and accent. If they looked upon him with distaste, attempting to reinstate the aristocratic-peasant social class system in France, then René strutted his Acadian heritage with pride. He'd be damned if he would bow down to anyone.

"What on earth are you wearing on your head?" the Creole asked.

René folded his arms defiantly across his chest. He'd left the comfort of his wife's arms for this harassment? "May I help you with something?" René asked, trying to keep the bitterness from his voice. This was business after all.

The man straightened, and began to remove imaginary lint from his sleeves. "I have a business proposition for you, if you're interested."

René wanted to offer the middle-aged man a chair, but the stables had never been a place where he conducted business dealings. "My home is only minutes away," René offered. "May I suggest we continue our conversation there? I could offer you some refreshment, some . . ."

The Creole waved his hand in front of him. "There's no need. I'll not keep you long. I'm interested in a race between my horse and several other gentlemen from New Orleans. I'm from New Orleans, you see."

"Really?" René hadn't meant the remark to sound so biting, but it emerged with quite a sting. The man ignored it and continued.

"I would like to have the racetrack for an entire day, to ensure privacy."

"That is quite difficult to do," René said, folding his arms across his chest. "I have races scheduled every day."

"I'll pay handsomely for it."

René laughed. "Yes, you will."

The Creole pulled out a large leather billfold from his waist-coat pocket. Inside René spotted a thick wad of currency. "I aim to pay you very well,'' the Creole said quietly, ''for more than just the use of your track.''

René stared at the Creole, searching for that familiar glint of greed that appeared in the eyes of the most unselfish men. He had seen it numerous times, men driven to desperate acts because of financial misfortune. If he had a *piastre* for every time someone had tried to bribe him, René could have easily quit the horse-racing business.

Ironically, the glint didn't appear. The Creole glared at him, his eyes cold as black steel, as if daring him to take the money.

''If you're insinuating what I think you are, then you best be on your way,'' René replied coldly. ''I believe New Orleans has many gambling venues that will happily take your money, but I, sir, run a reputable track.''

The Creole removed the money from the billfold and held it up in the light so René could see exactly how much money he was throwing away. What appeared to be hundreds of dollars waved before his eyes. René glanced at the money, more out of curiosity than want, than tipped his hat as politely as he could muster and turned to leave.

''Wait,'' the Creole called out.

When René looked back into the office, the Creole had deposited the billfold back into his pocket. He almost looked pleased that René had turned him down.

''I didn't mean to insult you, my boy, but I wanted to see where we stood.''

''Next time, ask the people of this town what kind of business I run,'' René said. ''Anyone for miles around, including New Orleans, would have told you I don't fix races.''

The Creole bowed politely. ''Again, I am sorry.''

René stood at a loss for words, something he wasn't accustomed to. Most men would have exchanged angry words or attempted to bribe him further. This Creole seemed more agreeable.

"I understand you have married," the man offered in an amiable tone.

"Yes," René answered guardedly.

"And she is an American, the daughter of the local judge?"

"Yes."

"I knew James Richardson when he lived in New Orleans. His daughter, Amanda, was only a child then. Is this the woman you married?"

René immediately came to life at the mention of his beloved's name. "Yes, it is. You must come up to the house. Amanda would be anxious to meet you."

The light mood that the Creole exhibited passed, and a shadow replaced it. *"Non, merci.* It is late and I have kept you away long enough."

René placed his hands at his hips, genuinely puzzled at the whole meeting. "Do you still wish to use the track? I board horses as well."

To further his amazement, the Creole placed a friendly hand on René's shoulder. "No, I have learned what I came here to learn."

The Creole moved into the darkness of the night, where a carriage and its driver waited. "There is one thing you can do," he offered as he entered the carriage's interior.

René closed the door behind him as the driver lit the carriage's lamp. The meager light cast an eerie shadow over the Creole's face.

"Watch your back," the older man cautioned. "I have witnessed a man named Henry Tanner slandering your name. If he acts on his words, you are in grave danger. I do not believe this man to be an honorable one. I doubt he will challenge you to a duel. *Vous comprenez?*"

René nodded that he understood. Henry Tanner was rumored to stab a best friend in the back if it meant he would win at cards.

"Give my best to Amanda," the Creole said as the carriage bolted.

"What is your name?" René called out, but it was too late. The mysterious Creole had disappeared.

Chapter Eleven

Ever since she had arrived at the Comeaux house that morning, Katharine had exhibited a most disagreeable nature. She snapped at the boys when they played a harmless joke on her by placing a small green lizard on the seat of her buggy. She politely accepted coffee from Colette, then barked orders to Amanda for more sugar and a clean spoon. Amanda tried to help her into the buggy when it appeared she was experiencing a spell of lightheadedness, but Katharine rudely pulled her elbow away.

Now that they were on their way to town, Amanda couldn't help but wonder why Katharine Blanchard, who'd never shared "company" with Amanda before, had suddenly become interested in her affairs. Disagreeably interested, she realized.

"I'm sorry," Katharine finally said after moments of silence. "I don't know what's come over me this morning."

"Perhaps you are not feeling well," Amanda offered, searching her face for sincerity. To her surprise, tears were forming in Katharine's eyes.

"Yes," she whispered. "I don't feel very well."

As a lone tear escaped down Katharine's cheek, Amanda felt certain Katharine would tell of her misery. A look of sadness and a want of friendship overtook Katharine's previous angry state, and Amanda reached down and took her hand. Katharine squeezed it tight, as if thankful for the companionship.

"I have done something terrible," she whispered.

Before Amanda could ask, she heard a horse quickly approaching from the woods next to the road. The sudden movement caused the buggy's horses to spook and rear. Katharine grasped the reins tightly to keep control over them.

Both women looked up anxiously at the inconsiderate rider, who grabbed the horses' reins from Katharine's grip and stopped the buggy.

"What on earth?" Amanda demanded, standing up to get a better look at the intruder. To her horror, Henry Tanner filled the saddle.

"Nice to see you again, Miss Richardson," he said sarcastically. "Or shall I call you Mrs. Comeaux?"

Fear consumed Amanda's being and she silently prayed someone—anyone—would be passing by. After searching the horizon and finding no one in sight, Amanda sat back down, trying to quickly formulate a plan of action.

"Henry," she heard Katharine say at her side. "You scared us to death."

"Did I?" Tanner said with mock concern. Moving toward Amanda, he leaned down in his saddle, making it impossible for her to escape his gaze. "I certainly wouldn't want you scared of me."

Amanda placed a gloved hand on her neck while she stared down at the buggy floor, trying to avoid Tanner's penetrating eyes. She could feel the wild beating of her heart pulsating through the veins in her neck. She had to think of something; she had to get away.

"There's no way of escaping me, my dear," Tanner said as if reading her thoughts. "You can marry whomever you wish, but I will always know where to find you."

Katharine stared at him, then pressed a handkerchief to her lips. "I think I will be sick," she said, this time crying freely.

"For goodness' sakes, Katharine, this is not the time," Tanner barked.

"She's ill," Amanda told Tanner, wondering how he could be so rude to a woman he barely knew.

"She's fine," Tanner answered. "I want to talk to you and I shall not keep you long."

Amanda's mind whirled. What could Henry Tanner possibly want of her now? He had done his damage, and because of her silence on the matter he should be grateful and halfway to Texas.

"I heard you concocted a nice little story about eloping with the Cajun man," he began. "So, it seems your father wouldn't be too keen on you inviting his overseer out for a secret moonlit ride, eh?"

"It wasn't like that, you know . . ."

"It was exactly like that, my dear." Tanner leaned in closer, his black eyes staring coldly into hers. "You asked for something and you reneged on it. Meanwhile, I'm the one on the losing end."

Amanda stared up at him, horrified. "I only asked for a ride to the ball."

"You asked for exactly what you received."

Katharine stopped crying, and the silence that followed began to swallow Amanda whole. She felt her nerve slowly fading. If only a farmer or a traveler would happen by.

"I want three thousand dollars by tonight," Tanner said. "I

want it delivered to this spot, to the abandoned cottage over there.''

Through the trees Amanda could barely make out the old Wiley homestead. When the old man had died, his neighbor, Reed Harris, had purchased the land from his descendants, used the accompanying fields, and let the meager house fall into disrepair.

''I don't have three thousand dollars.''

''Sure you do,'' Tanner said. ''You have a trust fund.''

''It's only a few hundred. And I can't remove that kind of money from the bank.''

''Find a way.''

''But . . .''

''Find a way,'' Tanner shouted, ''and have it here tonight or Pappy gets an earful.''

Amanda swallowed hard, resolving to keep her wits about her. ''You wouldn't dare tell my father, not after what you have done.''

Tanner smirked. ''I can fill your father's ears with all kinds of information about that opportunist husband of yours and his dealings at the racetrack. Your father will be quite happy to throw that no-good son of a bitch into jail and shut down his whole operation.''

''You wouldn't,'' Amanda said.

''Tonight, my dear,'' Tanner said with finality, pointing to the house. ''I expect you to deliver.''

Tanner threw the buggy's reins toward the women, and Amanda quickly grabbed them.

''One more thing,'' Tanner said, riding his horse up closer. ''Tell your husband about this, and I'll kill him.''

Amanda didn't breathe comfortably until she saw the shiny red bricks of St. Mary's Episcopal Church on First Street.

Katharine remained silent when Amanda took control of the reins and sent the horses bolting toward town. When they arrived safely, the two women looked at each other for the first time since the fateful meeting with Tanner.

She had to explain to Katharine. The woman must be horrified that Amanda knew Tanner well enough to give him money, or even worse, that she had been out in an unchaperoned carriage ride with him.

To Amanda's surprise, it was Katharine who appeared eager to talk. "Amanda, I can explain," she said.

Suddenly, it all made sense. Katharine had asked for her company so she would get Amanda alone in a secluded spot to meet Tanner. That was why they'd treated each other with such familiarity. They were friends. The way Katharine had defended him the night before, Katharine was probably in love with him.

Closing her eyes, Amanda tried to dispel the anxiety. Alcée had insisted T-Emile accompany them that morning, but both she and Katharine had talked him out of it. Nothing would happen, Amanda had argued, in broad daylight on a quick trip to town.

Katharine reached over and touched Amanda's arm lightly, but Amanda drew away. "I'm sorry," Katharine said. "He's only doing this for his sister."

Amanda shook her head. She didn't know which hurt worse, her continuing stupidity about men or that Katharine had fallen for the deceitful bastard and betrayed her. Deep down she wanted to warn Katharine, to explain how Tanner had compromised her, but her anger won out. "He doesn't have a sister," Amanda said bitterly, quickly descending the buggy and heading toward the sanctuary of the church.

When Amanda entered Franklin's oldest religious establishment, she was overwhelmed by the intense humid air pouring in from the windows. It was not yet noon, and her petticoats and camisole were already pasted to her skin. Her head spun from the heat, and she sought comfort in the first available pew.

Before she could reach her destination and mop the perspiration beading across her forehead, she stood face-to-face with Sally.

"Sally," Amanda said, grabbing her old friend like a drowning swimmer lunging for a preserver. "Thank heavens! I must talk to you."

"Oh?" Sally answered unemotionally. "Life not turning out the way you expected it, Amanda?"

Amanda stepped back and took in Sally's stern countenance. Surely, she couldn't be mad at her, not after all that had happened. If anyone had cause to be angry, it was Amanda.

"Sally, what have I done?" Amanda asked.

When Sally finally spoke, Amanda saw that her best friend was close to tears. Amanda instantly regretted not speaking to her sooner, explaining what happened that night with Tanner.

"How could you?" Sally asked, the hurt emerging in her voice. "If you wanted to elope with the Cajun racetrack owner, then so be it. But, asking me to arrange a rendezvous with Henry Tanner and making a complete fool out of me... I thought you were my friend."

"I am your friend," Amanda insisted. "It wasn't like that at all."

"I saw you with the Cajun in the market that day. I know exactly what it was like."

Amanda started to explain, but Sally instantly pressed a handkerchief to her nose and headed for the privacy of an empty pew. Amanda thought to go to her, to try and explain, until she recognized her friends congregated by the altar. Several of the American women Amanda had socialized with for years turned and stared. Even the minister, whom Amanda had met only at marriages and christenings, glanced at Amanda with curiosity. He must have heard of her scandalous elopement, she thought; the whole town must now know.

Amanda felt isolated, unwanted and threatened. Her heart close to buckling under the pain, she left the gaiety of the crowd and quickly exited the church, running toward home. As soon as she reached the sidewalk, a welcomed familiar voice sounded from behind.

"Miss Amanda," T-Emile said. "May I accompany you somewhere?"

Amanda nearly burst into tears upon sight of the young man. Instead, she bit her lip to keep her emotions inside and accepted his outstretched arm. "Please take me to my father's house," she whispered.

"Are you not well?" he shyly asked.

Amanda silently stared at the ground, but couldn't find the words. She didn't feel like talking, especially translating the words into French, and she knew T-Emile wouldn't press her. Silently, the pair walked down Main Street to her father's house. When they reached her home, Amanda released T-Emile's arm.

"I'd ask you in, but I really must talk to my father," she said.

T-Emile smiled as if a great weight left his shoulders. "That's fine," he answered a bit eagerly.

"You don't have to wait. René is expected later and he will see me home."

T-Emile appeared doubly relieved. "I have business in town," he said, surprising her with his sudden attentiveness. "I will be back in an hour in case you need me."

Amanda almost smiled at his concern. "Thank you," she whispered, and entered the house.

James couldn't pinpoint the exact moment the connection occurred, but he estimated it happened around Amanda's first birthday. Genevieve, as usual, had thrown quite a party, inviting all of her treasured theater friends to perform for her daughter. After the cake and presents, everyone began to sing songs around the parlor harpsichord, each one trying to outperform the other, their voices increasingly rising in volume.

What was it? James wondered as he stared out his office window, trying to recall that ominous feeling. It was almost as if something invisible had tugged on his sleeve, urging him to get up and leave the room. Or a thought had entered his mind and refused to leave. But he knew, at that very moment, that Amanda was not where she should have been and was in danger. He knew it before the kitchen servant screamed.

Amanda, an early walker, had followed the servant out the front door, heading for the street and an oncoming buggy. James hadn't thought logically what to do; he'd instinctively headed straight for his daughter, pulling her into his arms and tumbling onto the distant sidewalk, perhaps saving her life.

That parental instinct had not diminished through the years. He felt it again when Amanda silently opened the door and entered the hallway. That familiar anxiety, that inner knowledge that something was amiss, that his only daughter could be in danger, lingered between them. When she finally called his name, he knew he was right.

"What is it?" he answered hurriedly, meeting her in the hallway and examining her from head to toe.

"Father, I must talk to you," she said nervously.

James grabbed Amanda's shoulders and took a closer look. She wasn't physically hurt from what he could assess. "I'll kill him if he hurt you in any way, shape or form."

Amanda stared up at him puzzled.

"What did that son of a bitch do to you?" he demanded.

Amanda pushed his arms away and entered the office. She appeared willing to talk, but hesitant.

"If that Cajun did one thing . . ."

"It's not about René," Amanda answered.

"Then what is it?"

"It's Henry," Amanda said softly.

"Henry?" What the blazes did his overseer have to do with anything?

"Father, you have to get rid of him," she insisted.

Something deep in his gut pulled at him. It wasn't the Comeaux man after all. There was more to this story, just as Virginia had warned. "Why?"

Amanda turned slightly, but refused to meet her father's eyes. She kept moving a paperweight around his desk, as if trying to find the proper words. "I fear he will do something terrible to this family. He may be robbing us blind at this very moment."

James wanted to shake his daughter and make her get right to the point, but he knew that if she was harboring a secret about this man, it was best to take it slowly. "Why would Henry be doing that, Amanda?"

Finally, his daughter met his gaze. "He's in debt, Father. Haven't you heard?"

Of course he'd heard. Henry was always in debt. Every other month his overseer asked for an advance. But Henry's gambling problems couldn't have anything to do with Amanda.

"What he does with his finances is his business, Amanda, not ours," he answered a bit impatiently. "I must say I don't necessarily trust the man, but I keep a watchful eye on everything he does. He has no access to any of our funds, so there's no need to worry about him stealing."

"But, Father . . ."

"I had already planned on letting him go at the end of the summer, when I can find a new foreman. Henry and I have not seen eye-to-eye on matters with the slaves."

His answers refused to relieve the anxious expression on his daughter's face. "There's more," she said.

"What else has Henry done?"

Amanda walked toward the back of the room, staring out the window at the back garden's crape myrtles. "He has a reputation in town for compromising women."

The grip that caused his breath to quicken intensified. "Who?" he asked, both wanting to know and wishing he could retract the question.

"Women in town. Women from prominent families," she explained, then added softly, "people you know."

"I would have heard," James countered.

"Not necessarily."

"Why is that?"

"Women don't always talk about such things."

James was beginning to tire of the chase. "Amanda, if Henry has done something to a woman of this town, I must know about it. I can't go accusing him of . . ."

"He promised to take a woman to a ball and instead took her to Port Cocodrie in the middle of the night in the hope of bribing her father into marrying her."

The words had emerged without Amanda thinking of the consequences. She had promised herself she would give her father enough reasons to fire Henry without having to use herself as an example. But he'd kept prying, insisting on knowing more. Now she feared she'd said too much. Her father stood behind her, silent, as if absorbing the meaning of her words. Amanda prayed he would not inquire more.

"If he did this, as you say he did, then he would be married now," James said slowly. "I am not aware of Henry marrying anyone."

"It's true, Father. But Henry didn't marry her."

"And why is that?"

Amanda paused to catch her breath. "While he was off in search of her father, she met a friend and he brought her back to town." That should suffice, Amanda thought. The young lady in question could have sneaked back into town, no one the wiser.

"She never would have made it back into town before daybreak," James argued.

Amanda closed her eyes tightly. She was digging herself deeper and deeper into a hole, and she saw no relief. Why couldn't he just take her word? "Please, Father," she whispered in a pleading voice. "Fire Henry."

Amanda turned to look at her father, and found his gaze more crushing than all of Tanner's actions. Where she thought to find anger and blame, she found a man consumed by guilt, tears forming at the corners of his eyes. He appeared anxious to say something, but his emotions kept the words from emerging. Amanda never felt so ashamed of anything in her life. She wanted to beg his forgiveness, to admit everything, but words would not come either. Instead, father and daughter stood staring silently at one another while the parlor clock announced the passing moments.

Suddenly, a knock sounded at the front door.

"Oh, my God," Amanda said. "It's René."

Staring at the front door of the Richardson household for the third time that week, René adjusted his cravat and waistcoat. He felt like Joshua approaching the walls of Jericho. Sooner or later he would make enough noise and the walls between their nationalities would come tumbling down.

He should be feeling apprehensive, he thought with a smile. But after the kisses his wife delivered last night, René could think of nothing else. If she cared for him, her father was easily a surmountable obstacle.

When the door opened, a pair of deep aquamarine eyes met his. After a quick glance at the street behind him and the hallway ahead, René snaked an arm about Amanda's waist and planted a loving kiss upon her lips. She didn't resist, but she didn't return the kiss either. René looked down and found his wife's face grave.

"Don't worry," he said. "I can handle your father."

Amanda said nothing, but walked René to her father's office at the back of the house. René knew the home well. The first time he'd taken notice of every room, examining every painting, knickknack and servant. He'd wanted to familiarize himself with all the details of Amanda's life so that when they courted he would have points of reference. The second time, when he had come only to impart news of their elopement, nothing had registered.

On this occasion, René wanted to reassure her father. The man needed to know, even if René had told him twice before, that his daughter was in the best of hands, that René would face a dozen August hurricanes before letting anyone or anything hurt his beloved *petite chou*. The Judge had to understand that René was perfectly capable of providing a proper home for his daughter.

Amanda hesitated at the office threshold. René knew she was still skeptical about the meeting—even if he felt that her father was relenting—but her solemn demeanor made him wonder if something else had transpired that morning. When he looked over at the Judge and noticed his stern countenance as well, René began to worry.

"Has something happened?" he asked.

René's words made the Judge come to life. "Come in, my boy," he said, motioning for René to take a chair.

If the solemn mood didn't convince René that something was amiss, the Judge's familiarity sure did. René glanced back at Amanda, hoping she would speak, but she had moved to the back window, staring vacantly out at the back garden. Amazingly, the Judge ignored her.

"My cook is visiting family and my housekeeper has gone for coffee," James said. "I apologize for the inconvenience."

René was prepared for many things, but politeness was not one of them. What on earth could have happened? he wondered.

"You must come over for dinner," René offered. "My cousin Colette is a wonderful cook and she's used to feeding an army. You'd be more than welcome at our table."

René wanted to appear hospitable, but his offer sounded hollow. He again looked at Amanda for support, but her mind was elsewhere.

"Thank you, but Virginia has made do," James replied.

"Perhaps another time then," René said.

"Yes, another time."

Amanda seemed to finally acknowledge what was being said, and turned to join the conversation. "You and Gin must come out to the house one Sunday," she said softly to her father.

The Judge glanced at his daughter with what looked like pity. The change in the man was startling. "That would be nice," James said.

The housekeeper René had seen on occasion burst through the back door, announcing to all that she had returned. Both the intrusion and the informal nature of the woman made René's heart feel lighter. Even James and Amanda seemed to brighten at her arrival.

"I'm sorry I'm late," she said, entering the room. "Everyone seems to be at the market today."

René and James both rose. "Virginia," James said. "I'd like you to meet René Comeaux. Monsieur Comeaux, this is Virginia O'Neil, Amanda's former nanny and the head of my household."

René bowed politely, but not without first taking in her astonishingly brilliant auburn hair. Women with hair that color he nicknamed *baieonne,* referring to horses with chestnut manes. "It is a pleasure, madame."

Virginia placed her hands defiantly on her hips, but offered a cautious smile. "My pleasure, sir, would have been to know you before you became my charge's husband."

Without so much as a reaction, René responded, "It would have been my pleasure as well, madame, particularly since I have heard nothing but wonderful reports about you. Unfortunately, destiny has proven otherwise."

René shot James a sly glance, but James was not listening. This time, René was not alone in his concern.

"Has something happened?" Virginia asked.

"Why don't you and Amanda get us some coffee?" James offered.

René couldn't help but notice the chemistry between James and his employee. With one glance between them, whole conversations seemed to pass.

"Of course," Virginia answered. Taking Amanda's arm, she urged her from the room.

"But . . . I must . . ." Amanda insisted, looking imploringly over at René.

"I'll be fine," he said with a grin.

As the door closed behind them and the Judge's grave countenance remained unchanged, René began to doubt his words. James stood and walked toward the windows, staring out as his daughter had done. For the first time, René realized the room's massive drapes were opened and sunlight filled the usually darkened room. Before René could digest the information, James hurled a more impressive subject his way.

"What do you know about Henry Tanner?"

After years of dealing with vastly different kinds of people in his business, René learned one important lesson: When confronted with a difficult situation, take your time and try to reason with the confronter.

"He's your overseer, no?"

The grave appearance James exhibited turned to his usual

angry state. "Damn it, man. I know who Henry Tanner is. What I want to know is what has the man done to my daughter."

René breathed deeply, searching his brain for a resolution. He'd promised Amanda her "mistake" with Tanner would be their secret. But putting himself in the Judge's shoes, René felt it was a father's right to know. He couldn't help admitting to himself as well that having someone else worried about Amanda's welfare would be welcomed. If Tanner harbored ill feelings against René and Amanda, it would be to their advantage to have Judge Richardson on the lookout for trouble.

Still, he had promised Amanda. "Have you talked to your daughter about this?" René asked.

"Yes."

"And what has she said?"

"That Henry took her to Port Cocodrie in the middle of the night in an attempt to bribe me into their marrying."

Something in the way the Judge described the story made René doubt Amanda had bared her soul. He decided to proceed with caution. "She told you that?"

"Not in those words exactly," James said.

"In what words exactly?" René asked.

The Judge leaned toward René and glared at him. "You tell me."

René could almost feel the pain and suffering the man felt over the loss of control of his precious daughter. It was bad enough she had eloped with René, but now her father sensed she had been abused in the night by a man he trusted, a man he'd chosen to run his estate. René decided to follow his heart. "Henry Tanner took her to Port Cocodrie as you said."

The look of pain in James's eyes intensified. For the first time, René imagined himself a father loving someone as much as he did his wife. For the first time, he sympathized with the Judge.

"How?" James asked, dropping his shoulders from the weight of the news.

"I don't know the details. Amanda never offered much. I do know that she was taken there against her will."

James immediately stood and began to pace the room. "Of course she was."

"I'm sorry, I didn't mean to imply otherwise. It's just that Amanda has always insisted the whole affair was her fault."

James stopped pacing and stared at René. "Why on earth would she believe that? My daughter never would have done such a thing."

René shook his head in agreement. He didn't believe it either. "I don't know."

"And what was your role in all of this?"

"The father of the woman I adored refused me," René said with a grim smile. "I went to Port Cocodrie to seek refuge in a bottle of rum."

"Are you trying to tell me that it was a coincidence that you and Amanda found each other?" James half shouted.

"Yes, sir, that's exactly what it was."

James stared intently at René as if reading his face for sincerity. "And?"

"And the rest is history."

"You didn't have to force her to marry you?"

Now it was René's turn to stand. "I didn't force her to marry me," he answered a bit too harshly. He had vowed to remain calm during the interrogation, but the Judge had touched a nerve. "I wanted to bring her home, but if I had arrived in broad daylight, you would have had my head."

Surprisingly, the Judge laughed. "You have a point."

"I did what I thought was best," René continued.

"And you got what you wanted—my daughter," James argued.

"I won't deny that marrying your daughter was one of the

greatest pleasures of my life," René explained, this time in a calmer tone. "But she is well provided for, well protected, and seems to be very happy at my house. She will never want for anything as long as I draw breath."

"But does she love you?"

The fire that raced through René's veins was suddenly extinguished. "I don't know," he said softly, staring down at the hat held between his fingers.

"But you love her?" James asked in an equally quiet tone.

René looked up to meet James's gaze. It was important the Judge knew that, more than anything else spoken today, René was sincere in his affections toward Amanda. "I love your daughter with all my heart and soul," he said slowly and succinctly.

The two men stared at each other for several moments. Finally, the Judge broke the silence. "Marriages have been made on less than regard for one another. I suppose my daughter is a lucky woman."

René knew admitting error was difficult for a man like Judge Richardson. To relieve him of the embarrassment, René extended his hand. "Amanda is lucky indeed to have a father who cares as much as you do."

"What father wouldn't?" James asked proudly, but he accepted René's hand and held it tight before adding, "If you hurt one hair on her head, I'll have you hanged for sure."

René grinned broadly. The walls had finally fallen. "Yes, sir."

Again, James motioned for them to sit down. "Now, how about some coffee? We have a lot to discuss."

Chapter Twelve

Finally, the truth was at hand. Virginia sensed it when she walked into the house. Now Amanda sat silently before her at the pantry table, more guilt-stricken than the first day she had lunched with her father after the elopement. Something had happened, and Virginia was determined to get to the bottom of this insane affair.

As if reading her thoughts, Amanda spoke before the questions left Virginia's lips. "I'll explain everything," she said solemnly.

Amanda never got a chance. Both women literally jumped when Sally Baldwin began pounding at the back door.

"What in the world?" Virginia said, opening the door wide. Ignoring Virginia and rushing past, Sally headed straight for her best friend.

"Amanda, can you ever forgive me?" she said with tears fresh in her eyes. "Katharine told me what happened."

Virginia stood watching the two friends huddle in conspiracy, enveloping and comforting each other over the sad, secret event that no one understood but these two. Virginia had had all the mystery she could stand for one week. She placed a loving yet firm grip on Sally's shoulder and guided her toward an empty chair. When Virginia gave her a little push, Sally fell backwards into a seated position, while Virginia handed her a cup and saucer and moved the steaming pitcher of remaining coffee in her direction.

"There's sugar and cream," she said. "Help yourself, then wait your turn."

Virginia joined the other women at the table, folded her hands tightly together in front of her and waited for Amanda to explain.

"Perhaps I should start at the beginning?" Amanda asked softly.

"Try the moment that Acadian left you at the gate," Virginia answered.

Amanda sighed, glancing pleadingly in the direction of Sally, who returned her gaze with guilt-stricken sympathy. Then Amanda began her tale. "It all started with my birthday," she said. "I was afraid of becoming an old maid."

"You must realize I don't approve of gambling," James said sternly, looking over at René. "No daughter of mine will be married to a gambler."

"Your daughter is not married to a gambler, sir. She's married to a horse track owner."

"I suppose there's a difference?" James smirked.

"Absolutely," René argued. "I never gamble. I run a reputable track."

"You encourage others to throw money away on a senseless sport instead of earning it the hard way by the sweat of one's brow."

René leaned forward in his chair, maintaining eye contact in a serious, yet friendly, stare. "What others choose to do with their money is none of my concern. Foolish men who bet too frequently or cause disruption at my track are not allowed to return."

James rested his elbows on the velvet arms of the Queen Anne chair, linking his fingers together as was his habit when reviewing arguments in court. His mind digested the information cast his way, but it wasn't at all what he expected. All morning he'd anticipated an argument with this upstart Cajun, possibly angry negotiations over the size of Amanda's dowry. Instead, he found René amiably sparring with him, holding his ground with grace. No stranger to debates and the thrill of victory, James decided to push the case further. "Where are these men to go then, after being tainted with the allure of gambling?"

"I offer a sport, sir. I do not *lure* them with anything."

"But to win?" James said. "Surely, that is allurement indeed?"

"The odds of losing are always higher," René countered.

"So, you say that if a man was to lose enough at your race track, then he would be cured of the gambling disease forever."

René took a breath and briefly looked away. Like so many of the parish's lawyers and the eager men naive enough to challenge the popular judge in elections, René had been cornered, James knew, and he proceeded to deliver the final blow. "A man such as Henry Tanner?"

The muscles of René's jawline tightened. "Henry Tanner has not been welcome at the track for quite some time."

"Obviously, it hasn't deterred him from gambling."

René picked up his hat from the table and began turning it around in his hand. "I hardly see how I am responsible for Henry Tanner's abominable behavior. If my racetrack did not exist, Tanner would find another, of that I am sure."

James leaned in toward René, this time thinking more as a father than a debater. "Son, Henry Tanner would be relieved of his problem if there were no gambling halls at all. You must realize, respectable though your track may be, that you are part of a very large problem in this state."

When René did not answer, James pried further. "Is it a question of money?"

René stood up so fast he nearly disturbed the contents of the coffee tray sitting on the small table at his feet. "I stated my feelings clearly to you before, sir, the day you so rudely announced that your daughter would have nothing to do with me. I am fully capable of providing a home for Amanda."

Hoping to return the conversation back to a calmer state, James rose and reached for René's shoulder, but René moved quickly away. "I love your daughter, you must realize that by now."

"Yes, I . . ."

"I am hardly a man of need."

"Horse racing pays that well?" James asked.

When René glanced back at James, the Judge caught the semblance of a smile. "I only operate businesses that pay well."

"Ah," James said, motioning for them to resume sitting. He was beginning to understand. "You enjoy the sport of commerce then."

René tilted his head slightly. "I'm sorry?"

For an instant James remembered his wife's sweet face, uttering that exact phrase when he spoke English too difficult for her to comprehend. He quickly ignored the tug on his heart, and concentrated on the conversation at hand. "You enjoy making money."

Several moments passed before René spoke again. James feared the young man was losing his nerve or worse, inventing a lie to appease him. "Yes, sir," René said with a serious grin. "I enjoy making money."

"Then this can all be settled easily," James said. "You need a reputable profession and I need a new overseer. We can work . . ."

"That's very kind of you, sir, but I'm afraid I cannot accept," René interrupted.

James narrowed his eyes. "Why?"

"I do not wish to pass judgment, what you do with your own affairs is your business," René began.

"But?"

"I do not approve of slavery. I will not be party to it."

Until that moment, René felt confident he was at least winning the old man's respect. Now, as the tension-filled moments passed between the two men, he began to doubt they would finish their conversation on amiable terms. In St. Mary Parish, slavery remained a nondebatable issue. Those opposed to the institution need look elsewhere to reside. René never publicly stated his opinion on the matter, but he could never be master over people enslaved. He would consider selling the track, but never working on the Richardson plantation.

"I see," James finally said, his tone curt. "We'll just have to think of something else."

After several more awkward seconds, James leaned back in his chair again, signaling to René to relax as well. "You're right. I don't see you as an overseer type."

René picked up his coffee cup and drained the lukewarm contents in an effort to escape the piercing eyes of his father-in-law. The *cafè au lait* was delicious, but the *baieonne* had not returned with refills and he longed for another hot cup. Anything to keep his hands busy and eyes focused on something besides James's examining stare.

James reminded René of his own father, always scrutinizing him with contemplating gazes, as if trying to read something from René that René was unable to comprehend himself. His father too wished for him to leave the horse racing business, to return to Loreauville and a life of farming and cattle raising. René never dreamed of insulting his father, but farming was the last profession he'd consider.

"I can't quite put my finger on it," James said. "But I have a feeling your potential is underused. There's a career here that I'm missing. One that's perfect for you."

René sighed. God only knew what Judge Richardson would insist he do to maintain the reputation of his fine wife's family name. Alcée was right. He was going to be an American before he knew it.

James rose, extending his hand. "I must go. There is business I need to take care of at the plantation."

René rose too, immediately meeting James's handshake. "I'd like to join you if you don't mind."

"I do mind," James said. "I don't want my daughter widowed before her first week as a married woman is over."

All the kind phrases and warm smiles couldn't have mattered more to René than the Judge's last words. René knew he had finally been accepted; James's faint smile confirmed his feelings.

"I appreciate the thought, Judge," René said, "but I must insist on riding with you. You should not face Henry Tanner alone."

James instantly dropped René's hand and straightened. "Nonsense. I want you escorting my daughter safely home. I will bring the sheriff with me."

René nodded, glad his father-in-law had the sense to realize there was power in numbers. "Your daughter will always be safe with me."

James placed a paternal arm on René's shoulder and guided him toward the parlor doors. "You have a strong handshake, my boy," he said. "Have you ever thought of entering politics?"

* * *

Virginia nearly stopped breathing during Amanda's lengthy explanation, listening intently to every horrible detail. When Amanda finally arrived at the morning's meeting with Tanner, Virginia gasped, then expelled a deep breath.

"I have ruined you," Sally said between sobs.

"You have not ruined me, Sally," Amanda answered, stroking her friend's arm to soothe her. "You could have kept the part about me becoming an old maid to yourself."

The last statement made Sally cry harder. "I will never forgive myself. I have sent you off to a life with the Cajun racetrack owner."

Virginia covered her mouth with her hand and shook her head. "What are we to do?" she asked herself.

Thinking of René gave Amanda strength. Despite the threat of Henry Tanner looming in the distance, she still had her husband. The man she loved. "It's not as bad as all that," she began. "He has a nice home and a wonderful family. I've grown quite fond of them, actually." Just then Amanda remembered the passionate kiss she had shared with René the night before, and she smiled.

Her sly grin startled Virginia, who must have thought her momentarily insane. Virginia shot Sally a concerned look, and Sally stared back, equally confused.

"I've grown quite fond of René as well," Amanda confessed, a smile stealing across her lips.

Virginia made the sign of the cross. "Mary, Mother of God, she's fallen in love."

Sally's jaw practically hit the starched collar of her high neckline. Amanda laughed at them both. It was a pretty ironic turn of events.

"There was something between you two," Virginia said,

sending her a sideways look. "Meeting at the fence every morning, talking about Louisiana history."

"What happened at the market that afternoon?" Sally added. "After that mysterious meeting, I could have sworn you eloped with that man."

Amanda sighed. There was still so much to explain, but there wasn't time. "I'll tell all in great detail in due time," she said. "Now, you must help me find a way to get rid of Henry Tanner."

Virginia immediately rose and opened the back door, calling the stable boy's name. While she waited for the young slave to arrive, she wrote a note on a small piece of paper.

"The first thing your father will do is confront Mr. Tanner," Virginia answered as she handed the boy the note, instructing him to deliver it as quickly as possible to the plantation. "If we inform him that we are on to his game, he will more than likely leave town before the Judge arrives."

Amanda felt relieved that Virginia had thought of her father. She couldn't imagine Tanner challenging him, but then again, she'd never dreamed Tanner would have kidnapped his employer's daughter to pay off gambling debts. Watching her former nanny twist her apron in worry, Amanda wished with all her heart that her father loved Virginia in return.

"Perhaps I should bring more coffee in to the men," Virginia stated, hoping to stall James from his duty.

"It's cold," Sally offered. "And we have to decide about the money."

"How much do you have in your trust fund?" Virginia asked Amanda.

"A few hundred dollars."

"Withdraw it," Virginia instructed. "Then somehow get it to the spot Tanner talked of. If he has money in his pockets, he should have no trouble buying a ticket out of here."

"Virginia's right," Sally piped in. "We have to make it

easy for Tanner to leave town. Once he's gone, we can all breathe easier."

Fear and trepidation gripped Amanda's heart. It seemed too risky. She would rather the bastard rot in jail. Yet absent men don't tell tales. The most important thing, Amanda concluded, was to rid Franklin of Henry Tanner.

"All right," she said. "How should we do it?"

The three women leaned forward to make their plans, but all conversation halted at the unexpected sound coming from the hallway. It was the last thing Amanda imagined she'd hear in her father's house. Acadian René Comeaux was laughing.

As the two men entered the back parlor, all three women stared up in disbelief.

"I don't understand," James was saying to a smiling René, clearly at a loss over his amusement. "What is so funny about a career in politics?"

René stalled, appearing to formulate the right words. Amanda smiled. She knew what he was thinking. An Acadian never gets involved in American politics. Only René didn't know how to explain that to her father without insulting him. She decided to rescue him by rising and snaking her arm through his.

She tried to think of something witty to say, to move the conversation in another direction, but her father turned and caught sight of her, stopping the words in her throat. His light-hearted expression turned grim. "I expect you to see my daughter safely home," James instructed René.

"Of course," René said, gently placing a hand over hers.

"I will be at the plantation," James told Virginia before heading toward the door. "Do not wait dinner for me."

Virginia rose to say something, but James left the room too quickly. As she listened for the front door to open and close, Virginia twisted the corner of her apron into knots. Amanda too seemed to stop breathing.

"Do not worry," René said under his breath. "He will get the sheriff first. Now, let us go home."

This time, Sally bolted to her feet. "She can't!" Sally practically shouted.

René hadn't seen the young woman sitting at the far corner of the table. Amanda instantly reprimanded herself for forgetting her manners. "René," Amanda interjected, "this is my best friend, Sally . . ."

"Baldwin." René smiled as if he finally made the connection. "You look just like your . . ."

Sally rolled her eyes and sighed. "Like my brother?"

"Perhaps, mademoiselle, yes," René said. "But you are far more handsome than your brother will ever hope to be."

Amanda watched Sally blush as René sent her a dashing smile and a complimentary bow. *Politics,* Amanda thought, staring at her husband, who seemed to make everyone feel at ease. Of course. Why hadn't the idea occurred to her before?

"I must borrow your wife for an hour or two," Sally continued. "We have some charitable business to tend to."

René gazed down at Amanda with a concerned frown, and her feelings mirrored his. She had no intention of driving around town alone, with or without Sally Baldwin. Then she remembered her walk from church that morning.

"T-Emile is here with me," Amanda said. "He should be right outside the front door. He can join us in our errands."

René appeared disappointed. She knew that he, as much as she, was anxious to discuss the meeting with her father. "I'll be home as soon as possible," she whispered.

"You will return home the same time as me," René answered sternly. "I will be here in an hour to escort you home. I assume that is enough time for your charitable work?"

Sally sent Amanda a disapproving frown, but Amanda secretly welcomed René's company on the ride home. She felt infinitely safer with her husband than with a boy in his teens.

With a bow to Virginia, René claimed Amanda's hand and headed toward the front door. "I do have some business to tend to in town," he told Amanda before they reached the front of the house.

"Then it will be beneficial for the both of us." As hard as Amanda tried, the anxiety emerged in her voice. She wondered if René suspected.

He studied her hard, solemnly gazing into her eyes before leaning down and gently kissing her. Amanda's lips trembled at the touch of his, more from the fear of what lay ahead than the passion he hoped to evoke. René moved back. "What has happened?" he asked.

She hated lying to him, but she feared Tanner lurking around the next corner waiting to hurt her husband. She wanted the horror to go away, and the only solution was to get Henry Tanner out of town.

Amanda slipped a hand behind René's neck and lifted her lips toward his. As they kissed, René pulled her into his chest, holding her so close she could feel the dramatic beating of his heart. Thoughts of Tanner disappeared.

Horseshoes, René kept reminding himself, as he urged the ailing horse towards the blacksmith shop. It wasn't bad enough that the Vaughn horse refused to eat, but he was lame as well and in need of shoeing. René had promised its owner he would rally the horse to health, but other pressing matters were commanding his attention these days. Even now, all he could think of was Amanda's pert, upturned nose and her brilliant blue eyes just before she kissed him.

Would he miss the horse racing business? Or did anything else in the whole world matter besides being near Amanda? No, he concluded, horse racing was just a career. There were plenty of others. There was only one Amanda Rose.

Grinning at the image of Amanda in his arms, he entered the dark blacksmith shop. Before he could adequately assess the situation, an all-too-familiar voice sounded from behind.

"Well, if it isn't the Cajun," René heard Henry Tanner sarcastically exclaim. He was lounging by the far wall with two of his friends. The two men glanced his way, but didn't smile or acknowledge him.

René stopped before the blacksmith, who was working forcefully on a plowshare. René couldn't see Tanner, but knew by the sound of his voice that he was directly behind him.

"Look at that, boys," Tanner said, emerging from behind his horse and circling René so that they stood side by side. "A smile like that means only one thing. Could it be he's getting a little loving?"

René felt the blood rush to his temple, but knew he was outnumbered.

"American girls are quite a catch," Tanner continued. "Especially when they're loaded with sugarcane money."

"I've heard Texas is nice this time of year," René answered unemotionally.

The teasing smile disappeared from Tanner's lips and René straightened, bracing himself for an attack. "That's exactly where I'm going to send you, you bastard," Tanner hissed through his teeth.

The clanging of the blacksmith's hammer stopped abruptly and the large, heavily muscled man moved between them. "I don't want trouble in here. You two either take it somewhere else or I'll call the sheriff."

Tanner bristled at the mention of the sheriff, and sent the blacksmith a forceful smile. "There's no trouble here, Sherman," he said, slapping a hand down hard on René's shoulder. "We're old friends, aren't we, Cajun?"

René shoved his shoulder backwards, and Tanner's hand fell to his side. "We were never friends, Tanner."

"No," Tanner replied snidely, leaning in so close to René's face, René could smell the whiskey on his breath. "You and your old lady's horse track can go to Hell."

With that insult, René thought Tanner would pull back and leave. Instead, Tanner grinned again and moved in closer. "You know," he said with an evil glint to his eye, "she asked for everything."

Tanner fought to maintain his balance, but his eyes never left René's. "But what she really wanted most of all was what I gave her on that dark buggy ride down to the bay."

"You son of a bitch," René said bitterly. "I should kill you right here."

Tanner laughed, then leaned close, literally spitting out his words. "That won't keep her from calling my name when you make love to her."

René grabbed Tanner's shirt and flung him backwards, slamming his head against the far wall and knocking the breath from his lungs. The two companions pulled their pistols at his back, ready to come to Tanner's aid, but René's only focus was Tanner's face. "You stay away from me and my wife or so help me, God, I will rip you to shreds."

René tightened his grip on Tanner's shirt to cut off his air, determined to destroy the man. Tanner started choking, his arms flailing as he ineffectively reached for René's hold on his throat.

The two men cocked their pistols and voiced a variety of threats, but René refused to release him. Finally, the blacksmith's voice came through, urging him to let Tanner go before he killed the man.

With one sudden movement, René dropped Tanner to the floor. He fell choking and coughing, gasping violently for air.

René turned and angrily pushed the men aside while he headed for the street. As he marched from the blacksmith's shop, he heard Tanner's hoarse but determined threat.

"You can't walk away, Cajun," Tanner croaked. "I will get you back for this. If it's the last thing I do, I'll see you dead."

It took René the entire length of road back to the Judge's house before the blood retreated from his forehead. Never had he been so angry. But then he had never threatened to kill a man before.

He wanted to kill Tanner, though. He wanted to rid St. Mary Parish of that blight of humanity. More than anything he wanted to stop the words Tanner uttered from echoing in his mind.

She asked for everything.

René could quickly dismiss his accusations. Tanner would say anything to get what he wanted. But Amanda had admitted the affair was her fault on more than one occasion. What was it she had said when he found her at Port Cocodrie? She had looked up into his eyes and spoken the truth.

I have done something terrible.

When René came to fetch Amanda at her father's house, she appeared out of breath, but anxious to return home. They quickly made their good-byes and headed out of town. Feeling the blood still pounding through his temples, René chose to remain silent on the drive home. Surprisingly, Amanda did the same. Funny, he thought, that she didn't question him about his meeting with the Judge.

When they reached the farmhouse, René jumped down from the buggy and helped his wife to the ground. "I have to take the horse to the stables," he said unemotionally.

Amanda grabbed his hand and looked beseechingly into his eyes. She appeared as if she wanted to talk, but René was in no mood to listen. "Is something wrong?" she asked.

René didn't answer; he simply turned, mounted the buggy and rode toward the stables. Still suffering the aftereffects of his previous rage, René unbridled the horse and sent him into his stall, throwing the harness angrily against the opposite wall. Dropping defeatedly on to a bale of hay, René ran his fingers through his hair, then rubbed the back of his neck. The Judge had said it all too clearly the day René asked for Amanda's hand. Americans don't marry Acadians. They may make mistakes with other Americans, but peasant Frenchmen were out of the question.

"René?" T-Emile peered inside the stall, gazing curiously at his cousin. "Are you all right?"

René was in no mood for company. "What do you want?" he asked curtly.

T-Emile paused for a moment, then decided to enter the stall, sitting on a bale. "Is this about Amanda meeting Tanner this afternoon?"

What was merely a headache turned into an excruciating pounding between René's temples.

"I tried to keep up with them, I swear," the boy continued. "I was following them just fine, but Widow Pitre made me stop. A branch fell during the last thunderstorm and she needed someone to get it off her front porch. I couldn't say no. It was hard for her to get out her front door."

T-Emile gazed expectantly up at René as if waiting for a reprimand, but René had no idea what he was talking about. "What meeting?" René asked brusquely.

Small beads of sweat broke out on T-Emile's forehead. "Promise me you won't be mad."

"What meeting?" René repeated.

T-Emile quickly recounted the morning's events, apologizing profusely for not following Amanda better, the way Alcée had instructed him to do after the two women left the house. He described Amanda's meeting with Tanner at length, and how scared she appeared when T-Emile finally caught up with her at the church.

"Did she tell you what happened?" René asked, trying hard not to imagine the worst.

"No," T-Emile said. "She wouldn't talk about it."

The weight of his wife's unfaithfulness fell heavily on René's heart, and his head dropped forward against his chest. T-Emile stood staring, while René ran his fingers through his unruly hair. The throbbing in his head continued.

"There's more," T-Emile added.

His leaden heart began to ache, and René imagined his head splitting at any moment.

"After you left the Judge's house, Amanda and that Baldwin girl went to the bank," T-Emile explained. "She came back to the buggy with something wrapped in one of her handkerchiefs. Then they asked me to take them to that old deserted place where . . . What was that man's name?"

"Wiley," René said in a hollow voice.

T-Emile paused for a moment, studying René's grim countenance. "Are you mad at me?"

"No," René answered a bit too harshly.

"Are you sure?"

"Just tell the damn story," René practically shouted.

T-Emile moved back a few inches on the bale, and René instantly regretted barking at his cousin. "Just continue," he said, trying to keep his voice calm.

"Well, the Baldwin girl tells me that she and Amanda want to pick some herbs at the Wiley homestead."

René sent T-Emile a puzzled expression. T-Emile tilted his chin up slightly. "I understand more English than you know," he said.

"Go on."

"So the two women disappear behind the house and return to the buggy a few minutes later. Only they come back without the herbs and the handkerchief is missing. Odd, don't you think? That was the exact same spot where Tanner confronted Amanda."

René said nothing, only stared at the ground.

"I didn't say anything wrong, did I?" T-Emile asked, clearly anxious.

"Thanks," was all René could muster. His throat was dry and constricted, as if his swollen heart was blocking the air from his lungs. He rose and retreated to the stable office, closing the door behind him.

Sometime in the afternoon T-Emile left, but René had lost all track of time. When he finally noticed the sun approaching the horizon, he knew what he had to do. Before darkness settled in, he would make a trip to the old Wiley homestead.

Chapter Thirteen

Amanda watched the oncoming thunderstorms from the back gallery, counting the seconds between the violent flashes of lightning and the echoing claps of thunder. Within minutes the storm would be upon them. She had secured the items on the galleries, closed all the windows and brought in the children's playthings that were lying on the ground by the backyard well. With toys in tow, Colette had ushered Alex and Pierre to bed. T-Emile had retired early after an evening of shy glances and little conversation. Amanda thought they had developed a friendship, but T-Emile's actions tonight made her wonder if he wasn't just being nice on the buggy rides to town.

Or maybe something was wrong. She asked T-Emile, and he refused to answer.

Then René didn't come home for dinner.

Something *was* wrong, Amanda surmised as she stared out toward the stables. A serious storm was approaching and René was nowhere to be found.

"You better come in before it starts raining," Alcée said as he brought in the last tools from the fields.

"Where is he?" Amanda asked, trying to keep the anxiety from her voice.

Alcée pulled his hat from his head and wiped the sweat from his brow. "You know René. Always working."

"In weather like this? It's past sunset. What could he possibly do in the dark?"

Alcée placed the tools at the side of the house, and Amanda could tell by the look on his face that he too was concerned. "I'll go look for him," he said.

"Look for whom?" René emerged from the darkness, rounding the side of the house from the opposite direction of the stables. Both Amanda and Alcée had to turn to find him in the darkness.

"Where the hell have you been?" Alcée asked, confirming Amanda's fears that he was very concerned about his nephew. Alcée never would have used profanity in front of her under normal circumstances.

"Went for a walk."

As René neared, and his eyes met hers, Amanda shivered. Something was definitely wrong. His clothes were dirty and ruffled, not like him at all, and his expression was haunting, his gaze icy. He looked at her so intensely, she felt as if his stare could turn her to stone.

"What has happened?" Alcée asked, apparently feeling the same chill.

"Why don't you ask Madame Comeaux?" René answered unemotionally, never taking his eyes off his wife.

Alcée glanced briefly at Amanda, but she could not look away from René. Her heart lodged itself in her throat. It wasn't possible that René could have known about their trip to the Wiley homestead.

"I don't understand," Alcée said when neither René or Amanda answered.

Finally, René's eyes left Amanda's and he reached inside the breast pocket of his vest. He pulled out something soft and white and thrust it into Amanda's hands.

Startled by his sudden reaction, Amanda didn't comprehend at first what she held. It wasn't until Alcée spoke that she realized why René was angry.

"A handkerchief?" Alcée said.

In the midst of several bouts of thunder, Amanda gasped. The sound fell about the group with more intensity than the impending storm. She closed her eyes, wondering how she would explain this. Instead, René began to explain.

"You see, Alcée," René said between gritted teeth, "my wife has been secretly meeting with Henry Tanner."

Amanda swallowed hard at the accusation and instantly came to life. "That's not true."

René moved so close to her she could make out the bloodshot streaks in his eyes. "You must have thought me such a fool, my dear, to think you would have forgotten a man you eloped with. Did you honestly think I wouldn't find out?"

Amanda stepped back a pace, horrified. "I never eloped with Henry Tanner."

"You said it yourself at Port Cocodrie," René said.

"I never said I eloped," Amanda explained. "I asked him to escort me that night to a ball my father had forbidden me to go to. It was a secret arrangement only because of my father; it was never to be an elopement." As hard as she tried, Amanda couldn't keep the emotion out of her voice. She was close to tears.

"Maybe we should all calm down and talk about this sensibly," Alcée interjected as the thunder became louder.

"There's nothing to talk about," René said, his voice rising over the noise. "If you didn't elope, what the hell were you doing at Port Cocodrie with him?"

"My best friend Sally arranged for Tanner to take me to the ball at the Franklin Exchange," Amanda said, the tears beginning to fall as she recounted that horrific night. "She told Tanner there was no hope in my marrying. I was a Catholic and the Protestant men in town wouldn't marry me. She told him I was in need of a little romance. He took it the wrong way. He needed money to pay off a gambling debt and he thought I'd be happy to have him as a husband and that my father would pay for the marriage to take place."

"If that's true, then why have you been secretly meeting him?" René demanded.

"I haven't been secretly meeting anyone," Amanda continued through sobs. "He threatened me today. He told me if I didn't pay him three thousand dollars he would tell my father lies about you. And if I told you about our meeting today, he would kill you. So I took out what little money I had in the bank and placed it at that old house down the road. Sally and I hoped he would take the money and go to Texas."

Amanda hung her head in defeat. "I never meant for anything like this to happen," she said quietly, almost to herself. "I only wanted a kiss. And Katharine said Henry Tanner always kissed the girls on the buggy rides home."

Amanda raised her handkerchief to her face and cried freely. Alcée placed a loving arm about her shoulders and pulled her close.

"A kiss?" René repeated as the lightning overhead illuminated his face, now filled with hurt and regret. "You expected a kiss from Tanner?"

It all seemed so logical at the time. Now, the idea of kissing Henry Tanner was ludicrous. Her father was right. She was a naive girl who knew nothing about life. Amanda couldn't bear to meet René's eyes, so she simply nodded.

René raised his eyes to the heavens in exasperation. "Why didn't you ask *me?*" he asked incredulously, his voice filled with emotion.

Amanda looked at him then, knowing well the answer. Sometimes the most obvious solution to a problem is the hardest to achieve. "Because you're an Acadian," she said softly.

René stared at her hard, closed his eyes tightly as if to erase the words she had spoken, then smiled grimly and looked away. He shook his head slightly, then walked off into the darkness amidst the howling wind of the storm.

Alcée gave Amanda one last squeeze on her shoulders, then left to follow René.

Amanda stood frozen, watching the men walk out of sight. Out of the corner of her eye she recognized movement, and saw Colette and the children huddled on the stairs, obviously wakened by the shouting. Suddenly, she felt extremely tired and wondered if she would collapse on the spot. Colette must have read her mind, for her hands were quickly about her waist, leading her up the stairs to the sanctuary of her room.

While Colette helped her undress, the sobbing rose unbridled from Amanda's chest. Colette whispered something soothing in French as she pulled on Amanda's nightgown and tucked her into bed. Amanda's sobs continued unabated, so Colette sang her a ballad while softly stroking her hair. Amanda recognized the song as one her mother used to sing to her as a child. Closing her eyes, she prayed for sleep to end the unrelenting pain pressing at her heart.

Five hundred lousy dollars, Tanner thought with disgust, fingering the marks left on his throat by René. He'd told the bitch three thousand. Did Amanda really think she could dismiss him so easily, waving him off with change when the Richardsons were loaded with sugarcane money?

Maybe the Cajun put her up to it, Tanner thought. Maybe the stupid girl told René what happened, and he suggested leaving those few dollar bills at the Wiley place for spite. The two of them were probably laughing right now at his expense.

They won't be laughing much longer, Tanner decided, pulling out a pair of pistols from his traveling sack.

"What are you planning on doing with those?"

What once had been a welcomed affair was now becoming severely annoying. Tanner didn't know how Katharine had managed to find him at his friend's hunting cabin several miles out of town, but she sure as hell wasn't welcome.

"I don't remember asking you here," he said between gritted teeth.

"You're leaving," Katharine said, pointing down to his belongings that had been quickly thrust into a sack and a saddlebag.

"My, aren't we observant," Tanner said sarcastically.

"Take me with you," she demanded.

Tanner was in no mood for an emotional female. He grabbed Katharine by the arm and forcefully led her to the door. She grasped his meaning and began to protest.

"You must take me with you," she pleaded. "I'm with child."

The news caused Tanner to stop. Grinning down at Katharine, he said, "How are you going to explain this to Bernard?"

Katharine's eyes widened in shock. "You can't leave me. I'll be ruined."

Tanner urged her forward toward the door. "How awful for you. Now, if you don't mind, I really want you gone."

Katharine yanked her arm free and placed both hands flat against the door, staring back at Tanner as if daring him to throw her out. "I know you don't have a sister," Katharine said emotionally, fighting back tears.

Tanner had to laugh. Where did he find these women?

Before he could reach for her arm, Katharine picked up a pistol and pointed it in his direction. She really was an idiot, Tanner thought to himself, believing she could kill him with an unloaded weapon. He knew he would have to get physical.

"I know what you did to Amanda," Katharine said. "I know you kidnapped her and took her to Côte Blanche Bay in the middle of the night, that you wanted to blackmail her father. I know about the gambling."

The smile creasing Tanner's lips disappeared. He was growing tired of the chase.

"I'm going to tell the Judge everything," Katharine continued, her emotions breaking through her forced tough exterior. "Including how you took advantage of me."

Tanner had had enough. The worst week of his life wouldn't end. But he was going to make it end—now. He would have his three thousand by Monday. And these people causing problems were going to be eliminated. Starting with Katharine Blanchard.

Holding the bucket tightly with both hands, Alcée planted his feet firmly on the ground before emptying the water on top of his nephew's head. The water did its job. René bolted upright, staring wide-eyed at his uncle.

"Awake?" Alcée asked.

"What the hell do you think . . ." René began shouting.

Alcée brought up another bucket threatening. René immediately stopped talking, but the angry expression never left his face. Alcée leaned down on one knee to get a close-up look at his nephew. "The question, my dear boy, is what the hell are you doing sleeping out here?"

René ignored him, stood up and began picking the wet hay from his clothes. His actions were futile; the hay clung to him tenaciously. "Leave me alone," René grumbled.

"So she asked another man for a kiss. Have you looked into her eyes lately? Your wife loves you, you fool."

"Leave me alone," René repeated, louder.

"Don't do this, René. Don't hurt that sweet girl. She made a mistake. It's over now."

"Is it?" René asked with a sarcastic smile. "She's still an American and I'm still an Acadian. That's never going to change."

"Her father wouldn't let her associate with the French, you know that. I hardly think any of this is her fault."

"Her father made it clear *she* would not accept the affections of an Acadian."

"Then why did she wait for you at the fence every morning?" Alcée wanted to knock René's head against the wall. "She told me herself . . ."

"I was a novelty in a strange-looking hat."

"René, you know better than that."

René closed his eyes and rubbed his forehead between two fingers. Alcée recognized the gesture; René performed the same movements every time Alcée lectured him on working too hard. Alcée imagined his nephew was trying to build a wall inside his head to block out his words. Sighing, Alcée placed his hands on his hips and examined the stable rafters. "I don't know how to get through to you anymore."

René opened his eyes and shot him an icy stare. "Then don't."

Alcée shook his head and dropped the bucket. "Fine. It's your life." As he exited the stables, he left René with one last thought. "I'll let you explain this to your mother. She's waiting for you at the house."

* * *

As hard as she tried, Amanda could not seem to leave her bed. She rose several times that morning, but repeatedly returned. She managed to dress and fix her hair, but couldn't muster enough strength to venture downstairs. She couldn't face the painful, accusing stares of the household, especially René. Every time her eyes dared a glimpse of her smiling husband gazing down from the wall, her heart froze. Why, when she was so close to happiness, had it been snatched from her grasp?

Amanda heard a buggy arrive and Colette speaking excitedly with another Acadian. The buggy left, but she thought she heard a strange woman's voice on the downstairs gallery.

She didn't even try to listen in on their conversation, which, she suspected, probably concerned her. Her mind felt dead, oblivious to everything.

After a few minutes, Colette knocked on the door. "Amanda," Colette asked. "May I come in?"

When Amanda didn't answer, Colette entered, placing a motherly hand upon her forehead. "Are you ill, child?" Colette asked, sitting next to her on the bed.

Amanda stared off absently. "I'm very tired," was all she managed to say.

"There's someone here to see you," Colette said, straightening her clothes as Amanda had seen her do for Pierre. "I know you're not up for company right now, but I think Marie Comeaux can help."

Amanda glanced at Colette. "Marie Comeaux?"

A sweet, but somewhat guilty, smile broke free on Colette's face. Amanda knew wholeheartedly that Colette was a wonderful mother.

"Come downstairs," she said, gently moving the escaped blond strands of hair from Amanda's face. "I brought some fresh water with lemon and herbs. A few splashes and you'll feel and look like new.''

Amanda sat up and brushed the wrinkles from her bodice. ''Marie Comeaux?'' she asked again.

''Oui,'' Colette answered. ''I sent for her.''

Amanda wasn't quite prepared for René's mother. Her portrait upstairs made her appear petite and acquiescent. In reality, Madame Comeaux was small, her height and waist about the same size as Amanda's, but her presence was anything but passive. She sported coal-black hair, woven high around her head in a series of magnificent braids. Her incredibly dark brown eyes reflected her son's, boring intensely into Amanda as she entered the room. Her hands were placed defiantly on her hips, as if meeting Amanda might require defending the Comeaux family name. Even though the two women stood eye-to-eye, Amanda instantly felt three inches tall.

Madame Comeaux wore homespun cotton clothes: a brown and blue striped vest atop a sea-blue skirt and a light brown cotton shirt that tied at the neck. Hanging unused at her back was a *garde soleil,* or sunbonnet, which was popular among the Acadian women. Amanda couldn't help but think that sometime in the future, if there was a future, she might learn how they made such beautiful clothes.

''I suppose you know who I am,'' Madame Comeaux began.

Amanda bowed politely. ''Yes, madame. I am Amanda Rose . . .''

''Comeaux,'' the older woman added tartly.

Madame Comeaux continued her assessment, walking around Amanda to view all aspects of her. ''Colette tells me you understand French.''

''Yes, madame.''

Finishing her circle, Madame Comeaux smiled cautiously

when she again met Amanda's eyes. "My name is Marie. Madames and monsieurs are Creoles."

"I'm sorry, madame ... uh ..."

Marie seemed to comprehend Amanda's awkwardness, and signaled toward a chair. "Why don't we sit down and have a talk?"

Amanda chose the far chair and Marie sat next to her, never faltering in her discerning stare.

"My full name is Marie Rose Dugas Comeaux," she offered. "It appears we have the same middle name."

Amanda smiled slightly, still at a loss for words.

"Do you understand me?" Marie asked. "I'm afraid I don't speak a word of English."

"Oui, madame." Try as she could, Amanda could not break herself from habit. "French was my first language."

For the first time since they met, Marie appeared hopeful. "Oh? Why is that?"

"My mother was French."

Marie's eyes brightened further. "Would it be too much to hope for that you're a Catholic?"

This time Amanda smiled. *"Oui, madame* ... uh ... Marie."

Watching Marie formulate the next sentence, Amanda wondered if Marie was breathing. "Was it possible a priest performed the ceremony?"

Amanda nodded, and Marie immediately made the sign of the cross. The tense air that had permeated the room seemed to lift. Marie leaned over and grasped Amanda's hand between hers. "Now, tell me, dear, exactly what happened," she said.

Amanda recounted every detail from her father's flight from New Orleans and her mother's scandal to the moment she first met René at the fence. She explained why she had chosen Henry Tanner to escort her to the ball one week earlier and how René had rescued her at Port Cocodrie. She ended with the previous day's horrific meeting with Tanner and René's painful accusations on the gallery.

"You've had quite a week," Marie said after Amanda finished.

Amanda remembered René's grim, regretful face when she admitted she would not have asked an Acadian for a kiss. "The worst thing of it all," Amanda finished solemnly, "is that René believes me to be prejudiced against him. I'm afraid that may have been true."

Quietly, Marie brushed a blond curl from Amanda's face. "Do you love my son, Amanda Rose?"

Amanda turned and looked deeply into the eyes of the woman who had brought forth and raised the man she so dearly loved. "Very much," she said.

Marie smiled and planted a soft kiss on her forehead. "That is all that matters."

If only things were that simple, Amanda thought, as she rose and began to pace the room. "René will never forgive me."

"Have you told him how you feel?" Marie asked.

Stopping at the mantel, where she had watched Alcée performing his soulful ballads, Amanda sighed. For a moment she imagined never hearing those songs again, and her heart tightened. "No. I don't think he feels the same way."

This time, Marie laughed. "Do you mean to tell me that son of mine has not told you how *he* feels?"

When Amanda didn't answer, Marie stood and took her hands again into hers. "Do you not know that René approached your father with the prospect of proposing marriage?"

Amanda stared back at Marie, dumbfounded. Marie guided her back into her chair.

"I think I understand the problem here," Marie said. "Alcée wrote me a couple of days before Colette's letter arrived, saying that René had asked the Judge for your hand and the Judge had refused."

Amanda audibly gasped and placed a hand over her mouth.

"Your father told René that you would never consider marrying an Acadian."

Amanda's eyes widened. "Oh, my God," she exclaimed. "Is it true?"

"No!" Amanda said emphatically. "I would have been honored."

Amanda closed her eyes and recalled the day she had first witnessed René walking down Main Street. She'd spotted the broad, white hat first, but when the smiling brown eyes met hers, she'd literally stopped breathing. A fiery blush had permeated her face while an unknown force had insisted she raise her hand in greeting. And René had graciously accepted that hand, smiling down on her while planting a foot on the fence post and leaning forward to make her acquaintance. She remembered it clearly. It didn't matter what nationality he was. René always took her breath away.

No, Amanda thought with certainty, she held no prejudices. "I have been in love with him since the first day I met him," she whispered with a broad smile, the admission relieving the weight on her heart.

Marie squeezed her hand tightly. "Then tell him so."

Amanda tried to imagine exclaiming her love to René, but was too inexperienced to know where to begin. As if reading her mind, Marie patted her hand knowingly.

"I have an idea," she said.

Almost an hour passed since Alcée confronted René in the stables, and still Alcée's temper steamed. He was furious his nephew caused poor Amanda such pain, but amazed his anger continued so long. René had pinched a nerve.

"Alcée," a young voice shouted from behind.

Paul LeBlanc, the closest neighbor, had a house full of children. His oldest, Jean Baptiste, had ridden up on horseback carrying a red flag.

"Le bal ce soir chez LeBlanc," the boy said, announcing that the Saturday night dance would be at the LeBlanc house.

Alcée nodded, then thanked the young messenger. It was the host's responsibility to spread the message of the dance, and the only way to communicate with the area's Acadians was to ride horseback up one side of the bayou and down the other.

"And Alcée," Jean Baptiste shouted before turning to go, "Marguerite is visiting from Loreauville."

Alcée's eyes followed the boy as he disappeared down the road, but he comprehended nothing. The realization that he would see his beloved that night knocked the breath from his chest.

Her silky black hair, the way her dark eyes sparkled when she laughed, the feel of her cheek against his—it all came back mercilessly. *God, to smell her fragrance one more time,* Alcée thought, feeling his chest ache.

Now he knew why René had angered him so. He recalled how flippantly he had dismissed Marguerite's fears of becoming an old maid, laughing at her concerns for two years. Finally, she had had enough. Even when he'd promised to raise the money building a racetrack with René, her patience had dissipated. Paul LeBlanc's brother, François, took the opportunity while Alcée was in Franklin to court Marguerite, offering her a substantial farm. Had Alcée been more aware of her needs and less of his own selfish feelings, Marguerite might have married *him* instead.

Now, his fool nephew might be making the same mistake. Only, René's tragic flaw was pride.

Alcée sighed, then tried to resume a steady breath. He had to talk to Marguerite, make her realize how his life had ended when she wedded François. He prayed God would grant him another chance.

* * *

The whole house was abuzz with activity when René arrived from the stables. The boys were dressed in their good clothes for that night's *bal de maison* and were running up and down the *garçonnière* stairs as if to break them in for comfort. T-Emile was worried over his dress, complaining that women preferred men in long pants instead of the traditional britches he wore that stopped at the knee. In the midst of it all, René's father, Etienne, had lectured him endlessly on the responsibilities of marriage and insisted he return to Loreauville and a life of farming.

It was a miracle René had been able to enter his room, wash and dress without being stampeded.

Now that the men had changed into clean clothes, they gathered in the downstairs living room waiting for the women to arrive. Alcée kept asking Etienne about Marguerite's motives, whether she was considering him now that her mourning period was coming to an end, but René's father only shook his head.

"I told you," Etienne said. "She said she wanted a change of scenery, that's all."

"Perhaps the dance will get her into the right mood," T-Emile offered quietly, with a twinkle in his eye. "I heard tonight's *bal de maison* is in honor of René and Amanda's marriage."

René rubbed the bridge of his nose in frustration. That was all he needed, every Acadian from miles around congratulating him on marrying well.

"What about *her* father," Etienne asked René, returning to their previous conversation. "Maybe you could work for him? What does he do?"

René's parents lived in the neighboring parish, so Judge Richardson was not a familiar figure. Still, his father's question irritated him.

"I don't want handouts, Father," René grumbled.

"I'm not talking about him *giving* you a job," Etienne argued. "I'm talking about you working *with* him."

For a moment, his father looked lost in thought. "It's not anything illegal, is it?"

René laughed. The Judge was the last person he imagined doing anything beneath the law.

"You have to get out of the horse racing business, René," Etienne continued. "You can't have your wife living next to a racetrack."

You mean you can't have an American wife, René thought bitterly. Would he feel the same way if she was an Acadian?

"Yes, I would," Etienne interjected, reminding René that as far as his parents were concerned, his mind was practically transparent.

The lack of sleep, the earlier confrontation with Tanner and the knowledge that his wife probably did not love him weighed heavily on his heart. His father's endless lecturing was equally exhausting. René felt very tired. He wished he could return to the quiet comfort of his work, where facts and figures didn't break hearts and complicate one's life.

Suddenly, all talking ceased. Even the children stopped playing, silently staring at the back gallery. When René looked around T-Emile to view the source of everyone's amazement, he was equally stunned. Amanda entered the room, dressed in a blue and brown Acadian *cotonnade* skirt and vest, her silky blond hair hanging loosely down her back, tied with a bright blue ribbon. Her shirt was store-bought, but the image she generated was not American. In her dress, anyone would have mistaken her for an Acadian.

But regardless of what she was wearing, Amanda was breathtaking.

Etienne finally broke the silence. "You must be the wife my son has been hiding all this time," he said, taking her hand.

"I was furious when I heard he was married, but now I know why. You're beautiful. He's trying to keep you all to himself."

Amanda smiled. "Now I know where your son gets all his charm."

Her compliment couldn't have pleased Etienne more. He squeezed her hand and leaned in conspiratorially. "I taught him everything he knows."

Alcée stepped forward and silently planted a kiss on Amanda's forehead. "Your mother was a pale comparison," he whispered.

Etienne jokingly pushed Alcée aside. "Find your own girl," he said with a grin.

"Etienne Joseph Comeaux," Marie belted from behind the group, "I believe you are married to me."

Etienne acted as if he had been caught with his hand in the cookie jar. Everyone laughed at his expression. Until they witnessed Marie.

"My, my," Etienne said, gazing at his wife from head to toe.

"It's from Europe," Marie said proudly, swinging the silk skirt of the imported dress to and fro.

"Paris," Amanda added.

Etienne stared first at Marie, then Amanda. "Now, I'm thoroughly confused," he said with a grin.

"As well you should be," Marie answered, sending Amanda a wink. "Women should always keep men guessing."

Just then, Marie caught sight of René. *"Maman,"* René said solemnly, giving his mother a cautious kiss on her cheek.

"I should be angry with you," she whispered. "But I like her too much."

René glanced back at Amanda, who was watching the exchange carefully. Even dressed in homespun and home-woven fabric, she appeared so delicate, so fragile and so utterly captivating.

"Use your head, René," his mother warned, before she turned and took Etienne's arm.

The buzz returned. T-Emile announced that the buggy was waiting, and the children bolted out the front door, nearly knocking down everyone in their path. As they headed outdoors, Alcée began to interrogate Marie about why Marguerite had come. Etienne followed behind, shaking his head. Colette was busy gathering up food she had promised to bring, barking out orders to the children, who refused to listen.

René found Amanda in the same spot as before, as if she was waiting for a response from him. He didn't know what to say. Hell, he didn't know what to feel.

He merely held out his arm and escorted her out the door to their waiting family and the weekly *fais do-do.*

Chapter Fourteen

"So why do you call it a *fais do-do?*" Amanda asked Widow Pitre as they enjoyed their midnight gumbo. "*Fais do-do* means to go to sleep."

"Exactly," the widow replied. "Parents bring their children to the *bal de maison* and put the children under the watchful eyes of the grandparents in the *parc aux petits,* or the designated children's room. The children go to sleep and we dance all night."

Amanda well understood her last sentence. All the furniture in the small house was either pushed up against the walls or placed outside to offer as much dance space as possible. And dance they did. Alcée performed endlessly from the moment he arrived, and absolutely everyone took the opportunity to turn around the LeBlanc living room floor. They danced jigs, reels, waltzes, mazurkas and occasionally a *contradanse* resembling those Amanda had danced in Virginia. Alcée performed every type of song, from children's ditties when the young ones were still awake, to humorous songs the men preferred, to soft ballads for waltzes for doe-eyed couples. Even T-Emile braved his timidness to join Alcée on second fiddle for a song or two.

Now that midnight had arrived, everyone moved outside for the traditional gumbo. Amanda was thankful for the meal, for it finally gave her a chance to sit down and cool off in the late-night breeze. And as was everything else that night, the gumbo was made especially in her honor.

"Do you like it?" Widow Pitre asked for the third time.

"It's delicious," Amanda answered. She wanted to add that it was the best she had tasted, except for Colette's, but she feared the widow might think she was overdoing it.

Amanda had worried that the Acadians would not approve of her dress, her accent or the fact that she'd married René, but everyone opened their arms and welcomed her into the fold. She soon realized that they were more curious over who had finally forced ambitious René Comeaux to settle down than what nationality she belonged to. Being able to speak their language was a plus. For hours Amanda moved from one introduction to another, greeting everyone with a smile. And she steadfastly followed Marie's advice.

"Ignore him," Marie had told her earlier when they were dressing. "Flirt harmlessly with the other men, get to know the women. Enjoy everyone's company and let them enjoy you. Be the center of attention. Let René know you are incapable of being prejudiced against anybody. By the end of the evening, René will be dying to get near you. Then, and only then, must you tell him how you feel."

It was working so far, Amanda thought, until she sat down to dinner. Immediately, Cyprien Thibodeaux and Eraste Boudreaux, the men she had met days before at the track, sat down on either side of her, forcing René to choose another chair. She knew René was getting angry; he had been trying to get close to her for hours, and their action further irritated him. When he tried to sit across from her, Alcée grabbed the seat.

"You don't mind, do you, René?" Alcée asked innocently.

The three men exchanged discreet smiles, and Amanda wondered if they were enjoying themselves at René's expense. René was the successful one, the one always in charge, the richest Acadian among them. Tonight, they were going to flirt with his wife and watch him be annoyed. Tonight it was their turn to be in charge.

"You get to sit next to her all the time," Boudreaux quipped to René, who was forced to eat his gumbo standing up, leaning against the house's outside wall. "Give us a chance."

The men laughed good-naturedly at the remark, but Amanda knew René was not enjoying their sentiment. When he leaned forward to retort to Boudreaux's remark, an angry look crossing his face, Alcée interferred. "Did you know Judge Richardson caught Boudreaux and Thibodeaux stealing chickens?" he asked Amanda straight-faced.

"My father?" Amanda asked surprised. At her side several people laughed, making her realize Alcée was joking.

"The Judge sentenced them to death by hanging," Alcée continued seriously. "They built a gallows by the bayou, then placed a noose on Thibodeaux's neck. The doors swung wide open, the noose loosened and Thibodeaux fell into the bayou. He then swam away to the other side and to freedom."

Alcée paused to let the image sink into the minds of his captive audience. "Boudreaux stared at the Judge and at the noose, shaking his head," Alcée continued. " 'You better fix that noose, Judge,' he says. 'I can't swim.' "

Everyone listening began to howl while Boudreaux protested loudly. Glancing over at René, Amanda found he was not amused. Not even a smile seemed destined to cross his stern face. She wondered if Marie's plan was working after all.

"How did you two meet?" Thibodeaux asked, changing the

subject to appease his friend, who was still bristling from the joke.

"I was picking flowers one day for the dining room table," Amanda began. "René came walking down the street, gazing intently at the ground as if lost in thought. He was probably thinking of new ways to make money."

The group laughed at the reference. It was obvious they all knew René's overenthusiasm for commerce. Amanda saw from the corner of her eyes that René was frowning, but she forged straight ahead.

"When he looked up, and his eyes met mine," she continued, "I lost all logical thought."

"She was intrigued by my hat."

It was the first thing René had said that night. All eyes turned in his direction, but they found him as straight-faced as ever. He had placed the gumbo down on the ground at his feet and folded his arms defiantly across his chest.

"If you believe that," Amanda said, lifting her chin, "then *your* father's Judge Richardson."

The group began to laugh again, Boudreaux urging her on. "Tell us more," he said.

"I don't know what spell he cast on me," Amanda said more seriously, glancing up again at René. "But I braved the hot weather every morning, pretending to cut flowers on bushes that had none just so I could see him again."

A hush fell about the crowd accented by a few sighs of approval, and Amanda could almost feel the smiles of the people around her. But the only person she saw was René. He still refused to smile, his eyes never leaving hers.

"What I could never figure out," Amanda said quietly, "was what business he had in town every day that took him by my house."

"Is it so odd that an Acadian would stroll past the great

Judge Richardson's household?" René asked, a slight curtness emerging in his voice.

Everyone fell silent, and Amanda could hear the bullfrogs in the bayou's rushes several hundred yards away.

"I never noticed the nationalities of the men walking my neighborhood," she said.

Without his gaze leaving her face, René answered solemnly, "There was no business."

Amanda should have been thrilled at the news, that René indeed cared for her, walking past her house for no other reason than to have conversation with her. But the personable René she'd fallen in love with refused to return. He leaned contemptuously up against the side of the house, condemning her with his eyes. All Amanda could do was stare imploringly back, wishing that he still believed in her despite what seemed to be prejudice on her part.

Alcée sensed the awkwardness between them. He immediately rose and grabbed his fiddle. "I think it's time the wedding couple had a dance," he said.

The group mumbled their approval, Thibodeaux leading Amanda by the arm back into the house, and several women pushing René in as well. Alcée resumed his royal position in the northwest corner of the room and began playing *Jolie Blonde*. Amanda and René didn't have a chance to react to their closeness; they both turned to Alcée and voiced their disapproval.

"One more time," Alcée argued, raising his hands. "I promise I'll not sing the words."

Before they could digest it further, the lilting song began and everyone stared grinning at the couple who had fallen hopelessly in love over a white picket fence. René took Amanda gently into his arms and began leading her across the floor in a slow waltz.

For several minutes, neither one spoke. Amanda couldn't fathom what René was thinking; all she comprehended was the immense pleasure of once again being in his arms. She realized then she could not wait a moment longer.

"Why didn't you tell me you asked my father for my hand?" she asked.

René stiffened, glancing suspiciously down at her. After what seemed like an eternity, he finally said, "I thought you knew."

Amanda shook her head. "Your mother told me this afternoon."

She wasn't sure René believed her, for his scrutiny continued.

"René, I don't know what my father said to you," she continued, "but I don't share his opinions. How could I? I'm half French."

"Half Creole," René interjected, and Amanda felt as if she had moved two steps forward and three steps back.

"That's not fair."

A grim smile edged its way at the corners of René's lips. He turned so he faced her directly, and tilted his head downward as they continued to turn about the room.

"Be honest with me, Amanda," he said sternly. "If your father had agreed, would you have married me?"

Before he could finish the sentence, Amanda answered confidently, "Yes!"

René jerked back slightly, clearly surprised at her answer. But by the doubtful expression on his face, she knew he wasn't yet convinced.

"Why would I have waited for you every morning if I didn't care for you?" she asked.

"Care?" René asked, frowning. "You said yourself last night that you didn't care for Acadians."

"It wasn't a matter of caring," Amanda whispered heatedly. "I had no choice. My father never would have allowed it. Yes, I asked Henry because he was an American. Do you think I could have asked you? I defied my father going to that ball.

Imagine how disobedient I would have been asking you to escort me."

René continued turning around the dance floor, but said nothing. "Make no mistake, René, I would have been honored. But I was strictly forbidden to associate with the French."

Still René said nothing, staring over her shoulder lost in thought. Taking in a deep breath, Amanda knew it was now or never. "I love you," she whispered.

A light sparkled in the dark depths of his eyes and he stood taller, as if a great weight had been lifted. She sensed a smile lingering behind his still-stalwart expression.

"I always was in love with you," Amanda continued. "Only I never let myself believe it. It seemed like such an impossibility at the time. And I always imagined you had a girl somewhere."

At that last thought, René finally grinned, shaking his head. "There was never anyone but you," he breathed so passionately, Amanda felt a lightning bolt all the way to her toes.

The song ended and René smoothly turned Amanda around while bowing, as was the custom at the end of a dance. Amanda curtsied, then drew herself as close as polite company allowed. She wanted so desperately to touch him.

René returned a look that also spoke of desire, and Amanda wished with all her soul they were anywhere but in a room filled with people. Suddenly, a thought came to mind. A sly, deceiving, ingenious thought.

"May I have the next dance?" Thibodeaux asked, as he reached for Amanda's elbow.

"Please forgive me," she said, offering a sweet smile, "but I'm really not myself. I feel a headache coming on. Perhaps I could sit this one out?"

René moved in closer, clearly concerned. "Why didn't you tell me you were ill?"

She almost laughed. She never expected René to fall for the

lie as well. Marie was right about the power women had over men.

"It must be all the excitement and dancing," Amanda stated, fighting back a smile.

"It is still terribly hot," Thibodeaux said. "What you need is some fresh air."

"Fresh air on a buggy ride home," René added, taking her arm and gently leading her to the front of the house.

They made their farewells, politely thanking Celestine LeBlanc for her hospitality and heading for the door before Amanda realized she was on her way home and to her first night as a bride. The blood racing through her veins was enough to give her a headache for sure.

While René asked Paul LeBlanc for a ride—leaving the larger wagon for the family to use later—Amanda spotted Marguerite by the side of the house placing dirty dishes into a wash bucket. Marguerite had helped the LeBlancs with housework all evening, and Amanda didn't remember seeing her dance once. Amanda approached her quietly. The dark-haired woman looked up at Amanda, her coal-black eyes emitting a warmth like that of a hearth on a cold winter's day, and she presented a shy smile. Amanda took the opportunity to place her hand in hers.

"I'm sorry we haven't been able to talk," Amanda began. "I was so looking forward to knowing you."

Marguerite's eyes brightened. "Perhaps another time," she offered.

"I do hope so," Amanda said. "I have heard so much about you."

"Oh?" Marguerite looked unraveled. "I can't imagine from whom."

Amanda squeezed her hand. "Can't you?"

Just then, Marie appeared and gave her daughter-in-law a loving hug. Turning to René, Marie planted a motherly kiss on

her son's cheek before sending them off to the buggy.
"Brandy," Marie whispered to René. "A glass of brandy will
do wonders."

"What?" he asked, but his mother merely waved good-bye.

René helped Amanda into the buggy, placing her between
him and Paul, who held the reins. Since there was no moon
and visibility was nil once they left the house, Amanda snaked
an arm through René's and placed her cheek against his taut
upper arm. Paul sang a favorite ballad on the ride home, one
Amanda would have cherished on any other occasion. Tonight,
all she fathomed was the broad shoulder on which she rested
her head and the delicate kiss that arrived so silently on her
forehead.

Their house had been left in darkness, so Paul and René felt
their way to the oil lamp left conveniently by the hitching post.
Once the lamp was lit, the men entered each room, lighting
more candles and lamps until they could make their way around.

"I'll help you light the upper floors," Paul said. Word had
gotten around among the Acadians about Tanner's threats
against René. Amanda knew Paul was looking out for his friend
and neighbor. She felt safer knowing he lived a quarter of a
mile down the road. René checked his rooms while Paul looked
in on Colette's quarters. Amanda followed quietly behind.

"I'll quickly check on the garçonnière and then I'll be on
my way," Paul said, tapping his hat politely to Amanda.

"Merci," René answered. He turned to Amanda, and for the
first time that evening she felt hope. The smile that beamed
from his handsome face was warmer than noon in August. He
cupped her face with his large hands, delicately stroking her
cheek with his thumbs. "Is there anything I can get you for
your headache."

"No, thank you," Amanda said in a hollow voice. His actions
were doing funny things to her breathing. "But René," she
added, stopping him in his tracks, "I don't have a headache."

* * *

René whistled as he watched Paul LeBlanc ride out of sight. *Brandy. Brandy would do wonders.* Funny, he thought, how parents seemed so unintelligent when one was young. His parents had gained so much knowledge since he left home five years ago.

He smiled at the humor of it and grabbed two glasses and the brandy decanter. He wanted to leap up the stairs to his waiting bride, but he told Amanda to get ready for bed and God only knew how long women took doing such things. He whistled *Jolie Blonde* climbing the stairs and walking through his bedroom—hopefully soon to be Alcée's again—giving Amanda fair warning he was getting close. René knocked at the door, and an anxious voice granted him admittance.

Amanda had stripped to her nightgown, a light cotton shift that buttoned at the front and left her arms bare. Her blond curls flowed freely about her shoulders. She sat upright on the bed, the cotton sheet held tightly between her fingers as she held it up against her chest. All the intensity of unrequited desire emerged within him, and he thought he would explode on the spot.

"What have you brought?" she asked, and René knew she was nervous by the sound of her voice.

"Brandy," he said, sitting across from her on the bed. Slowly, he began to remove his boots. "My mother thought it might help."

"I can't drink liquor," Amanda said, wide-eyed.

"It's not liquor, it's brandy."

Amanda smiled slightly, and René wondered if he was wrong. Alcohol was never his forte. "Are you sure your mother said . . ." she asked.

"It will help you relax."

Amanda looked at René hard and nodded. She loosened her

hold on the sheet and let it fall in her lap. "I guess I'm a little nervous."

René slipped his hand around her cheek and brushed his lips gently across hers. She instinctively put a hand on his shoulder when he drew near, then moved her hand around his neck, sliding her fingers through the soft brown curls at his nape.

René moaned at the touch and moved closer. He placed his other hand at her waist and drew her against him. He could feel the roundness of her breasts and her heart beating rhythmically against his chest. He deepened the kiss until he tasted all of her, at the same time exploring the curves of her back and the upper soft reaches of her thighs.

When his hands moved the gown upwards, exposing more and more of her legs, Amanda jerked back.

"I'm sorry," she instantly said. "I really am nervous."

"Don't be sorry, my love," René said, moving back. "All brides are nervous on their wedding night."

René reached for the glasses and began filling them with the dark brown liquid. "This will help," he said, offering Amanda a glass of brandy.

Amanda took a quick look at the drink before her, then tilted her head back to drink it whole. René stared in shock as his nondrinking wife devoured an entire glass of brandy in one swallow.

"Are you out of your mind?" he asked when the effects of what she had done suddenly hit her and she began coughing.

"Aren't you supposed to drink it that way?" she asked, her face turning a beet red. "My father drinks whiskey like that."

René deposited his glass and the rest of the brandy on the night table and began patting Amanda on the back. "*Men* drink whiskey that way, not women. You're supposed to sip brandy."

"Oh."

When the color returned to Amanda's face, René had to smile. His wife clearly was a mystery. Just when he thought she was a naive flower, too inexperienced to know better, she surprised him with the bravery of a conqueror. Then, at times like this, he felt destined to protect her from life's harsher realities.

"I'm sorry," she reiterated.

"Will you stop apologizing."

The brandy began to affect her, for her eyes became glassy and her movements seemed more relaxed, more fluid.

"I'll stop apologizing," she said with a sly grin, "when you start kissing me again."

René didn't need encouragement. He linked both his hands around her waist, pulling her close as he planted loving kisses over her face and down her neck to her shoulders. Amanda didn't resist this time, moving whenever René demanded more space at her neck. When he began unbuttoning her gown, her breathing quickened, but she didn't protest. René drew back then, gazing deeply into her azure eyes while he slid a hand inside the bodice of her nightgown, cupping the sweet magic hidden underneath. He quickly found what he was searching for, squeezing the nipple gently between his fingers as his mouth descended again upon hers.

Amanda eagerly met his lips, her tongue meeting his. Fighting the urgency in his desire, René slowly lowered Amanda down against the pillows, while his kisses laid a trail down her neck to her exposed breast. He took her in his mouth then, feeling Amanda's fingers groping madly through his hair, his tongue circling her nipple, forcing it taut. His hand moved down to her thigh, sliding upward, taking the gown with it.

When he parted her thighs, she was moist and ready for him. He slid a finger gently inside, hoping to ease his wife's pain when they were finally joined. She murmured a slight protest, reaching for his hand, until René moved his thumb forward and found the soft, raised fold of skin. As he began to stroke, her body arched in response.

"Oh, my God," Amanda cried, tightening her hold on his hair, her hips lifting toward heaven.

René's lips never left her breast as he continued to massage the tiny pressure point. Amanda moaned continuously, her breathing becoming more rapid while deep shudders echoed through her body. Finally, she arched her hips stiffly and pushed René's hand away.

"No more," she whispered.

René gazed up at her then, so magnificently beautiful basking in the mist of passion. She opened her eyes, still sated by the effects of the brandy.

"I never knew . . ." she whispered.

René smiled and nibbled at the tip of her chin. He wanted her so badly he imagined the buttons popping from his trousers. But he had to take it slow. He'd die before he'd hurt his precious love.

Amanda raised herself up on her elbows. "What about you?" she asked so sweetly, he nearly took her on the spot.

"I don't want to hurt you," René said softly, brushing the dampened blond curls from her cheek.

Amanda stared at him thoughtfully while her hand moved across his face stopping to graze his lips. René grasped her hand tightly against his lips, savoring the inside of her palm.

Suddenly, Amanda moved her hand away. She picked up the glass at the bedside table and once again drank it whole.

"What are you possibly thinking?" René started, as she again began to cough.

This time, Amanda didn't answer. She placed the glass down, took a moment for the liquor to leave her head and fill her veins, then began unbuttoning René's shirt. René thought to stop her; after all, it was up to him to be the teacher tonight. But the touch of her long delicate fingers undressing him was too delicious to resist. He watched her as she bit her lower lip, concentrating on the matter at hand. God, how much he loved his wife.

When the shirt opened freely, Amanda hesitated.

"Touch me," René whispered. "And promise me you won't run away."

Amanda giggled and blushed at the mention of that night in his bedroom. But she did as she was told. Her fingers combed their way through the fine brown hairs of his chest, lingering slightly at his own nipples. René thought he would lose all control of his senses.

Taking a deep breath, Amanda reached down to unbutton his trousers. After the second button, however, she turned crimson and stopped.

"Let me," René said.

He turned toward the far wall and discreetly removed his pants, coming back to bed underneath the sheet. Amanda removed her gown and worked herself underneath the sheet until they found each other. René could no longer control himself. He snaked his arms around her while Amanda moved her arms about his shoulders. They kissed passionately while their bodies melted into one.

Again, René lowered his wife on to the pillows, his lips never leaving hers. She parted her legs, offering herself to him willingly. While he devoured her mouth with his, deepening the kiss as he pulled her hips toward his arousal, he slowly entered. Amanda reacted immediately, gasping at the intrusion and clenching her eyes shut in fear.

"Look at me," René instructed.

Amanda gazed at him, trusting. René brushed back her hair from her cheek, then placed his hands by the sides of her face.

"I love you," he said in English.

"*Je t'aime,*" she whispered back.

René entered her again, but Amanda never strayed her eyes from his. He felt her stiffen, but her hands contradicted her body's natural reactions by drawing him closer. He was deep inside her when he felt her relenting. She swallowed hard when her breathing quickened, and stared lovingly into his eyes. It was all he could do to hold back.

Soon, their bodies began to beat a rhythm all their own. They moved together in unison, a passion bound in love. René felt the burning intensifying. He wanted to shut his eyes, to release the tension, but he held on, delving into the blue depths of his wife's eyes.

"It's coming back," Amanda said heatedly.

Before René could comprehend her statement, Amanda shut her eyes, arched her hips forward and moaned. Her hands, only moments ago grabbing at the flesh on his back, reached up and over her head to grab the headboard. While her teeth bit into her lower lip, she shuddered violently, tipping her head back with a passionate sigh.

René felt the waves flow over him as he released his own blazing need. He called out her name as Amanda's hands found him once more, holding him so close he couldn't fathom where he began and she ended. They lay there for quite some time, kissing and caressing, until René moved over on to his back and pulled her tightly into his chest.

Before sleep finally washed over him, René imagined heaven could not possibly be as sweet.

Chapter Fifteen

James didn't know which was more disconcerting, Tanner disappearing or the overseer's cottage ransacked, its contents left in scattered remnants. Apparently, Tanner had caught wind that the Judge was wise to him or his creditors were growing impatient. The only consolation, James figured as he surveyed the splintered mahogany of the bed frame and the down feathers littering the floor, was that Tanner, in all probability, was fast on his way to Texas.

The slaves couldn't hide their excitement when James informed them of Tanner's disappearance. As James drove the carriage back into town, he could hear the music ringing out over the cane fields and the hearty laughter of the men, women, and children who shared his land. Their merriment tugged at his heartstrings. He had never heard their laughter before, nor ever been conscious of whether they were happy or not. He'd always considered them fortunate to have food and a place to live.

Have I been dead to life all these years? he thought. *Was I so preoccupied that the happiness of everyone around me was sacrificed?*

James immediately thought of Virginia and how only recently he'd learned of her marital situation. How miserable she must have been when she first came to work for him, so newly widowed and without family. She took care of their every need, nurturing Amanda's wounded heart and maintaining a household without complaint, when all along her own heart must have been breaking from the loneliness.

He couldn't lose her now. It might be his own selfish nature speaking again, but James couldn't bear living without her. How could he awaken each morning without Virginia's cheerful greeting at breakfast, without the constant lectures on his poor eating habits and her opinions of his judicial business?

There would be no more campaign consultations, no more parental discussions regarding Amanda. No more of her soft, ruddy complexion that lit up brilliantly when she smiled. No more admiring the way her silky auburn hair escaped its prison of pins and cascaded down in tendrils at the end of the day. No more chance of tasting those sweet, prominent lips that had eagerly met his that morning in the foyer.

The thought exploded through his mind, causing him to almost lose his balance on the buggy seat. *Dear God,* he thought, *I'm in love with her.*

Virginia stirred the simmering stew for no other reason than to give herself something to do. Most of the families in town, including the Americans, preferred gumbo, a Louisiana twist on the French bouillabaisse, only with New World ingredients and highly seasoned with spices introduced by the Spanish. Virginia had heard gumbo was filled with contributions from several nationalities: filé from the Indians, okra from the Africans and the basic *roux* from the French. Still, until the Irish had a stake in this melting pot of a soup, she was going to cook a good old-fashioned Irish stew.

It had been half a day since the Judge left, and her stomach tightened at the thought. Mr. Comeaux said James would contact the sheriff, but what was taking them so long? Midnight was approaching. She sent a prayer to the Virgin Mother and began stirring again.

"Don't tell me you saved dinner for me?"

Virginia nearly dropped her spoon as James crossed the threshold of the kitchen door. She wanted to hold him, to feel his arms about her to convince her he was all right. Instead, she turned back to the stove and discreetly made the sign of the cross.

"You weren't worried about me?" James asked, his voice sounding almost seductive. He moved so close, Virginia swore she could feel his breath at the back of her neck.

"Of course, I was worried about you," she answered, giving her best defiant retort so he wouldn't guess her true feelings. "I wouldn't want to not get paid this week."

James slid his hands on to her waist and slowly turned her around so that they faced one another. "Is that the only reason?" he asked.

Say something witty, Virginia instructed herself. *Say something smart.* When James's eyes gazed into hers, as if searching for some hidden meaning, suddenly Virginia's tongue turned to stone.

"I need to ask you something," James began. "And I want you to be completely honest with me."

He's so serious, Virginia thought nervously. *And so near.* Why was he making it so hard? If he only knew how much she wanted to be close to him, he would probably stand in the other room to carry on a conversation.

"Do you care for me?"

Virginia knew she heard wrong. "I beg your pardon?"

"You heard me," James said, brushing a red thread of hair from her face. "Do you care for me?"

"Of course I do," Virginia answered, trying desperately to keep the emotions from her voice. "I have always cared for you and Amanda."

James shook his head and smiled again, that same endearing smile that always made Virginia's heart flutter. He was alarmingly attractive tonight, Virginia thought, with his blond hair wild about him from the buggy ride home and his shirt opened unusually at the neck. One more smile and she would lose all self-control.

"Virginia," James said, grasping her hand in his, "I want to know if you care for *me.*"

Virginia's heart stilled and all logic left her. There were no more witty remarks, no clever verbal barriers to protect her. "Yes," she answered softly. "I have for quite some time."

As the words left her lips, Virginia felt a great weight leaving her chest. She knew what was coming, but the burden of the secret was more than she could bear. Regardless of James's reaction, the wound had been flushed and would now be allowed to heal.

To her amazement, James smiled. "I was hoping you would say that."

Before Virginia understood what had transpired, James reached into his breast pocket and removed the diamond ring he always lovingly kept attached to the chain of his father's pocket watch.

"This was my mother's," he began. "It was too simple for my wife; she preferred a more pretentious piece of jewelry to show off to her friends. But I have always been partial to this ring. My father and mother were very happy."

James placed the ring on Virginia's hand, which was now

shaking considerably. If she wasn't mistaken, the room itself was beginning to spin. "I have to sit down," she whispered.

"Of course." James quickly pulled out a chair and helped her into it. To her equal amazement, he took the opportunity to kneel before her.

"Virginia O'Neil," he pronounced proudly, "I am probably the most disagreeable man you have ever met. I have a terrible disposition, a stubborn nature, and I work too much. But if you will do me the honor of marrying me, I promise I will make you the finest, most faithful husband to ever grace the great state of Louisiana."

The dizziness passed, but Virginia knew she was crying when she felt a tear roll down her cheek. She tried to speak, but could only nod instead. "I promise to be a good wife," she managed to whisper.

James smiled as he took her face in his hands. "You already have been."

They kissed softly, Virginia gingerly reaching down to touch his face. As her fingers led a gentle trail down his cheek, James moaned and reached up to intercept her hand and passionately kiss the inside of her palm.

Virginia hoped for more, but James suddenly stopped, taking a moment to clear his thoughts. "We should make arrangements for you to stay somewhere until the wedding."

"I could stay with Marsha McKinley," Virginia offered, although she dreaded leaving her home and the man she loved, who finally loved her in return.

"You should pack," he said solemnly. "I can take you there tonight."

Always doing the right thing, Virginia thought as she stared into the incredibly rich blue eyes of the man kneeling before her. But she recognized the passion lurking behind his gaze, the sexual need tearing at his proper countenance. She recognized it as her own.

"It can wait till tomorrow," she whispered.

Before she could regret her wanton remarks, James lifted her from the chair, kissing her passionately as he carried her from the kitchen and up the stairs to his room.

Just before dawn a lull had descended over the dance floor at the LeBlanc house, and small groups of people stopped dancing and began milling about in the doorway, talking quietly while they sipped their cool drinks. The enthusiasm prevailing before the midnight gumbo had waned. With René and Amanda gone, and all discussion about their marriage exhausted, there was little excitement left to the dance.

For the thousandth time that night, Alcée searched the room for Marguerite. She was usually helping with the cleaning or assisting in pouring everyone drinks, but never inside. Unless he took a break and stepped outside the house, Alcée wasn't able to even steal a glimpse of the coal-black hair and penetrating eyes of the woman he loved, let alone talk to her.

A few more songs and he would call it a night, Alcée decided. One way or another he would get close to her.

Between songs, Alcée saw Marguerite bring in a pitcher of water to the young girls congregating by the side of the make-shift dance floor. She kept her head down while she filled their glasses, as if purposely refusing to meet Alcée's eyes. Alcée had tried to remain aloof during the evening, consciously making it appear that her presence at the dance made no difference to him, but her current disinterest unnerved him. Besides the years of unrelenting pain tearing at his heart, Alcée felt the heat rise in his temples. He wanted an answer and he wanted it now.

He wiped the sweat from his brow and began the waltz, a slow mournful tune he'd composed years before, a song born from the pain of a broken heart and an intense longing that was never to be satisfied. Alcée had written the song for Marguerite's wedding, but the tune had not been created for the couple being joined together that day, but rather to show how love could never be denied or destroyed. It was the perfect choice for lovers, deeply sentimental, passionate and moving, even though only Marguerite and Alcée knew its true meaning. Marguerite had cried through the entire piece, and for sometime afterwards. He had wanted her to cry, to realize she was ripping his soul in two by severing their love. He'd wanted her to know just how much he would always love her.

Alcée watched Marguerite pause as she filled the last glass. He saw her tremble slightly as the violin wailed its lament. He studied the silken braids pulled tightly behind her head, released into rivulets of black curls down her slender shoulders. He slowly absorbed the curves of her waist and the soft roundness of her skirt. He remembered how well her figure fit into his embrace, how her fingers lovingly rubbed his back in response. The sweet, seductive taste of her generous lips that so easily pursed into a frown when things didn't go her way.

Alcée wanted to cry out, to release the aching pressure suffocating him all these years. Instead, he closed his eyes and transferred the powerful emotions threatening to tear him apart into his music. He furiously worked the bow across the strings, and began to sing. The original words had described how his life had ended when she chose another, but that he wished her well. Tonight he added how the years had not lessened the pain in his heart, that he would never love another until his dying day.

"My soul died the day you married," Alcée sang. "And my life has since ended. I walk the world a lonely man."

Alcée was so intent playing the song, he failed to notice Marguerite moving to the center of the floor between the waltzing couples. When he opened his eyes at the last strain, his violin strings still humming from the beseeching tune, Alcée saw Marguerite standing before him, tears streaming down her face.

The couples stopped and stared at Marguerite, and Alcée heard someone mention retrieving Marguerite's in-laws. Before the messenger left the room, Alcée moved quickly to her side, placing a cautious hand at her waist in case she fainted. When her eyes, filled with a mixture of pity and desire, met his, Alcée lovingly wiped the tears away. Only the buzz of commotion, some semblance of reality, kept him from taking her into his arms.

"I have to see you," he whispered heatedly. "I have to talk to you."

"I can't," Marguerite whispered back.

Out of the corner of his eye, Alcée saw her in-laws walk through the door. "Meet me at the stables in an hour," he said before they reached her side.

The LeBlancs immediately put their arms about her, asking what had transpired, but Marguerite refused to talk, her gaze never leaving Alcée's face. She swallowed hard, trying to keep the tears at bay.

"I played the song I wrote for her wedding," Alcée told the mother when she glanced accusingly in his direction. "Marguerite is remembering François."

Marguerite finally looked away, turning the corners of her lips down in her typical childish pout, the simple action Alcée always found so charming. He closed his eyes to calm the passions pulsating through him. He had to have her, or he would die for sure.

"It's time to retire," Monsieur LeBlanc instructed Marguerite. "Sleep will do you good."

Alcée wanted to appreciate the LeBlancs' comfort and support, but they remained a symbol of the man who'd stolen Marguerite's heart from him. Now they were the ones taking her away. As the LeBlancs began to lead Marguerite from the room, he felt the anxiety rising in his chest. He couldn't bear another night without her, or at least not knowing how she felt. Just when he thought he would burst from the pain, Marguerite quickly met his eyes and very gently placed a hand over her heart. A second later she was gone.

He wasn't sure if he was imagining the gesture, but suddenly Alcée had hope. He began to quickly clear the room. "Time to go home," he announced, and amazingly found only a couple of objections. Usually, the Acadians demanded he play past dawn.

Paul LeBlanc handed Alcée his pistol, loaded and cocked. Alcée moved outside to a clearing and shot the pistol into the air. *"Le bal est fini!"* he exclaimed, the traditional announcement marking the end of the dance.

When Alcée returned, most of the people had retrieved their sleeping children and disappeared into the night. Through the intense darkness, Alcée could hear the wagons rolling away.

Alcée walked the short distance from Paul LeBlanc's house to the stables and waited. Sitting anxiously on a bale of hay, wondering if Marguerite would even think of joining him, he played a soft tune to serenade the horses. Mary's Blessing neighed in approval.

"Aren't you afraid you'll scare them?"

It was the first full sentence she had spoken to him in more than five years. The heavenly words fell about him like a soft misty rain.

"God, I missed you." Alcée tried hard to keep his emotions in check, but five years of grief had destroyed his self-control.

Marguerite moved closer to the lantern, and Alcée instantly reached for her. Before he could slide a hand around her cheek, she withdrew and looked away.

"I came to tell you I can't meet you tonight," she said.

Alcée laughed nervously, the fear of her leaving emerging in his voice. "But you are meeting me *here* tonight."

"I didn't want you waiting here all night for me," Marguerite said without looking at him. "I have to go back now."

Without forethought, Alcée grabbed her waist and pulled her toward him. He moved his other hand about her to keep her from escaping. "Why did you come all the way from Loreauville if you didn't want to see me, to talk to me?"

"Your parents asked me if I wanted to come with them," Marguerite answered, wide-eyed at his actions. "And since the LeBlancs were visiting their family, I thought I would join them."

"Join them?" Alcée almost shouted. "You make it sound like a social outing, while you waltz into my life and ignore me. Do you take pleasure in tormenting me?"

A lone tear fell down Marguerite's face, but she refused to wipe it away. "I never meant to hurt you," she whispered.

"How did you imagine marrying another man would not hurt me?" He hadn't meant to sound so menacing, but the pain bore too deep.

Marguerite pushed her arms through his and broke away. She turned and gazed up at the ceiling of the stables, wrapping her arms tightly about her chest. "Why haven't you married?" she asked, visibly fighting back the tears.

"Would that have eased your guilt?" Alcée asked. "If I had married?"

"I only want you to be happy," she said as a tear freed itself.

Alcée slid his hands about her shoulders, burying his face in the mound of braids and curls. "Make me happy, Marguerite," Alcée whispered before turning her around and taking possession of her lips. She didn't resist. Instead, Marguerite clung desperately to his lapel, crying softly while Alcée kissed the tears from her cheeks and chin. When he began to kiss the soft, tender reaches of her neck, she wound her arms about his neck and pulled him close.

"I can't help myself," she said softly.

"Then don't," Alcée answered, but it was too late. Marguerite drew away.

"Is it money again?" he demanded angrily, tired of the game.

"No."

"Look around you," he insisted. "I have more than enough."

"It's not money," she said through her tears.

Alcée anxiously rubbed the bridge of his nose, remembering how René had made the same gesture only that morning. Slowly, enunciating every word, he asked her, "Then what is it that keeps you from me?"

Marguerite closed her eyes and swallowed. "I am barren."

Alcée stared at her, perplexed.

"I cannot have children," she added. "I was married five years and bore no children."

He didn't mean to laugh, but the idea that something so simple was keeping them apart, that she indeed cared for him after all, made his heart light.

"It's not funny," Marguerite said. "How can you laugh about such a thing?"

"Children," Alcée said, still unable to keep from smiling. "This is about children?"

Marguerite stared at him dumbfounded. "I can never give you a son. You will never have a namesake. No one to carry on the generations."

Alcée very gently took Marguerite's hands and pressed them to his chest. The smile disappeared, replaced by a serious countenance. "I love you more than life itself, Marguerite Hébert LeBlanc. I can live without children. I have, and will have, more than enough nephews and nieces to care for. But I cannot—I repeat, cannot—live without you."

Marguerite said nothing, but her eyes told Alcée her answer.

She moved her hands from Alcée's grasp, then quickly slid them up to wrap them around his shoulders. Alcée wasted no time in reciprocating, meeting her lips with all the unleashed passion of five very long, very lonely years.

Chapter Sixteen

Amanda woke to find the sheets cold and a slight chill in the air billowing through the open windows. As she retrieved her discarded clothes in the early morning light and pulled them quickly over her head, she recognized that late summer feeling of hope.

It always amazed her how autumn first appeared in Louisiana. Instead of the trees turning colors and dropping their leaves in a climate where shawls were required, it simply became merely hot instead of unbearably hot. Until as late as November, they could not hope for significantly cooler weather, but residents delighted in the slight drop of temperature nonetheless.

Amanda assumed René had headed for the stables for the morning chores, until she heard movement on the front gallery. Emerging from the sanctuary of mosquito netting, Amanda made out René's tall figure leaning against the railing as he stared thoughtfully across the fields.

"A penny for your thoughts," she said, sliding an arm about his waist and resting her head against his right shoulder.

René instantly pulled her close and planted a kiss on the top of her head. Amanda snuggled, taking in his manly scent and brushing her cheek against the soft white cotton of his shirt. *The world could disappear at any moment,* she thought, *and I would be happy staying in this position forever.*

"I have to tend to the horses," René whispered.

Amanda closed her eyes, dreading letting him go. "I know," she said. "But promise me you won't race horses today simply because it's cooler."

A deep laugh emerged from his chest while his fingers raised her chin up so that his smiling eyes met hers. "Wild horses couldn't drag me away from you today," René said. "I shall feed them and return immediately."

"Couldn't you ask T-Emile to go?"

René's smile deepened. "What did you have in mind, Madame Comeaux?"

A deep, fiery blush spread about Amanda's face, but before she could respond, René cupped her cheek and kissed her passionately. Amanda took the opportunity to reach an arm around his neck and pull herself tightly against his broad chest. The horses would have to wait.

Just then, someone coughed. Amanda and René moved apart to find an embarrassed Alcée walking up the front path.

"Well, isn't that a sight," he said.

"I'd say the same for you," René quickly replied. "You look like you slept in the stables last night."

Alcée averted his eyes and began beating the hay and dust from his clothes. For a moment, Amanda thought he looked guilty.

"I fed the horses," Alcée said, still refusing to look up at them. "You can go back to bed. I'm going to start the coffee."

When he disappeared inside the house, René turned and

kissed Amanda again, hoping to pick up where they'd left off. But Amanda's thoughts were elsewhere.

"Alcée was acting strange, don't you think?"

René moved to her neck and began nibbling. "Uh-huh."

"Why would he be so dirty if he only fed the horses?"

Reaching her earlobe, René took a friendly bite. "Don't know."

"You don't think he was in the stables with Marguerite?"

René stopped and looked up. Amanda could almost see his logic at work as he deliberated on the past conversation. When a side of his lips turned up in a sly grin, Amanda knew she was right.

"I'm going to talk to him," she said, leaving the gallery.

René tried to grab her hand but she was too fast. "Can't it wait?" he implored.

Amanda stuck her head over the threshold sporting an equally sly smile. "No, it can't."

When Amanda finally finished her toilette, pulled on all the necessary garments and arranged her hair in an acceptable fashion, she quickly left for the back kitchen. René was close behind in his dressing; he had insisted on lying on the bed while she completed her wardrobe. The wicked man watched her every move with a satisfying smile. Remembering the moments made her breath quicken.

Still, she was on a mission. She had to know.

"So, what happened?" she immediately asked Alcée as she turned the corner into the kitchen.

Alcée laughed before he acknowledged her. "You don't waste time, do you, Madame Comeaux?"

Amanda liked both the sound of her name and the congeniality of his voice. She hoped he was finally accepting her as family.

"Did you talk?" she kept prying. "Is anything resolved?"

Alcée smiled. "She did ask what things I had been saying about her to René's new wife."

"I'm guilty," Amanda admitted. "Did it help?"

Again, Alcée laughed, this time nodding his head. "Yes, it helped."

He turned away, continuing to gather up the cups and saucers for breakfast until Amanda grabbed his arm. "Alcée," she insisted. "Do I have to beg it out of you?"

Alcée sighed, placed the cups down and wiped his hands on a kitchen rag. "We are going to be married in a month's time."

Amanda let out a soft squeal of delight and threw her arms about him. She immediately realized how improper the action was, but Alcée returned the hug.

"I always wanted a little sister," he said with an affectionate squeeze.

"I always wanted a big brother," she responded.

The two held each other for a brief time until footsteps were heard on the cobblestones leading from the house. "From one man's arms to another," René exclaimed behind her.

Amanda turned to find her husband staring at them accusingly, a sly glint in his eye. "And to think you were the one who said American girls were nothing but trouble," he teased his uncle.

Alcée grinned and placed a loving hand on each of their shoulders. "I wish you both the best of happiness," he said.

Amanda moved toward René, who wound his arm about her. "He's getting married," she whispered to him.

Amanda watched as René's eyes lit up, a smile exploding across his face. He grabbed Alcée and hugged him tightly.

"Now, don't get too excited," Alcée said, breaking away. "She's still in mourning and we have to keep this a secret for another month."

"I shall not breathe a word," René agreed, still beaming from the news. "Your secret's safe with me."

"What secret?" Colette asked as she appeared in the doorway.

Before Alcée could interject, René announced proudly, "Alcée's marrying Marguerite."

Alcée cringed as Colette gave an ear-splitting shriek.

Breakfast with the Comeaux and Dugas families was just as Amanda imagined. Everyone talked at once, each one trying to be heard over the noise, and the food continuously made its rounds about the table. The children ran excitedly around the room until they became disruptive, and then Colette quickly shooed them outside. And every few minutes, a pause would descend on the group and most of the eyes would fall on the newlyweds and Alcée. Then almost instantaneously, everyone would begin talking about René and Amanda's future and the upcoming wedding.

Amanda always wanted a big family. Staring at the faces surrounding her, the people who graciously accepted her as their own, Amanda realized she finally had one.

A gentle hand softly caressed her cheek. "What are you thinking about?" René asked, pulling her back to the present.

"How much I like your family," she whispered.

René smiled proudly and leaned in closer. "You may be surprised at this, but I like your father too."

"My father?" Amanda asked, clearly surprised. Then, looking up at the figure in the doorway, she repeated, "My father?"

Everyone momentarily stopped talking to gaze at the Judge standing before them, his hat held politely in his hands. Etienne Comeaux immediately stood and introduced himself. But if the Judge's presence at the house wasn't shocking enough, his response clearly was.

"It is a pleasure to meet you, monsieur," James replied in French, accepting the man's hand.

Etienne then introduced Marie, and James bowed, offering a cordial sentence or two of introduction, again in French. Amanda glanced toward René, and found his reaction mirroring her own. Alcée had dropped his jaw in amazement.

When Marie invited him to coffee, James accepted, and Amanda wondered if there would be no end of surprises. The Judge extended a hand to René, who introduced him to Alcée, Colette and T-Emile.

"I'd like to offer my apologies, my boy," he said to T-Emile, who seemed frozen to the spot. "I behaved rudely the other day. My daughter's family is always welcome in my house."

James planted a kiss on Amanda's cheek before he sat down next to René's parents. Amanda finally closed her mouth and swallowed, but she still wondered if she were dreaming.

"My daughter is in shock," he admitted to them. "She has not heard me speak French in ten years."

"I must say I am surprised as well," Marie said. "I didn't know you were bilingual."

"I studied in France as a youth," James explained, "and worked for many years in a Paris exporting firm. When they expanded overseas to New Orleans, I helped them open the business."

"I thought you were in government work," Alcée said.

"I came to New Orleans around the time of statehood," James answered, accepting a steaming cup of coffee from Marie. "American and French businesses were having a difficult time getting along. The municipal government hired me to be an intermediary since I was familiar with trade and spoke both languages."

"That must have been quite a challenge," Etienne said.

James laughed good-naturedly, a sound Amanda hadn't heard in years. "More than you know."

Suddenly, tears welled in Amanda's eyes. This was the father of her youth, the laughing man with a hundred stories to tell, the affectionate man who adored his daughter. A man who braved the scorn of a prominent Creole family and his own, yet returned home smiling every day with kisses, chocolates and humorous tales.

If she could find a better life, then so could he. Perhaps a score of grandchildren would help erase the pain. A man could be born again from the ashes of rejection and grief.

"Tell them about the Marquis," Amanda said, trying to keep the emotions from her voice. "Tell them how you met General Lafayette."

James gazed lovingly at his daughter. Amanda knew meeting Lafayette, George Washington's aide-de-camp during the American Revolution, had been the highlight of his life. She remembered how proud he had always been recounting the story.

"You met Lafayette?" Marie asked, amazed.

"I was one of the dignitaries who welcomed Lafayette to New Orleans," James began. "I only spoke with him briefly, but it was an honor I will never forget."

"Tell them about his sword," Amanda urged.

James smiled at his daughter, relaxing back into his chair. "Lafayette was never seen without his sword during all the festivities. While we were dining at the banquet in his honor at the John Davis Hotel, Lafayette told me it was the same sword given to him by Benjamin Franklin."

Amanda tapped René lightly on the arm to get his attention, then whispered, "He was one of *our* Founding Fathers." René resumed listening to James's story, but Amanda could see the smile curling at the sides of his lips.

"Laced within the sword's ironwork were illustrations depicting the fraternal union between France and America," James continued. "When he visited the United States in 1825, Lafayette showed it with pride to anyone who asked. As we dined, he told me it represented the invaluable friendship that existed between France and America, a friendship he held dear to his dying day. Did you know he named his only son George Washington Lafayette?''

"Yes, I had heard," Etienne said.

"I told him that despite our differences, and our mutual stubbornness, the Americans and the French did possess a remarkable force when they worked together," James said. "If it hadn't been for the French influence in the American Revolution, we might not have won. And I believe the French were inspired by our actions to establish liberty in their own country.''

"And the Battle of New Orleans," Amanda interjected.

"Yes," James said, patting her hand. "I told Lafayette not to worry about the difficulties between our cultures here in Louisiana. I gave the War of 1812 as an example. It was immediately following the Louisiana Purchase and the Americans and French were distrustful of one another, to say the least. But there was one thing they despised more than each other, the British. Together, we could not be defeated.''

"And here we are all together," Alcée said with a twinkle in his eye. "One big happy family.''

He hadn't meant any harm, but Amanda feared her father would not see the humor in his statement. To her added amazement, James raised his coffee cup and offered a toast.

"To Amanda and René," he said, and the others followed his lead.

"To Louisiana," Etienne added, "and the freedom of us all.''

The Judge stayed for more than an hour, enjoying the hot coffee, baked bread and fresh fruit. Most of the conversation revolved around Etienne and Marie, but Amanda was thankful to merely sit and watch. She had never seen him in such good spirits.

When James finally said his good-byes, he asked if she and René would escort him to his buggy.

"It was a pleasure meeting your parents," he said to René as they left the house, "but I must confess I came here with another purpose." James's smile disappeared as he placed his hat on his head. "I have some bad news," he told them.

What could possibly be bad news after the week she had experienced? Amanda wondered. What more could have happened?

"Katharine Blanchard was found murdered last night," James began.

Amanda shuddered involuntarily and placed her hand over her mouth.

"Katharine Blanchard?" René asked. "The American friend who visited?"

While Amanda nodded, James continued. "Apparently, she was a friend of Henry Tanner's. She was seen coming and going at the plantation this past week." James sternly looked his daughter in the eye. "Did you know about this?"

"Sally Baldwin said he had escorted her to a ball," Amanda practically whispered. The fear of Tanner had abated during the past twenty-four hours, but now returned full force. "The day I rode with her to the church, she spoke to him as if they were on cordial terms."

"You saw Tanner this past week?" the Judge asked.

"Friday morning," Amanda said, waiting for the outburst.

"Friday morning," James began to shout, then thought better of it. Trying to keep his anger at bay, he asked, "Was this the last time you saw Katharine?"

"Yes," Amanda said.

James grew silent, staring thoughtfully at the ground.

"Do you suspect Tanner of this crime?" René asked.

"We haven't been able to find him," James answered, sending a chill through Amanda. "He is either fast on his way to Texas or waiting to make a move of some kind."

A silence fell about the trio, and Amanda heard the children playing pirates on the other side of the house.

"I want you both to be extremely careful," James instructed them, his voice taking on its usual paternal tone. "Don't ever be alone. Stay near other people, populated areas. Don't venture anywhere by yourself."

Both Amanda and René assured him they would take extra precautions, but Amanda couldn't help feeling comforted that her father was concerned for René's safety as well as her own.

James turned to walk toward the buggy, then stopped abruptly as if he forgot something important. "Oh, there is something else."

Amanda waited for the additional piece of news, but when her father hesitated, she feared another dose of ill tidings was on the way.

"I uh . . . I have . . ." James smiled at his inability to form words. If Amanda wasn't mistaken, a blush began to spread about his cheeks. "I have asked Virginia to marry me," he finally said. "And she has agreed."

Amanda's jaw fell open for the second time that morning, and she stood staring, at a loss for words.

"That is, of course, if you approve," James added.

Amanda threw her arms around his neck and hugged him tightly. Her father was going to be fine after all. "Of course I approve," she said. "It's about time."

"Some of us need a little encouragement. Someone to open the curtains and let some light into our lives." James tightened his hold on Amanda, pressing his cheek lovingly against the blond curls. "I love you," he whispered.

"I love you too," she said.

When he released her, René extended his hand. "The *baieonne?*" René asked. "The one with the bright red hair?"

"Yes," James answered, staring thoughtfully down at their united hands.

"I wish you the best of luck and all the happiness in the world," René said proudly.

"Thank you, my boy," James said, placing a friendly hand on his shoulder. "With a handshake like that, I wish for you a long career in politics."

Amanda giggled, and René sent her a puzzled look. "Not you too?" he said.

"You would be great," she agreed.

"Think about it," James said before entering the buggy. "You're a natural. Most politicians would kill to have your kind of charm."

René placed an arm about Amanda's shoulders. "We'll see," he said.

James whipped the horses to action and the buggy started toward the road. "Next Saturday," James shouted back to the couple. "The wedding is Saturday."

Amanda watched the buggy slowly disappear from sight, still shocked by the morning's revelations. When she gazed back to René, in the hopes of finding someone to share in her astonishment, she found him frowning, a pensive look on his face.

"You really would make an ideal politician," Amanda said. "But if you're not interested, my father would not mind you saying so."

"What?" he asked absentmindedly. René dropped his arm and walked silently toward the path leading to the stables. His unusual silence unnerved her. A shudder passed down her spine, as if Henry Tanner was breathing down her neck.

"Is something wrong?" she asked, hoping the fear she was experiencing was unfounded. René silently stared at the horizon.

Behind them Alcée emerged from the house, a grim expression on his face as well. The two men exchanged glances, but said nothing. Amanda held her breath as they both looked back toward the stables.

Then Amanda heard the noise. The sound was hard to discern at first, but by the time it was repeated they all knew what it was. It was the cry of an animal in the jaws of death.

"Dear God," she whispered, at the same time recognizing the faint smell of smoke riding toward the house on the wind. "The stables are on fire."

Alcée shouted for his family and they all bolted into action. Everyone grabbed pots, pails and anything big enough to hold water and ran toward the stables. Even the children did their part, bringing up the rear with water jugs and their fishing pails.

Amanda fell back to help Pierre, but René instantly grabbed her wrist and pulled her forward.

"Stay with my family," he shouted. "I'll take care of the boys."

René picked up Pierre and followed the group down the path. When they made the clearing, everyone paused momentarily as the red, violent flames of the fire became visible.

"The well is several feet behind the western wall," Alcée shouted to Etienne, who was leading the pack.

Picking up her skirts, Amanda joined the parade of water from well to building, never taking a moment to wonder if the fire was abating. Like everyone else, Amanda kept her head bent down, concentrating only on moving water from one place to another.

No one spoke as they each placed their pail on the ground, pumping water from the well, then quickly running back to spray the water against the side of the building. After several trips, Amanda failed to comprehend who was by her side as she ran from one place to another. When the footsteps sounded from behind, she imagined it to be any one of the family members.

She threw her pail beneath the spout and began pumping furiously. If only the well wasn't so far away, Amanda thought, then the trail of water would be faster. If only there were more people.

Suddenly, a fear gripped her heart, an unsettling feeling that whoever was standing behind her was not welcome. She kept pumping, knowing her anxiety was unfounded. After all, who else would it be besides family?

The pail filled just as the thought of Tanner causing the fire raced through her mind. Amanda moved to turn, to face the presence at her back, but never got the chance. As she briefly caught an image of Tanner's menacing face, she felt a lightning pain at the back of her head and her world turned instantly black.

Chapter Seventeen

René dropped Pierre at a reasonable distance from the fire and bolted inside. While the others ran water from the well to the building, René released each horse one by one, covering their eyes to lead them from the burning stables. The poor Vaughn horse had been the closest to the fire and never stood a chance. René covered his own face with a horse blanket to avoid the awful smell of its burning flesh.

With the last of the horses rescued, René grabbed the saddles lining the wall furthest from the flames. He started for the office, but Alcée intercepted him.

"Get out of here," Alcée shouted. "The building's going to collapse."

René felt the burning in his lungs, and followed his uncle into the clearing. As he looked back at the stables, René realized all hope was lost. The fire burned with such a ferocity, the heat tinged his skin even though he stood several hundred feet away.

"There's nothing we can do," Alcée said, letting his empty bucket hit the ground at this feet.

"Tell everyone to stop," René said. "Tell them it's useless."

Alcée walked to the line of people emerging from the woods and the well and began to relay the information. René watched as first Marie, then Etienne and T-Emile caught up to Alcée, dropping their pails at the news. Alexandre stood to René's right, and Colette was at the building throwing water on the stable's wall with Pierre. René scanned the horizon and found no one else. In the distance, he heard the sound of horses galloping away.

The knowledge hit him like a lightning bolt.

René yelled to Alcée, but Alcée only looked back puzzled, too far away to hear anything over the noise of the fire. René reached Colette first and grabbed her anxiously. "Where is Amanda?" he shouted.

Colette looked back over her shoulder. "She was right behind me."

For a moment, René hoped he was mistaken, that the thought of Tanner setting fire to his stables to steal his wife away was absurd. He ran toward his family and the woods, praying Amanda would emerge from behind a tree. But the closer he got to Alcée and his parents, the more he feared the worst. His mother turned and called Amanda's name.

"Where is she?" René yelled to the group.

Alcée shot him a worried glance that caused René's heart to stop beating. Silently, Alcée ran toward the woods, René at his heels.

Her pail sat by the well, filled to the brim, but she was nowhere in sight. To the left were marks in the dirt as if someone had dragged another person away. René followed the path to the dirt road that led to the LeBlanc house. There the marks disappeared, but wheel tracks made it clear a horse and buggy had just passed.

René felt his chest constrict. He forced himself to breathe. He knew he had to think, to formulate a plan, but the thought of Amanda stolen away by a murderer was more than he could bear. René leaned over, placing his hands on his knees. He had to concentrate.

"I've sent T-Emile for the Judge," he heard Alcée say behind him. "He'll have the sheriff and every man in town after him."

René took a deep breath and straightened. "Where's Mary's Blessing."

Alcée grabbed his arm as he headed back toward the stables. "You're crazy if you think you can face Tanner alone. He'll kill you."

"Then so be it," René said, pulling his arm free.

"What good will you be to her if you're dead?" Alcée shouted at his back.

René spun around hard, sending Alcée a determined stare. "Not if I kill him first."

When René hit the clearing, the other members of his family were still searching the area anxiously for Amanda. T-Emile was saddling one of the horses he'd managed to round up.

"Tell the Judge I have gone to Port Cocodrie," René yelled to the youth as he helped him on to the horse. "Tell him to send some men to the bay, but have him comb the area in case I'm wrong." T-Emile said nothing, but kicked the horse into action and rode away.

René then scanned the horizon until he found what he was looking for—the fastest horse in St. Mary Parish. He moved cautiously toward the mare, careful not to spook the horse, which was already scared from the fire.

"Come on, Mary," René coaxed. "We have a job to do and I can't do it without you."

As if the horse could read his mind, she cooperated, letting René pass a rope around her neck and lead her toward a saddle.

René instantly tossed the saddle onto her back and tightened the girth. Mary's Blessing stood poised, waiting to take action.

"Where are you going?" Etienne called to René.

"Amanda is in trouble," René said before mounting. With those final words, René rode off toward the south, and the dark waters of Côte Blanche Bay.

Philip leaned against the pub's wooden post along the outside of the building, careful not to appear too attentive. He had watched the men's movement to and from the ship for almost an hour, and finally realized their business. He took another sip from the cheap rum he'd purchased, wincing as it burned a path down his throat. Philip despised poor liquor, not to mention seedy port life, but he knew he must appear as one of the merchants enjoying a little libation after finishing an exhausting day of exporting goods, when money flowed freely in his pockets.

The men took no notice of him, and began discussing their next course of action. Philip glanced down at the ground, pulling his hat low about his face but leaning an ear in their direction. He was just about to learn their destination when the sounds of a horse riding in from the north blocked out all conversation.

"*Merde*," he muttered to himself.

The interruption caused the men to look up and notice for the first time that others were in hearing distance. They boarded the ship and disappeared. Philip angrily turned toward the source of the noise, wanting desperately to give the intruder a solid piece of his mind.

As the man headed toward the light of the inn, Philip noticed something familiar in his gait. He knew it was only a matter of time before he followed her here, but Philip was surprised that René dared venture to Port Cocodrie by himself. Philip staggered toward him, wrapped an arm about his shoulders and pretended to be very drunk.

"It's about time you got here," he shouted into René's surprised face. "I hope you don't mind, but we started without you."

René tried to move him away, but Philip held tightly to his arm. "Play along," he whispered, leading René into the pub.

The saloon's patrons were few due to the early afternoon hour. A couple of Americans sat by the back wall, talking loudly and laughing, and a lone boatman sat to their right eating a dinner of fish stew and ale. All three men looked up as Philip and René entered the pub.

"Relax," Philip whispered, then gave him a hard slap on the back. René fell forward slightly and sent Philip an angry glance.

"Two rums," Philip shouted to the bartender in his heavily accented English.

The bartender pointed to the bottle of rum Philip grasped in his right hand. "Oh," Philip said with a drunken laugh. "Give us two more anyway."

He turned and grabbed René's shoulders again, pulling him into a chair as far from the others as possible. He fell into the opposite chair and began laughing again, while the bartender placed two glasses of rum before them. Philip threw the man a coin in payment. "Keep the change," he said.

When the bartender was out of earshot, René sat forward. "Just what the hell is going on?"

Philip raised his hand in caution and handed René the glass. René eyed it suspiciously, then accepted it. Philip tapped his glass against René's and offered a toast. *"A votre santé."*

René furrowed his brows, and Philip imagined the boy was beginning to think he really was drunk. "I don't think you understand . . ." René began, dropping the glass to the table.

"I understand that these men are watching us," Philip said

quietly, "and if you don't drink that rum they will get suspicious. If you want to help her, you'll follow my lead."

René's eyes intensified. "Do you know where she is?"

"Drink," Philip instructed sternly.

René took a deep breath, smiled as if enjoying himself and tilted the glass back.

"Another round for my friend," Philip yelled to the bartender. Quietly, he added to René, "She's in the inn on the third floor."

René immediately rose to leave, but Philip grabbed his forearm and pushed him back into his chair. The bartender brought another round, eyeing the two carefully. "Thank you, my good man," Philip said, offering up his best smile and placing another coin in the man's hand. "My friend is new to the area, just arrived from the Opelousas Poste. I'm trying to show him a good time."

The bartender grunted and left, this time without glancing back. "Listen closely," Philip told René. "There's a boat docked out back. If I'm not mistaken, it's Captain Marenga's ship out of the West Indies. He's a man with a price on his head in the States. Deals in the black market and slavery. White slavery, if you know what I mean."

René's eyes grew large, and again he tried to rise. "Hear me out, son. If you want to save Amanda you must think with your head and not with your heart."

"Just tell me where she is," René whispered heatedly.

"Tanner has her in the inn, but probably not for long," Philip explained. "I was eavesdropping on the ship's men until you came barreling in here. Because of you I was unable to hear where they are heading."

"They're not heading anywhere with my wife," René said so intensely, Philip felt the gooseflesh rise.

"Your head," Philip warned him again, "use your head. She's surrounded by many men, including Tanner, and the ones on the ship will not be happy losing such a prize. They're rough men, René. They would just as soon kill their own mother as kill you.''

René said nothing, staring down at the glass in his hand. "I have a plan,'' Philip said. "Are you interested?''

"Who are you?'' René asked. "First you try to bribe me at my stables; now you're willing to help rescue my wife against a pack of cutthroats.''

Philip couldn't but help smile at the absurdity of it all. "I am Philip Vanier,'' he said softly.

Several seconds passed before René finally responded, apparently understanding the connection. "What is your plan?'' he asked.

"Amanda is on the third floor,'' Philip began, "but Tanner has two men on watch at the front entrance. My room is on the first floor, at the end of the hallway, next to the back set of stairs. While I entertain the men at the front entrance, you enter my room through my open window and sneak up the stairs.''

René nodded as he considered the instructions. "I need a gun.''

"I have one underneath my coat.'' While Philip refilled both their glasses with rum, he slid the pistol beneath the table to René's lap. René accepted the weapon and discreetly placed it within his own waistcoat.

"*Bon,*'' Philip said. "You're using your head. But be careful. It's half-cocked and loaded.''

René nodded unemotionally. "Are you ready?'' he asked, rising.

Philip joined him, stretching lazily. "I think you're right, my friend,'' he said loudly. "We need some women.''

Philip hoped René had the good sense to play along, and was grateful when the young man smiled. "Only a hag would like the sight of you now!'' René joked.

"In my condition, I wouldn't know the difference," Philip joked back.

The two agreeably left the saloon, stumbling along the path that led to the inn. When they were safely out of reach of the saloon's intruding lamplight, Philip pulled René aside and pointed toward the end of the building.

"My room is the second from the end, the one with the torn curtains," he said. "Wait a minute or two for me to get the attention of the man at the door, then try to make it up the back stairs."

René agreed and turned to leave, but Philip grabbed his sleeve once again. "Use your head," he warned René in a tone that was now devoid of all merriment. "We all want her safe, but you will fail if you let your heart think for you. Remember the saying, 'Fools rush in.' "

After testing to make sure the pistol was safely lodged inside the waistband of his trousers, and hidden by his waistcoat, René headed off into the darkness. Philip prayed his plan would work, and that the boy would take his advice—for the sake of them all.

Philip took a deep breath and staggered to the front of the inn. A tall American with a rifle stood guard at the door. The dark-haired man, missing several teeth, was distinguished by a scar running across his left cheek up to his unclean hairline. He studied Philip thoroughly.

"My dear man," Philip said as he climbed the front stairs. "Are we expecting the President?"

Toothless remained silent, and Philip wondered if the incredibly ugly man was doing his job or just didn't understand the joke. Philip pointed the bottle of rum toward his rifle. "Are we keeping something out or keeping something in?"

The American frowned. Perhaps it was his accent. "Why the rifle?" Philip finally asked.

"I'm looking for someone," the American mumbled.

Philip looked worried. "Do I have reason to fear? I'm staying the night in this inn."

"Doubt it," Toothless replied. "It's a private fight."

Philip raised a hand to his chest in relief. "Thank goodness, my man. On that news, I think I shall have another drink."

Raising the bottle to his lips, Philip made two important observations: René crossing the hallway and reaching the back stairs, and the American licking his lips as he watched Philip drink. After pretending to take a sip from the bottle, Philip handed the rum to the other man. Before the American could accept the gesture, another armed man appeared from around the corner of the building. "What the hell do you think you're doing?" he shouted.

"Just a sip," the toothless man replied.

"Who is this?" the other man demanded, pointing to Philip.

"Another patron of the inn," Philip said, bowing politely.

"He's French," he said to the toothless man. "You know the rules."

"He ain't the Cajun," Toothless said.

"How do you know?"

Toothless gazed at Philip thoughtfully. "He's too fancy-dressed."

The other man slapped Toothless on the arm. "You know the rules. He's French. Blow the whistle."

Toothless hesitated, still gazing longingly at the bottle of rum. Philip started to say something witty, something to throw them both off track, but Toothless quickly raised the whistle to his lips and appeared ready to blow. Philip moved instantly, sending a fist into the man's ribs, knocking the breath from his lungs.

Before Philip could formulate his next move, however, he heard a crack at the back of his head and a flash of pain before he disappeared into darkness.

* * *

Somewhere in the black night a light came on, and Amanda hoped she was not dead after all. She heard voices, laughter, the sound of a bell like those used on ships. Seagulls. Water beating against a shore. *This couldn't be the afterlife,* she thought, *with such familiar earthly sounds.* The pounding pain that continued at the base of her skull was not something that would follow her into heaven.

She tried again to rise, but the pounding intensified. She willed herself to a seated position, fighting the nausea rising in her chest. Slowly, she raised her head, careful not to make any sudden moves to set the room spinning once more. Within minutes, she was sitting up, her back resting against a wall.

I can do this, she commanded herself, feeling the tears well up. *I will do this.*

Looking around the meager room, Amanda tried to make sense of what had happened. She remembered the *fais do-do,* the smile on Alcée's face when he played *Jolie Blonde* at the LeBlanc house. Her father speaking of the Marquis de Lafayette. Water at a well.

Gazing toward the wall where light was streaming in through the open window, Amanda suddenly recognized the painting. A ship with an English flag sailing among high waves, its bow sporting a scantily clad woman. She had seen it before. At a time when there were sounds of the sea outside the room.

Dear God, Amanda realized with horror, *I am in Port Coco-drie.*

Instantly, she remembered the fire, the screams of the horses as they kicked at their stalls. She recalled the fear that had raced through her veins when Tanner's face came into view. And something that landed hard on the top of her head.

I will get through this, she insisted, rising from the floor, her back flat against the wall for support. *I have to get away.*

"Going somewhere?" a voice sounded from behind, a voice Amanda knew only too well. She dared not look around for fear of fainting. Instead, Henry Tanner emerged from the shadow of the doorway, standing before her with a rifle in one hand.

"Why did you bring me here?" Amanda asked, trying to keep her voice calm. "What could you possibly want from me now?"

His cold black eyes stared down at her unemotionally, while the thin lines of Tanner's lips rose in a smirk. "I thought we had a deal, darling Amanda. You wanted romance, and I needed three thousand dollars. Only now, the price has risen."

"You're crazy," Amanda said, inching away from him along the wall, heading for the open door. The thought of Katharine strangled by this man constricted her voice. "I only asked for an escort to a dance. I never dreamed you would take advantage of me."

"Nonsense," Tanner said, following her. "You asked for it all, and now I expect to get paid."

"My father will make arrangements," Amanda continued as she felt the threshold beneath her fingers. "You only need to speak to him."

Tanner laughed as he slammed the door shut before her. Leaning down so close to her face Amanda could smell the whiskey on his breath, Tanner said sarcastically, "Don't worry, my dear. If your father shows up, I'll be glad to do the talking."

Amanda shut her eyes, willing the horrid man from her sight. She knew he lingered in front of her when his hand slid down her cheek, around her neck to the bodice of her gown. "I think perhaps it's time I collected interest on you as well," Tanner said. "If William McDuff can raise the debts, then so can I."

While Tanner's hand fumbled with the top buttons of her dress, Amanda heard a whistle being blown on the ground floor. Thankfully, the noise caused Tanner to divert his thoughts. She opened her eyes to find him rising and moving away, a smile dancing on his lips.

"If your father doesn't grace us with a visit," he said, reaching for the gunpowder and pouring a small amount in the gun's pan, "then maybe your Cajun husband will."

Amanda heard the hallway's wooden planks giving way to a person's footsteps. Someone was nearby. Help had arrived. She screamed seconds before Tanner slapped her hard across the face. But instead of being furious with her actions, Tanner grinned and raised his rifle at the closed door, cocking it slowly and taking aim.

"Your Cajun should arrive any minute now," he replied. "Thank you for that."

Still reeling from the burning slap and the bump at the back of her head, Amanda tried to sit up and concentrate. She had to do something quick. She heard the footsteps moving down the hallway, heading straight for the door in the line of Tanner's fire. If René had indeed followed her here, he wouldn't stop to think. His only aim would be to save her, no matter what trap he was walking into.

As the footsteps halted on the other side of the door, Tanner set the gun at his shoulder. Amanda saw the doorknob move slightly. If she yelled, he would bolt inside. But if she said nothing, he would surely be killed.

"Stupid Cajun," she heard Tanner utter.

Realizing her advantage in knowing French, Amanda yelled her instructions. "Move away from the door," she shouted in French.

The gun exploded, sending a blaze of fire across the room. The ball blew apart the wooden door, and Amanda heard the sickening sound of a body fall on the other side. Through the smoke and splintered remnants of what remained of the door, Amanda recognized the *cotonnade* shirt Marie Rose had lovingly made for her son. René lay dead on the hallway floor, blood covering his head and shirt.

Everything began to spin again as Amanda screamed and rushed toward René. She felt Tanner's arms pulling her back inside, but she refused to be afraid, pounding him with her fists and clawing his face with her nails. Tanner hit her hard across the face, a blow forceful enough to make her stop yelling. She began sobbing, falling to a defeated heap on the floor.

"Bitch," Tanner yelled at her, wiping the blood from his face. "You're going to pay for that."

Tanner grabbed her wrists while raising her skirts to her waist. Amanda knew what was coming, but she no longer cared. René was gone. And it was all her fault.

Use your head. The thoughts flowed through René's mind, seeping into his silent mind as if in a void. *Only a fool rushes in.*

He was hurt; somewhere he was bleeding profusely. He felt the warm liquid ooze down his face, burning his eyes. His head must have stopped the bullet, he thought, for he could hear nothing and most of the blood appeared to be covering his face. He had to be dead. No one could have withstood a direct shot at that close range.

Then René remembered Pierre's fall from the oak tree last spring, the blood pouring across his forehead in a stream. They had all feared a busted head, only to find a gash the size of a small fingernail.

René moved his fingers and found them in working order. He slid his hand along his trousers, brushing aside the fragments of wood until he found his pocket and the handkerchief inside. Raising the cloth to his face, he wiped the blood from his eyes and found the blood's source. Right above his right ear the bullet had grazed his skin. He was alive. And he still had time.

If Philip's words of advice were not enough to convince him, the pain searing his forehead sure did. He had no choice but to use his head, he thought grimly. The pain wouldn't allow him to think of anything else.

Except dear Amanda. He remembered her scared scream and her warning just in time for him to move to the side of the door. He would concentrate on saving Amanda, and kill anyone in his path.

René fought the desire to lose consciousness as he rose from the floor. Through the hole in the door, he made out Tanner's back. The bastard was removing his jacket and shirt while Amanda lay weeping on the floor before him. She would not cry for long, René vowed.

He entered the room slowly through the doorway, pulling the pistol from his waist and placing it at arm's length at the base of Tanner's skull. René could hear nothing, but saw Tanner stiffen when he pulled the lever to a fully cocked position.

"Get your damn hands off my wife," René said slowly and succinctly.

René knew Tanner heard him, but God, why couldn't he hear himself? The world had gone eerily silent, except for the incessant thunder reverberating through his mind.

Tanner swung around and laughed. He said something with a cocky smile on his face, but again, René heard nothing. It was just as well, René thought. He had to concentrate. Use his head. René stared relentlessly at Tanner, his eyes never leaving his face.

Tanner glanced behind René and smiled again, as if he wanted René to believe his men were behind him. René continued to stare at him, refusing to take the bait. If there were men at his back, René still held the gun to Tanner's head.

Tanner leaned back slightly, still smiling his wicked grin. He said a few words to René, but René's arm never faltered.

Then Tanner said something that registered. "Shoot him," René read from his lips.

For a moment, René doubted his safety. Still, he held his ground, his eyes locked in a duel with Tanner's.

Suddenly, a blast came from behind. Even though his hearing had not fully returned, René could detect a pistol firing. A vibration rocked the floor, but as far as René could tell, he stood unharmed.

Tanner's eyes grew wide with fear. If his men had followed him to the room, René assumed someone or something had interfered. Tanner's eyes betrayed him; he was caught and he knew it.

Panic, you son of a bitch, René thought as he watched Tanner eye his pistol on the side of the bed. *Reach for it.*

Tanner lunged toward the weapon. In the instant Tanner made his decision, René fired his pistol, the smoke of the gunpowder filling the room. As the air slowly cleared, René saw Tanner's body lying motionless on the floor, a bullet hole through his forehead.

The danger abated, René felt the blood rushing from his head. He fell to his knees as the strength slowly waned from his limbs and the pain intensified. The room began to spin, and he felt an angel grab him and hold him close. As she stared down at him with eyes the color of a summer sky, he saw her form three words.

He couldn't hear himself repeat them, but he said them nonetheless. "I love you too."

The pungent fog of burnt sulfur surrounded him, and René turned to find James grabbing his arm, a look of concern on his face and a smoking gun in his free hand.

"We're undefeatable when we work together," René said, sending him a grim smile just before the room faded to black.

Chapter Eighteen

"I don't understand," Amanda said, her heart and head still pounding from the fear. "What was Uncle Philip doing in Port Cocodrie?"

The Judge sighed, placing a hand at her temple. "All in good time, Amanda. Now, you must rest. You've had quite a shock. We could easily arrange a room for you . . ."

"I'm not leaving him, Father," she insisted.

"Your father's right," Philip said, holding a wet cloth to the back of his wounded head. "We will have time to explain later."

Amanda stared at the door leading into the room where James had carried René. The town's physician had been called, and for more than twenty minutes he had been attending to René's wounds.

"It appears that I have plenty of time," Amanda said grimly.

"He is going to be fine," James said.

Amanda turned and gazed at the man who had amazingly

metamorphosed within a few days' time. Only a week ago he'd angrily dismissed her marital worries, retreating into his darkened parlor and slamming the door on both her and the subject. Only a week before she'd first considered being escorted to a ball with Henry. Amanda shuddered at the thought of the man who now lay dead on the third floor of the Port Cocodrie Inn.

Without knowing that James had risen and come to her side, Amanda felt his arms wrapping tightly about her. "It's over now," James soothingly said, kissing the top of her head. "It's over."

Amanda snaked her own arms around her father and placed her cheek against his warm, rough lapel. *If only that were true,* she thought. *If only the doctor would tell them René was going to be all right.*

"Will you all ever forgive me?" she asked him.

"Someone once told me there was never a problem without a solution," James said, repeating Virginia's favorite saying with a slight smile. "I think it's time we moved on."

The door opened and the physician emerged from the darkened room. Before he could utter a word, Amanda heard René calling out for her. Without forethought, she lunged past the doctor and headed straight toward his bedside, never caring about revealing petticoats as she climbed onto the bed. René sat up and eagerly cupped her face, while Amanda's fingers traced the length of his bandage.

"Are you all right?" René asked her, his eyes searching her face for signs. "Has he hurt you in any way?"

Amanda shook her head, a tear escaping her eyes when she realized how deep the gun blast had penetrated the side of René's head. "Can you hear me?" she asked, afraid there would be no answer.

René planted soft kisses on her cheeks while his fingers

reached into the blond curls that escaped their hairpins and were lying loose about her shoulders. When he didn't answer, Amanda feared the worst.

"Yes, I can hear you," René said softly, holding her face close to his. "I'm fine."

"Of course you are," James said, placing a comforting hand on René's shoulder. "We will do everything in our power to get you well."

"You're a hero now," Philip said, coming around the side of the bed to shake his hand. "Because you used your head."

"René," Amanda said, "I'd like you to meet my uncle."

"We've met," René said, giving Philip's hand a firm shake.

Amanda gaped at first René, then Philip. When she began a series of questions, Philip held out a hand.

"Later, *ma petite*," Philip said, then turned to James. "You were right. He does have a good handshake."

"Hero," James repeated thoughtfully. "Now, you must run for office, my boy. You could win any election you choose."

René gazed back at Amanda. "Is he talking about what I think he's talking about?"

"Politics, my boy," James continued while Amanda laughed at René's grim expression. "After what happened today, you could have your choice of positions. As long as you don't choose the parish judgeship, of course."

"Nonsense," Philip interjected. "He's going into the importing and exporting business with me. I could use a sharp mind."

"Gentlemen," Amanda said firmly. "What René needs now is some rest."

The Judge again placed a fatherly hand on his shoulder. "I think Amanda is right," he said. "We should leave you two alone for now."

"An astounding idea," Philip agreed. "Let us leave the

newlyweds to themselves and seek some company in the nearby
pub.''

"So, it wasn't an act after all," René said to Philip, sending
him a sly grin.

Philip winked, then reached into his coat pocket and pulled
out a small wrapped package. "A wedding present," he said,
handing the package to Amanda. "This is all the rage across
America. You would know that if you lived in a civilized
city." Philip shot James a teasing look, and James grimaced
halfheartedly while he waved off the remark. Amanda couldn't
help wonder when the two estranged men had become reunited.

Philip's expression turned more serious as he gazed back to
René. "I think you will find it very interesting, *mon ami*. Very
interesting indeed."

James grabbed the smaller, dapper man by the arm and led
him toward the door. "It's time for that drink, Philip," was
the last remark Amanda heard before her father left the room
and shut the door behind them. When she looked back, René
was staring at the package in her lap.

"It looks like a book," René said.

Uncovering the wrapper, Amanda read the words on the
cover. "*Evangeline* by Henry Wadsworth Longfellow."

"The American poet?"

Amanda knew what René was thinking. She couldn't fathom
why René would find this American writer any more interesting
than she did. Until she read the opening pages.

She hugged the book to her chest and smiled, then gazed
into the loving brown eyes she had found so entrancing when
they had first stared at her over her front picket fence. She
didn't explain.

Amanda looked down at the story of a peaceful people who
were brutally exiled from their homeland. A story of a forgotten
people and two lovers separated in their Diaspora. The story

of the ancestors of the man she so dearly loved. And she began
to read:

> This is the forest primeval,
> The murmuring pines and the hemlocks . . .
> A Tale of Love in Acadie, home of the happy.

Epilogue

January 1853

"How do you stand on the governor's threat to publish names of legislators who fail to attend sessions? By God, we have crops to tend to and businesses to keep."

René cringed inwardly as he watched William McDuff, the senior lawmaker from Port Cocodrie, offer a quasi-friendly hand to the freshman legislator while attempting to sway him to his side. One thing René had learned after four years as a state representative was that Louisiana legislators were no better than hungry alligators.

"You mean you have pub hours to meet, isn't that right, Bill?" René asked the stocky, balding legislator, who paled at the comment.

"Now, René," McDuff retorted, "we all know the only reason you're siding with the governor is because Paul Hébert is a Cajun."

René smiled at the remark, remembering the early morning buggy ride when Amanda had insisted that only when Acadians voted and ran for office would they be represented in government. He had to admit she was right and that Paul Octave Hébert, the second Acadian governor in ten years, was a welcome sight.

"You must be René Comeaux," the freshman legislator said in a thick Southern accent, sounding his name as "Coe-mox" like so many other Anglo-Saxon Northern Louisiana legislators.

McDuff laughed. "Coe-mo," he said, slapping the freshman lawmaker, who was several years his senior, hard on the back. When the freshman sent him a hardened look, McDuff called out to another legislator and hurriedly moved on.

"They'll eat their young if they have a chance," René said as he watched the man leave.

"My apologies, sir, for mispronouncing your name," the freshman legislator said.

"No harm done," René said, offering his hand.

"Benjamin Whitley," he said, accepting it. "And it's a pleasure to meet such a famous man. Your story has reached us in Monroe."

René unconsciously adjusted his cravat. Even after four years, René could not get used to being labeled a hero. "Any man would have done the same."

"Perhaps," Whitley replied.

"Is your family here for the swearing in?" René asked, hoping to change the subject.

The man's eyes grew dim and he looked away when he spoke. "My wife's been dead some years now. My children have small children and couldn't make the trip."

René patted the man's back, much as McDuff had done, but this time in a friendly and sincere manner. "Then you must come home with me. I have more family than I know what to do with."

René and Amanda had rented a two-story town house in Baton Rouge for the legislative session, three blocks from the newly created Capitol Building. As was usual for a Louisiana winter, the cold weather had been interrupted by a brief warm spell and the camellias had been fooled into blossoming. The air was filled with the scents of the upcoming spring and the sounds of the busy Mississippi River traffic.

The two discussed current politics as they walked, and found they had plenty in common, even though their worlds and cultures were many miles apart. Honest and well-meaning men like Whitley, René concluded, were what made politics interesting. That and the unique opportunity democracy offered to duel verbally. The Judge had been right after all. René excelled in his new career.

Before the men reached the front walkway of the town house, two small children, one sporting a head of dark brown hair and the other as blond as a daffodil, bolted across the threshold. René immediately knelt and ushered his children into his arms, rising and bringing the giggling tykes with him, their little legs dangling.

"Where's your mother?" he asked Cecilia, the oldest.

"Where else," Alcée answered from the doorway. "She and Marguerite have been inseparable since we arrived."

René turned toward the street, and found Ben lingering uncomfortably behind. "Mr. Whitley," he said, hoping to make his guest feel welcome, "this is my Uncle Alcée."

Alcée offered his hand in greeting. "My pleasure, sir."

"Benjamin Whitley is a new legislator from Monroe," René explained. "He's never met an Acadian before."

The older man became visibly embarrassed. "Is it that obvious?"

"Don't worry, Mr. Whitley," Alcée said with a smile, leading the gentleman into the parlor. "Some of my best friends are Americans."

As the men made their way into the house, three small children darted through their legs noisily. René released Cecilia and her brother, Jean, so they could join their cousins.

"And you have another on the way?" René incredulously asked Alcée, who shrugged and grinned.

James and Virginia were Ben's first introduction, and he seemed glad to meet people whose first language was his own.

"The Judge is on his way to New Orleans," René told him. "He and Virginia hope to make peace between the French and Americans, and reestablish the single form of municipal government."

René then introduced Ben to Philip, his partner of four years, and his parents, Marie and Etienne. T-Emile and his new wife and child were in town for the occasion, and Alexandre was thrilled to make Ben's acquaintance to practice his English. Pierre, René thought as he announced Ben, was now taller than anyone in the family, including René.

The two finally made it to the kitchen, where Amanda, Marguerite and Colette were busy preparing a special meal to celebrate his second term. René again made his introductions, sneaking a kiss with Amanda when Ben turned and politely bowed to Colette, pausing a little too long at their introduction.

"It's a shame the governor was too ill to make the ceremony," Amanda said, carefully watching the interaction between Ben and Colette. "I would like to have met him."

"You will," René said, snaking an arm about her waist and pulling her close, breathing in her sweet smell. Four years and two children, and her image still excited him as if it were the first meeting.

"He likes her," Amanda whispered. Before he could ask who, Marguerite ushered them all into the dining room for supper.

Later that evening, as Amanda and René looked in on the

sleeping children and pulled their discarded covers up to their chins, René asked her what she had meant.

"Just that," Amanda replied. "Your Mr. Whitley's in love with Colette."

"That's ridiculous," René said. "He couldn't fall in love that quickly."

Closing the door to a crack, Amanda gazed up at him and smiled. "You did."

"That was different," René insisted.

"How?" Amanda asked, placing her hands on her hips defiantly.

"I spoke your language," he said.

Amanda laughed, the soft giggle René found so irresistible. "That's debatable," she said.

René pinched her chin lightly while his eyes twinkled.

"Did you see how Colette responded?" Amanda continued. "She couldn't keep her eyes off him."

"You're imagining this," René said, shaking his head. "They will never be able to communicate."

"Some things don't need words," Amanda answered, pulling on the lapels of René's waistcoat so that their bodies met. After René leaned down and delivered a slow, lingering kiss, Amanda added, "Besides, he told me so himself."

"Told you what?" René asked, moving his lips down the soft reaches of her neck.

"He asked me if it was difficult being in love with someone of a different culture, an Acadian to be specific."

René moved back to take in her full countenance. "What did you say?"

"I said it was no problem at all."

René stared into the pools of blue that had been his undoing. He couldn't imagine loving anyone more.

"You're right," he said before claiming her lips once again. "No problem at all."

AUTHOR'S NOTE

Jolie Blonde, translated from the French meaning "beautiful blonde," was first recorded as *Ma Blonde Est Partie* or *Jole Blon* by Cajun music recording pioneer Amédée Breaux in 1928. Today, the sad waltz about unrequited love is considered a favorite among Cajuns and Cajun music lovers. It holds the time-honored distinction of being known as the "Cajun National Anthem" and being the most requested Cajun love ballad in Louisiana.

ROMANCE FROM FERN MICHAELS

DEAR EMILY   (0-8217-4952-8, $5.99)

WISH LIST   (0-8217-5228-6, $6.99)

AND IN HARDCOVER:

VEGAS RICH   (1-57566-057-1, $25.00)